D1005629

The Serpent's Bite

Also by Warren Adler

American Quartet
American Sextet
Banquet Before Dawn
Blood Ties
Cult
Death of a Washington Madame
Empty Treasures
Flanagan's Dolls
Funny Boys
Immaculate Deception
Jackson Hole, Uneasy Eden
Madeline's Miracles
Mourning Glory
Natural Enemies
Never Too Late for Love
New York Echoes
New York Echoes 2
Private Lies
Random Hearts
Residue
Senator Love
The Casanova Embrace
The Children of the Roses
The David Embrace
The Henderson Equation
The Housewife Blues
The Sunset Gang
The Ties That Bind
The War of the Roses
The Womanizer
The Witch of Watergate
Trans-Siberian Express
Twilight Child
Undertow
We Are Holding the President Hostage

The Serpent's Bite

Warren Adler

Stonehouse Press, New York, NY
September 2012

Published by Stonehouse Press

Distributed by Greenleaf Book Group LLC

For ordering information or special discounts for bulk purchases, please contact Greenleaf Book Group LLC at PO Box 91869, Austin, TX 78709, 512.891.6100.

Design and composition by Val Sherer, Personalized Publishing Services

Cover design by Greenleaf Book Group LLC

ISBN 13: 978-1-59006-044-5

Publisher's Cataloging-In-Publication Data
(Prepared by The Donohue Group, Inc.)
Adler, Warren.
  The serpent's bite / Warren Adler. -- 1st ed.
    p. ; cm.
  "September, 2012."
  ISBN: 978-1-59006-044-5
  1. Dysfunctional families--United States--Fiction. 2. Family vacations--Yellowstone National Park--Fiction. 3. Interpersonal relations--Fiction. 4. Yellowstone National Park--Fiction. 5. Selfishness--Fiction. 6. Domestic fiction, American. 7. Psychological fiction. I. Title.

PS3551.D64 S47 2012
813/.54   2012937022

Part of the Tree Neutral® program, which offsets the number of trees consumed in the production and printing of this book by taking proactive steps, such as planting trees in direct proportion to the number of trees used: www.treeneutral.com

Printed in the United States of America on acid free paper

12 13 14 15 16 17   10 9 8 7 6 5 4 3 2 1

First Edition

TreeNeutral®

For Jonathan

How sharper than a serpent's tooth it is
To have a thankless child!
—Shakespeare, *King Lear*

Thank you for purchasing *The Serpent's Bite*. For a limited time you can go to

www.warrenadler.com/serpentsbite1

for a free download of one of Warren Adler's best selling books.

Chapter 1

⸺⟫⬥⟪⸺

They crossed the asphalt road into the trailhead, slipping seamlessly into the alien world of the wilderness. To Courtney Temple, the abruptness of the change was daunting, and she worried that its suddenness might trigger a panic attack and abort her participation in this eccentric attempt by her father to effect a family reconciliation.

Only the snorting of the mules and horses and the occasional sound of their metal shoes clopping on stone broke the initial eerie silence. Soon the atmosphere of audibility transformed, as her mind grew attentive to the birdsongs, insect buzz, and the rustling cacophony of breeze-brushed leaves. The July sun poked brightly through the tree branches like a roving beam, forcing an occasional painful squint through the lenses of her sunglasses.

Courtney was on the third horse in the string, behind three heavily laden mules and Harry McGrath, their outfitter leading the pack, and Tomas, the Mexican wrangler riding behind him. Harry had placed each of the horses on a domination scale known only to himself. Courtney's horse was named Bubba, and he was steady as a rock as he lumbered slowly forward with what seemed like a sense of bored equestrian indifference. Behind her was her brother Scott, his long legs perched awkwardly in their stirrups, and behind him, their father, who had required a helpful boost from Harry to get his leg over the cantle bag and his butt on the saddle.

Courtney felt an odd sensation of elation as she observed this sign of her father's aging after their four-year hiatus, as if it were a prologue to his decline and demise, the latter a wished-for outcome, the timing of which had often intruded on her thoughts. But aside from this show of diminished strength, his features seemed more youthful than she remembered. Puzzled at first, she realized on closer observation that he had had the bags removed from under his eyes, and his teeth were obvious implants, white and too perfect for a man of his years.

His complexion, too, seemed clearer, another obvious repair, probably by chemical means. His hair, once prematurely gray, had now miraculously turned to rusty brown. There was only one conclusion. The man had had a deliberate makeover. Why? The reason seemed obvious. It was an outcome that had already filled her with dread. There was a woman in the picture. He was well over his widower's mourning. In Courtney's mind the imaginary woman was certain to be a dangerous predator, a transforming competitor in the coming inheritance stakes. Whoever she was, she had become an instant enemy.

Not that Courtney was certain that he had changed his will to shortchange what was once their promised inheritance. Once, he and their now-deceased mother had proudly revealed that his two children would share equally in their largesse when they both had passed on. Had he cut them out or reduced their take after their rift and estrangement over the past few years?

She suspected as much but couldn't be certain. Was this trek a test for her and her brother? Was it worth the discomfort to find out? Was there a new wrinkle, a new demanding woman in the picture?

They had checked into the motel in West Yellowstone the evening before but had not had dinner together, since they had all arrived at different times. In the morning, they had breakfasted with Harry before leaving for the trailhead but had little chance for anything but the banal and polite chatter of a traditional family reunion.

Their father had greeted her with an affectionate hug that seemed oddly incongruous with the bitterness of their last argument and the long aftermath of the four-year silence that followed. He was equally affectionate in greeting her brother Scott, and both she and Scott had returned the gesture with propriety as if nothing had happened to split the once-unbreakable bond.

Throughout breakfast Harry did all the talking, outlining what they were to expect during their seven-day, fifty-odd-mile trek on horseback. They listened in silent concentration as he showed them the map of the journey and reeled off instructions reminiscent of their earlier trip. Their father had arranged an abridged replica of the original family trek, which had lasted ten days.

Harry seemed to offer a more detailed introduction than she remembered twenty-odd years earlier. A dirty-nailed finger traced their future journey on a wrinkled, much-used map of the Yellowstone area. He sounded more like someone eager to continue selling, as if he was still uncertain that he had made the deal. His voice seemed to have become rougher over the years, and his weathered complexion had the look of ancient parchment, out of which peered pale blue eyes surrounded by tiny rivulets of red.

She figured him for about sixty, a man well sculpted by the harsh outdoors and bad habits. His facial skin was florid, with bands of rough red mantling his nose and cheeks. There was a permanent indentation midway on his forehead, undoubtedly made by the band of his stained and misshapen cowboy hat, an apt symbol of his authentic Western bona fides. It struck her that he was trying hard, too hard, to reach for good humor and to portray himself as still young and vigorous. About him was a stale odor of dried sweat and boozy breath, larded with the obvious scent of the chewing tobacco that had yellowed his teeth.

In his explanation, he made a historical point that she did not recall, informing them that the Thorofare Trail, which they would partially follow, was the route taken by the Washburn party who first tracked the Yellowstone. The report of that journey had convinced politicians that two million two hundred thousand acres had to be preserved, and as a consequence, Yellowstone became the first national park in the world. He noted, too, that they were heading for an area just outside the official borders of the park, known generally as the Teton Wilderness, more than a half-million acres of unspoiled land.

It sounded as if he was trying to validate his knowledge like some chamber-of-commerce booster, and they all listened politely and nodded as he spoke.

"Here's where we're going," he said, following the trail with his finger as he informed them that they would be heading through the southeastern edge of the park, an area of high meadows in the Absaroka Mountain Range. He paused and looked up.

"Lot of this was burned out in '88 but it's mostly come back, though you can still see the residues of the burn."

Harry explained further that they would be traveling on trails along Yellowstone Lake, "the biggest mountain lake in North America," then returning over backcountry trails with spectacular views.

"No Eagle Pass," Courtney interjected, suddenly remembering its hazardous trail.

He rubbed his jaw and laughed.

"As your Dad and I agreed, no Eagle Pass."

"Now that was something," their father said. "Remember Mom's attitude? She was petrified."

"God, yes," Courtney said, remembering the narrow switchbacks and deep canyons.

"Scared the living shit out of me," Scott said.

"Hate to be dependent on a four-legged creature with a small brain," Courtney said good-naturedly. She was determined to be pleasant and ingratiating. She was, after all, a professional actress. "And I'm slightly uncomfortable living with my heart in my throat."

Their father chuckled.

"Tell you the truth," Temple said. "I'm a little too old for that kind of fear."

He was about to go on but aborted his remarks, obviously remembering his violation of the outfitter's age limit.

"Actually it was the shortest route of return during that last trek. That was a lot longer than what we plan this time. Of course, it's your nickel and your choice. Anyway, this I can promise, we'll see lots of critters, big and little, elk, moose, cougars, mountain lions, bison, deer, big-horn sheep, brown bears, and, I don't want to scare you…grizzlies, biggest carnivore in North America, and what you didn't see last time you were here, wolves." He pulled a face, sighed, and shook his head. "Damned wolves. Totally screwed up my hunting business. Maybe we're at the tail end of an era. Stupid government and those goddamned tree huggers."

Courtney exchanged glances with her father. There was an ominous tone to his remark, a flicker of both anger and anxiety. Although she had no passionate political leanings, she was exposed to the usual Hollywood mindset that leaned heavily liberal, assuming that most people felt this way. Not that she really cared one way or another. Actually, she was nonpolitical, except when it mattered careerwise.

"I thought bringing the wolves back was a good thing," her father said.

"For the wolves maybe, but not for us outfitters. We make most of our living hunting during season. The wolves are taking all the elk and moose calves. Anything they can find, especially the babies. The young ones kill for sport. Fucking ecology freaks." He coughed, looked at Courtney. "Sorry, but they just don't get it. Won't be elk or moose left to hunt in a couple of years. Maybe some brown bears. The wolves are everywhere now and…," he lowered his voice and turned toward her father as if he were confiding some vital information. "Not only the wolves, Temple. Fact is the grizzlies are invading. Endangered my ass. Tough bastards, big feeding machines, need lots of range space. I used to do my business out here in the wilderness without being armed, which is illegal. No more." He lowered his head and shook it sadly. "You'll see 'em. I guarantee that. We take precautions. They come smelling around for food, we hang it high. Remember the meat pole? Can't be too careful. They'll as soon as eat you as any piece of raw meat. Don't worry, though. We'll be watching. One gets ornery around me or my clients, I'll blow his fucking brains out, government or no government order, prison or not." He stopped abruptly, as if he had gone too far.

It seemed obvious to Courtney that he was disturbed, angry, and deeply depressed about the situation in general, adding to her suspicion that things were not going well for Harry. He was a long way from the Harry of twenty years ago. This man was obviously suffering, perhaps facing the end of his career and way of life. He was definitely not the strong, confident, rugged figure she remembered.

"Not to worry," he said, perking up, transparently trying to restore confidence and allay fear. "I'll bring you back safe and sound and give you the best damned adventure of your lifetime." He turned to Courtney's father. "Just like last time. Right, Temple?"

"That's what I'm hoping," her father said, nodding and offering a tight smile. It could not mask his concern.

"What do we do if one…you know…say a wolf or a grizzly pays us a visit?" Courtney asked. She felt genuinely frightened, remembering the famous story by Jack London about fending off wolves.

"Wolf doesn't go after humans."

"And grizzlies?"

"Hell, you remember your grizzly lesson," Harry chuckled. "Just don't get in his space. If you do, don't run. Assume the fetal position and play dead, and don't look the big bastard in the eye or threaten him in any way. And above all, don't go near the cubs if it's a female. And remember, he's a foodie and needs lots of protein to feed his bulk."

"Just lay there?" she asked. "And if that doesn't work?"

"Just pee in your pants," Scott said.

"Is this trip necessary?" Courtney asked with humorous sarcasm.

"Haven't lost anyone yet," Harry laughed, continuing. "Hell, we're here for adventure. Maybe I advertised the dangers too hard."

"Adventure, yes," Scott said. "But I wasn't planning an early demise." He winked at Courtney. "Not just yet."

"Not on my agenda either," their father said with a chuckle.

"Looks like I made it sound worse than it is. Just remember, you're in my care. And if any of those big bastards start something funny, I'm fully armed and loaded and can take down one of 'em in a couple of well-placed shots. You're under my care and protection. I've got more than thirty-five years of outfitting under my belt. My job is to bring you back safe, healthy, and happy and give you an experience to make conversation for years. Right, Temple? Did I deliver before?" He was getting repetitive.

"Sure did, Harry. And here we are back at the old cigar stand. It's been on my memory reel for two decades," Temple said. "I'm looking for at least another couple of decades to tell the story. Fodder for my dotage." He was cautious about talking about age now.

"I could do without the grizzlies," Courtney said, forcing herself to maintain the light tone. "And I'll take your word for it about the wolves."

"Actually I'd like to see at least one of both," Scott said.

"If I have to, I'll hire 'em," Harry replied, obviously hoping this banter would bond them closer. "Actually I can guarantee you won't be disappointed."

"Thanks a lot," Courtney murmured.

"You're as safe with me as a baby in a cradle," Harry said. Observing him, a faded version of his old self, did not give her much confidence. An image of old homeless drunks that infested Santa Monica popped into her mind.

She wondered how many times he had gone over the same ground with others, whetting their expectations with projections of danger. All part of the show. He was simply manipulating one's expectation in pure Hollywood fashion. As for her and her brother, adventure was hardly the reason for their participation. In stark terms, for them it was all about money.

"We're going over trails that are the furthest point from a road in the continental United States. And that includes logging roads," Harry added, embellishing the expectation further.

Occasionally Courtney's mind drifted as she stole clandestine glances at her father and brother. She had almost given up hope that sentiment and nostalgia would one day force her father into a reconciliation mode.

From his friendly and affectionate attitude, she was encouraged to believe that he might again be willing to reverse course and restore his earlier generosity in financing his darling daughter's great dream of celebrity and stardom. As for the inheritance, she would find subtle ways to press him toward revelation. Was it still in effect as once revealed? A two-way split?

Her brother was another matter. She hoped that his weakness and his often-wobbly conscience would not gum up the works.

On the drive to the trailhead, following the two big horse trailers in one of their rented cars, with Scott driving, her father beside him, and Courtney in the rear seat, they maintained a protocol of polite chitchat as if they had made a pact with each other to hold back intimacy until they grew more comfortable with their new proximity. Once on the journey, thrown together for hours at a time in the vastness of the wilderness, there would be no way to avoid conversation and, hopefully, intimate exchanges, a prospect she viewed with both anxiety and optimism. Opportunity knocks, she assured herself, and despite all hardships, she was determined to take full advantage of it.

She noted that her father carried a digital camera on a leather strap that hung on his shoulder, which surprised her. Apparently in the four years since she had seen him, he had become familiar with computers. Noting the camera, it brought back memories of the many slides he had taken of their last trek, which he often showed to visiting friends on their old carousel projector. It was always a highly detailed showing, a soup-to-nuts portrayal of what became the family's quintessential great once-in-a-lifetime adventure.

Both at home and in his jewelry salon in Manhattan's diamond center on Forty-seventh Street, he had blown up pictures of the trip, one of all four of them side by side on their horses, with the jagged peaks of the Absaroka Mountains in the background. The pictures graced one of the walls of the jewelry salon and served as a conversation piece for customers, especially those very rich ones who kept and rode horses. In their spacious Riverside Drive apartment, she recalled one picture prominently hung that showed them around the campfire, arms around each other, smiling at the camera as if, indeed, this was their happiest family moment. It might have been. Certainly their father thought it was. For her and Scott it was a lot more.

Noting the way her father had greeted them both, she grew even more hopeful that something momentous and wished-for would happen between them, a regeneration of parent-child dynamic, resulting in the genuinely copious gesture of generosity. Show me the money, she begged silently. For her this meant the longed-for freedom from financial stress, her principal objective. She was determined to focus all her energies and persuasive powers on that one goal. Be wary of any high hopes, she cautioned herself, having learned the primary lesson of an actor's audition: expectations that were too high often made for deepest disappointment.

Leading the mules and following behind Harry, riding a black horse, was Tomas, a runty deeply tanned bony-faced Mexican of clearly Indian extraction, with a surly look and a rare, joyless smile that displayed three gold-toothed front dentures. His features, shaded by a large, curly brimmed, sweat-stained cowboy hat, seemed expressionless, although his dark eyes betrayed a feral alertness that struck her as a studied attempt to appear deferential. He wore a dirty red bandana knotted around his neck and fancy worn snakeskin cowboy boots. His jeans featured a large shiny silver belt buckle embossed with crossed six shooters. She figured it was his own Mexican version of a movie cowboy.

At the trailhead as they unloaded, Harry had introduced Tomas to them as the cook, wrangler, and jack-of-all-trades.

Tomas acknowledged the introduction with a tiny indifferent nod.

"Knows his business. Right, amigo?" Harry said, nodding toward Tomas.

"*Si,* Señor Harry," the Mexican muttered.

"Only one helper?" their father asked, his expression skeptical. "Last time there were three. I think we talked about this. We had agreed on two."

"Hell, this little Mex can do the work of three," Harry said, brushing off the accusation. "Wait'll you taste his grub."

"But I thought…," their father began, politely protesting. "We talked of two people helping. Wasn't that part of the deal?"

He was acting true to form, a perpetual questioner, detail-oriented and persistent, a man who needed to know what was behind every action. She speculated that their father was paying top dollar. A consummate businessman, he expected true value for his money.

"I know my business," Harry said with annoyance, his eyes narrowing. "We have two less helpers than last time, Temple, because the trip is shorter."

"I know," their father pressed. "I thought we had covered this in our conversations. Didn't we agree on two helpers?"

"Trust me, Temple," Harry said, visibly exasperated.

Courtney was certain that her father was telling the truth.

"What I promised was one helluva trek, and I aim to keep that promise. As for this fuckin' Mex, you'll grow to really appreciate the sumbitch. He's one smart spic. When he's not working, he reads all kinds of book shit. No kidding. Does the work of three. I swear it. You'll see that I deliver what I promise. Besides, you came to me because I gave you one hell of an adventure a few years back, and by God, I'll do it again."

"I'm sure you will, Harry," their father said with some hesitation. "I just thought—" He broke off the argument, glanced at Courtney, and shrugged. "Too late" his look suggested. Harry quickly changed the subject.

"You check the weather report, Tomas?"

"*Si*, Señor Harry. Weather good now. Coupla days maybe rain."

"Nights cool, days comfortable?" Harry prompted.

"*Si*, Señor Harry."

"Still...," her father began, again showing an attitude of polite deference, his surrender not quite complete. She remembered his persistence when an idea consumed him. "It wasn't quite what we agreed."

Despite his persistence, she could see he was surrendering reluctantly.

"Trust me, Temple," Harry said again, his face reddening, selling hard now. "I've been at this for more than thirty-five years."

His résumé was getting repetitive.

"I know how many people I need to create a great wilderness experience. Believe me, this little fuckin' Mex is great. Been with me on what?...more than a dozen treks, winter and summer. Knows his stuff. Great cook. Wait'll you taste his stuff—biscuits, dumplings, corncakes. You ain't ever tasted better trout than the way he fixes it. And what that sumbitch can do with meat and potatoes! Man's a natural. Hell, he knows more ways to cook up chili than any man alive. Great wrangler, too. A lot smarter than he looks. Sumbitch obeys orders. Right, Tomas?"

"*Si*, Señor Harry," Tomas muttered without expression.

Harry lowered his voice and chuckled.

"Thinks he's the Mexican John Wayne. Right, amigo?"

"*Si*, Señor Harry," Tomas replied with a joyless laugh, as if it were part of their regular routine for the benefit of clients.

"Show him your Duke Wayne walk, Tomas," Harry ordered the Mexican.

Tomas smiled thinly on cue and did a passable imitation of a John Wayne walk. Like a trained monkey, Courtney thought, feeling a rising level of disgust. Her father shook his head and turned away.

"Sumbitch, ain't that something?" Harry guffawed, slapping his thigh, then with a wave of his hand he signaled the Mexican. "Let's move 'em out."

As Tomas began to unload the horses and mules from the trailers, Harry bent closer to her father and offered a stage whisper.

"Knows on which side his bread is buttered, Temple. Works his fuckin' wetback ass off if he knows what's good for him."

Temple shrugged, obviously offended by Harry's treatment of the Mexican, although he made no comment. It was obvious that Harry McGrath was not the sure-footed confident outfitter of two decades ago; he exuded an air of desperation.

Harry's hair had turned chalk white, he had bulked in his middle, and the once-handsome tan and burnished face was a map of prunelike wrinkles, but his cerulean eyes, like blue pools plunked in a network of red wiggly lines, seemed tired and less alert than Courtney remembered. There was a boozy effluvial mist that enveloped and moved with him like a cloud, despite efforts to disguise it with some clove-scented mouthwash or lozenge, which only made the odor more pronounced.

Hair of the dog, Courtney thought. The guy is a drunk. She guessed he might be on the wrong side of sixty, and his desperation suggested someone far past his prime, barely hanging on. She had never forgotten his earlier admonition on that long-ago journey that his guided trek through the wilderness was "short on luxury but long on adventure," and she was certain that the slogan continued to describe what they could expect, only more so.

His girlfriend then, the cook on their first trek, was apparently long gone from his bed and board. Courtney recalled, too, that there was another person, a blonde teenager who acted as wrangler. There was one other, a quiet skinny kid who was an all-around helper.

She speculated that this reduction in personnel was quite obviously a sign of lean times for Harry's outfitting business, which he had pretty well confirmed earlier. She recalled that her father had remarked that the first trip had to be booked a year in advance, which did not seem to be the case for the new one.

Harry had greeted them with what struck her as exaggerated enthusiasm, although she suspected that his memory of them, after more than two decades of similar treks with different people, was, at best, vague. Oddly, her own memory of that earlier trip had deepened as she forced her recall. It was, indeed, a glorious and loving time with genuine affection between parents and children and a hopeful and, as it turned out, naive optimistic outlook. There was also the other, she mused, with a brief glance at Scott.

There had been an element of real danger in the earlier trek, although Harry had not dwelled on such possibilities during his introductory remarks then. She did remember one caveat: the necessity of holding the reins of the horse, which, he pointed out, was the horse's preprogrammed steering mechanism. If the reins are dropped and the pressure eases, he warned them, the horse might suddenly feel out of control and panic, exposing the rider to be dangerously unseated by low branches or bucked off by a sudden burst of speed. And, of course, she could not eliminate from her bag of fears, an encounter with a hungry predator like a grizzly.

A ranger had visited their campsite on their earlier trip and, with deliberate relish, recalled a then-recent episode involving a grizzly that had devoured a half-digested peanut-butter sandwich in the belly of a female trekker, in a lip-to-stomach nosh that killed the poor woman. She had never forgotten that story. On that previous trek they had encountered evidence of grizzlies but, thankfully, no intimate visitation.

A lightning strike also presented a danger. A bolt could be attracted to a horse, which, as Harry explained then, was ninety percent water and ten percent metal, making it a prime target for a strike. When a thunder-and-lightning storm intruded, they had been forced to dismount. As it turned out, they had been lucky, since a bolt had actually felled a nearby tree and missed their party by a mere couple of feet. She did not relish Tomas's weather prediction of an impending rain.

The most dangerous event was their return to civilization through the ten-thousand-foot Eagle Pass, with its twenty-three narrow switchbacks traversing sheer drops into deep canyons. Some of the path was so narrow that Harry had ordered them to dismount and lead the horses by their reins. Her mother had been close to hysteria, but they managed, through false bravado and encouragement, to keep her moving. More than once she had stopped, closed her eyes, and squatted on the trail, unable to proceed without considerable cajoling on their part.

A misstep meant a fall into a canyon hundreds of feet below and certain death. Such apparent danger had salted the earlier adventure, especially in retrospect, and kept it in Courtney's memory along with the now legendary sense of family bonding that had become a quintessential event for her parents.

Thankfully, her father had eagerly agreed that the Eagle Pass adventure would no longer be part of the new trek. That earlier trek had, indeed, been a family-bonding experience, a powerful and nostalgic loving memory, and forever a conversational focal point. For her and Scott, the experience was far more explosive than mere bonding. Their parents hadn't a clue to what had been unfolding right under their noses.

Apparently her father still believed strongly in the bonding power of the old memory, and Courtney clung to her speculation that this new trek was designed as an unabashed attempt by him to bring the broken family back together and undo the corrosion that had set in since. For her it was strictly business. Show me the money, Daddy. For that, she would act the part of a loving, caring, devoted daughter, contrite over past offenses and eager to repair any misunderstanding. She was convinced that Scott would play his own assigned role in this little drama for less contrived reasons.

In pursuit of comfort and authenticity, she had come well prepared, with padded bicycle pants to cushion her crotch and butt, a straw cowboy hat with a stampede string, cowboy boots, long underwear, a miner-type flashlight that fitted over her forehead for tent reading, mosquito spray, extra supplies of sunblock, and plenty of ibuprofen and vodka.

Her father had called her out of the blue, catching her on her cell. At first, as she had done on his previous attempts to contact her, she was tempted to hang up. But years had passed, and she had always held out hope of a change in his attitude and generosity. Perhaps, as had been her prediction and her wish, he was obviously resurfacing for an important reason. She hadn't heard his voice in four years but its tone had lost none of its authority.

"Don't hang up, Courtney," he said. "Hear me out."

He quickly sketched out his proposal.

"Too weird for words, Dad," she told him initially. He persisted, selling hard.

"It'll be fun…like last time."

He had made more-than-two decades sound like yesterday.

"Almost, but not quite. Just six days instead of ten and only one camp instead of two like last time. Surely you remember." He was purring with good will and excitement. "I've lucked out and gotten a tentative booking with the same outfitter, Harry McGrath. He's still in business and apparently in great demand. He had a cancellation. He gave us a great time then. Remember? Maybe it will give us a chance to get to know each other again."

"Renew auld acquaintance," she said, with a touch of sarcasm.

If he caught the implication, he tactfully ignored it.

She turned it over in her mind. Perhaps it was the moment she had been waiting for.

"Maybe we can be a family again," he said.

She knew he believed it implicitly. This had always been his perception of what family meant, handed down from his own parents who had brought him up, an only child, in what was apparently a cocoon of smothering love. In his mind, it was all about Mom and Dad and the children, devoted, caring, one for all, all for one, an impregnable family fortress. Had she once believed that as well?

Somehow it had all gotten diluted by false expectations, by disappointment and disillusion, by passion gone awry, by dreams gone haywire, by bad luck, and by economic necessity. She prided herself on her insight into her father's psyche but had miscalculated her own ability to manipulate his generosity. Was this an opportunity for a second chance to play the loving daughter and invade his pockets?

"I'm not sure, Dad."

She decided to play hesitant and uncertain. Not too fast. Show restraint.

"I haven't been on a horse since that time," she said, stalling, searching her mind for further options, seeking just the right word and truthful gesture to react to this sudden reentry of her father into her life after four years. His attitude seemed enthusiastic with no sign of either hostility or remorse, as if nothing had occurred to break the old fatherly bond. Her sense of time vanished, and she felt like the dissimulating teenager again, Daddy's perfect innocent angel, the promising ingénue, a role she had played with gusto and great early results.

Her opening gambit was to show daughterly concern.

"You sure you can hack it, Dad? I mean healthwise."

She remembered vaguely that he had been diagnosed for high blood pressure, a condition that supposedly caused his mother, her grandmother, to die early of a cerebral hemorrhage.

"I've been working out like a demon. I'm in terrific shape."

"Doesn't high altitude affect high blood pressure?"

"Under control," he answered. "I take pills."

Her solicitousness seemed a knee-jerk reaction. Why such lingering concern for his health when her fondest wish was otherwise?

"You're over seventy," she said.

"Not by much," he corrected her.

She knew he was being disingenuous. He would be seventy-five in December.

"I wouldn't broadcast that," he said. "Granted that the outfitter has a sixty-years age limit. Besides, I'm fit as a fiddle. And I don't look my age."

"You could be taking a risk."

She hoped he would interpret her concern as genuine. Actually it opened up possibilities.

"I can handle it," he murmured. "Old is not as old as it used to be."

She supposed it was meant to be a joke, and she giggled appropriately.

"What about Scott?" she had asked, deflecting the conversation.

Her brother, younger by a year, thirty-seven now, was locked in another compartment of estrangement, although he did contact her occasionally. What they had in common was the same complaint: their father's unwillingness to open his purse and the status of their inheritance.

At one time, their father had been generous, more than generous. As an older dad with a lucrative business, he had the means to be generous. Then, abruptly, his businessman's experience kicked in, and he had closed the spigot. For their own good, he had alleged. Granted, he might have been right, especially in the case of her brother, whose passion was more commercial than artistic and, to be honest, a lot less intense.

For Courtney, her obsession was her ambition. She yearned for celebrity status as a movie star, knowing she had the drive and talent, although she had passed what was the traditional age of breakthrough in the twenties. So far, she had not made much of a career dent, which did little to dampen her determination. There was the occasional tiny television part or extra role in a commercial crowd scene and the occasional free turn on one of the many live stages in Los Angeles.

Still, despite all the setbacks, all the failures, all the rejections, all the pain of not being called back from auditions, and the lack of getting a respectable agent or manager, she remained unalterably committed to her pursuit, no matter what. Unfortunately the lack of her father's funding was a devastating setback for her career plans and the maintenance required for her to keep going. Giving up was not an option.

The joint financial issue with her brother, and the only real discussion between them on the rare times when they talked by telephone or communicated briefly by e-mail, was how to get this spigot reopened. So far they had both failed miserably. Courtney had bolted. Scott had not, maintaining a tepid telephonic relationship with his father. But then, he was always the weaker and needier sibling.

There were other matters between them that were buried too deeply to ever resurrect in dialogue, although she knew they were ever present in their consciousness and, like all histories, could never be erased.

"Scott is coming," her father told her on the phone. "But it's all contingent on your presence."

"Why mine?" she had asked, playing the innocent.

"It's either a family thing, or it's not."

There it was again, the family thing, a good sign. She wondered if it meant that he had succumbed finally to the guilt of separation. She had hoped it might kick in again one day.

Many times, down on her luck and desperate, she had invoked family ties, but he had ceased to respond as Big Daddy with the checkbook, which had become her not-so-secret characterization. Often she had begged, cajoled, tried every arrow in her quiver of manipulation, but the string had run out finally in a conversation she had with her father at her mother's funeral. That had been the breaking point—until now.

Her father's reaction to her plea had struck her as an odd disconnect. He was a man to whom charity was gospel. Often he would help a homeless person, dropping paper money in his cup, and his list of contributions covered a large array of causes. In his lexicon of compassion, it meant "giving back," a posture getting increasingly difficult for her to understand. His politics were liberal, and his feeling for others, she supposed, genuine. He was vocally against persecution, injustice, and unfairness in all its forms.

And yet, from her perspective he had become far less sanguine about "charity" for his children. She did acknowledge that it was an unfair presumption, since he had been tremendously supportive and generous to both his children in the past. But she saw herself now in her midthirties practically destitute. He had cut her off, her brother as well. For a man who bled for the underdog and thought of charity as "sharing," she characterized his attitude toward her financial well-being as cruel and unjust, and she had dismissed him as a fucking hypocrite.

She knew, of course, that she was hardened by failure and disappointment, and there was some limit to parental supportiveness, but her dream of becoming a movie star was still as strong and obsessive as ever and permitted no surrender, no negativity, and a ruthlessness that she felt absolutely necessary.

By blood and tradition, she considered her father's money her and her brother's entitlement. She had grown up with the certainty that sooner or later it would be theirs. He and their mother had, in the days before her death and their estrangement, often reiterated that he had made arrangements to divide his estate between her brother and herself. Could he ever muster the will and endure the guilt of cutting them off from their inheritance? Hell, he had already cut off her enabling stipend, why not the other?

What she wanted was to get her hands on some of it now. Before their estrangement she had tried every trick in the book to get him to increase her stipend, to gift her more money, to settle a regular lifelong lavish income on her. Not to part with it in the hour of her greatest need was heartless, selfish, and mean-minded. Pursuing her dream needed nourishment and heavy maintenance, financially and emotionally. All right, she had not succeeded, not yet, but her dreams and ambitions were as fresh as ever. The spotlight and celebrity beckoned. She knew in her heart that they would come to pass.

Perhaps she was spoiled by memory. Once he had been proud of her choice, had encouraged her. Always the dutiful father, he had attended all her high school and college performances, fueled the dream, kept her going. In an odd way, she had long ago acknowledged that his and her mother's cheerleading was partially responsible for enabling her pursuit of this obsession.

During her student days, she had played many of the Shakespearian female roles and had been heralded as a brilliant talent with an assured future. Her Lady Macbeth was dubbed "extraordinary" by a stringer from the *New York Times* who wrote a compendium of reviews of student productions. She had also gotten standing ovations for her Juliet and Desdemona. She knew in her gut she had the right stuff and was dead certain that one day she would grace the giant screens of moviedom. She deserved it.

Critics in her school newspapers and later reviewers of small live theatrical productions had lauded and lavishly praised her talent and beauty. By any standard she knew she was a beautiful well-made woman, tall, curvaceous, sexy, naturally curly-haired, with large hazel eyes peering at the world over high cheekbones.

If she had not achieved her rightful destiny, she reasoned, she simply needed more time for others to discover her. What she needed most was money to fund her enterprise.

Her father's earlier support had been massive. A dozen years before, she and her then live-in boyfriend Hal Bender, whose moviemaking fantasies were as deep-seated as her own, put together an independent movie with her as the star, actually a horror-genre movie that was at that time a good calling card for career promotion.

Ruthless and predatory in hindsight, Hal had her manipulate her father into putting in the two-million-dollar financing to make the movie. Her father was still in thrall to her ambition, and it was not difficult to persuade his participation. They were, after all, a family of proven means, and although there was gratitude in his investment, there was no guilt in it. Hal assured him that he might triple his investment or more, but she knew that his real motivation was the help he would be giving his daughter.

He had bought her a two-bedroom condo in a good neighborhood in Santa Monica, which she had sold later to make up for the movie's budget shortfall, a fact that she had withheld from her father at the time. But then she was under Hal's spell, and her ambition had—as it would again and again—clouded any rational business judgment.

Unfortunately, the story line for the movie was too derivative and, as writer, director, and producer, Hal was both unskilled and feckless. Nevertheless, she had been reasonably satisfied with her performance, and in the private showing to their parents she had noted the tears in their eyes, signs that assured them that their little girl had made it to stardom. The picture was a monumental failure resulting in the loss of her father's two million, her condo, and of course, Hal, who blamed it all on the powers that be in the business that didn't know quality when they saw it.

They parted in anger, each convinced the other had destroyed the project. Hal had gone on to a brief career as a director of porno films, and a few years later had disappeared somewhere into oblivion, joining, she supposed, the vast army of failed film wannabes, dead certain of their massive talent but unable and unwilling to continue the struggle. Although totally convinced of her own talent, she refused to count herself among their ranks and took pride in her endurance.

Her father, although he eventually had forgiven her for foolishness in losing the condominium, did not replicate his financial contributions, which slowly dwindled as time went on, despite her appeals. She did manage some bit parts in television, but it was never enough to sustain a decent lifestyle, certainly not one she was used to as a child. Nevertheless she soldiered on, totally committed, suppressing any inhibition that stood in the path of her pursuit. So far, despite frequent humiliations, insults, and abuse, despite every wile she could muster, weathering depression and flirting with cocaine and alcohol as a typical show business enhancement to sociability, she slogged ahead, likening herself to a thoroughbred with blinkers that ran her best race as a mudder.

Nothing could thwart her belief in her superior talent, and she would brook no negativity on that score. Despite within hailing distance of forty, she had kept her body tight with hard exercise and could, with clever makeup, appear ten years younger. She was, of course, considering the surgeon's scalpel, but that took money, and the lack thereof had become her secondary obsession.

In the years she had been cut off from her father's largesse, she had taken temp jobs, modeled at convention shows, and waitressed to keep herself financially viable, although she had maxed out on all her credit cards. Occasionally, a last-minute plea to her father was answered, but his contribution was never enough, and as time went on she began to harbor dark thoughts about him.

She had long ago lost any daughterly devotion for him. She now hated him. Worse, all guilt about hating him had vanished. She wished him dead. That is if he had preserved the provisions he had promised.

She had eschewed any deep relationships with men, although she dated for jobs, meals, and sex, in that order. In the latter category she had mastered the art of speedy culmination or a faked orgasm, especially when the partner of the moment was undesirable, which was most of the time.

There were exceptions, but the conditions had to be right and required her to dredge up one particular image deep in memory. She didn't need a man to get off on that one.

Her experience with Hal and his exploitation of her had made her cautious, and she had learned how to deaden any emerging hint of emotional attachment.

Unable to move her father to generosity, despite every form of persuasion and guilt trip she could muster, she could always eke out some money from her late mother when she was alive. She might come across, within limits, from her own cache of secret cash. But when her mother's health had broken, and she retreated from guilt to self-interest and physical pain, she no longer responded to Courtney's need.

Money, money, money. It was now her mantra. To pursue her dream, she needed the nourishment of money to support her increasingly heavy maintenance expenses. Over and over this drumbeat repeated itself in her thoughts. But her mother was dead now, and she had blown it at her mother's funeral four years earlier, further opening the abyss between her and her father. They had not spoken since.

"Think of it as an adventure and an opportunity," he told her on the phone, announcing the trek and avoiding any mention of their long silence. After all, he had been silent on his side as well. Although at the very beginning of their rift, he had made repeated contact attempts by phone and letter. She answered none of them. Let him wallow in his guilt. If he wants the trappings of his children's love, let him pay for it.

Opportunity! The word was pregnant with optimism. Opportunity for what? For bonding, reevaluating, coming together after years of estrangement? Translated it meant he might reconsider his largesse, come to grips with his tight-fisted indifference to her plight. Scott, she was sure, had consented for these very same reasons. He had been sought out as well. His bottom-line agenda was the same as hers. Money! Every enterprise he had touched had failed.

"Maybe recapture the moment," she had told him hopefully.

"Yes. I'd like that Courtney."

"So would I," she lied. Fuck the moment. It was all about money.

"I'm in," she said.

"Great. I'll send you all the details."

"And don't forget the airplane tickets, Dad," she had added.

"Of course."

"And some out of pocket. I'm stretched as usual."

"I'll do it."

So matter of fact, she had thought, as if their angry words four years before had not been uttered. Since then, he had turned off the money spigot. She had been on her own, and a tough struggle it was.

In all that time she had remained hopeful that his sense of fatherhood might one day miraculously kick in, fueled by fond memories and gnawing guilt. Had it? She hoped so, and knew she was up for the role.

Chapter 2

⟿⟾

Courtney hadn't been exactly diplomatic to bring up the subject of money yet again on the day of her mother's funeral. They had come back from the cemetery to the Riverside Drive apartment where she had grown up. Desperation does not always allow exquisite timing. Perhaps, she had reasoned, seeing her amid the trappings of her childhood would trigger in her father nostalgia and generosity and recall the loving nature of their early relationship.

All the relatives were there: aunts, uncles, cousins. She had tried her best to appear dutiful and affectionate, acting appropriately in her role as the grieving daughter of the deceased, demonstrating devotion, embracing her father during the service both in the chapel and at graveside. She felt certain she was making a dent, recounting sentimental memories of their early days together when she was "Daddy's little girl."

It was not an easy chore for her, since, by then, she had grown to resent bitterly his ungenerous attitude. Secretly, she supposed she hated him and had fervently wished that he, not her mother, had died first. This resentment of her mother's having the gall to precede him in death was the real reason why she had not bothered to attend her mother's bedside during her last days.

She had used the cover of "urgent business," meaning she was up for a big part, as an excuse to keep her away. It was the language her father understood. Business was business. When nothing materialized, she deflected his disappointment by hitting the usual hot buttons of his fatherly yearning for her success. At this point, the ploy was considerably weakened by overuse, but it seemed to have placated him for the moment.

Observing her father in his grief, she realized that she had made a tactical mistake. She might have used the visit to her mother's deathbed to show him, even in the face of his diminished generosity, her daughterly devotion. Realizing she would have to quickly change gears, she saw an opening in this new venue. Mourning was a time of vulnerability. In his pain, her father looked ripe for the plucking. Hell, she was an actress. She could play any part, especially the grief stricken. For an actress it was an essential instrument in her toolbox.

In that tight little group of family mourners she was a celebrity, a Hollywood star in their eyes. It made her stomach tighten to hear them voice their admiration, sprinkled with their pity and condolences offered at close proximity through herring-tinged breath.

A lavish spread from Zabar's filled the dining room table, a nod to the Jewish after-death ritual, triggering memories of her grandparents' demise. She had long ago tossed away any religious connotation in her life and rarely thought of her Semitic roots.

The memorial experience did bring back a rush of nostalgic thoughts of her mother, who she supposed she had once truly loved with a child's nonjudgmental and naive sentiment. Her mother had been a quiet woman who worked with Courtney's father in his jewelry salon, operating out of an office suite in the Diamond District. Her grandfather had started the business, and Courtney's father had worked at it since high school, inheriting it on her grandfather's death.

Her father had, she knew, other aspirations. He had majored in art at Columbia and was also devoted to the violin. Whatever youthful ambitions he had harbored were long repressed. Somehow he had rechanneled his ambition and made the decision to join his father, choosing money and comfort over art.

He had done exceptionally well financially. By her brother's calculation, the man was worth in the neighborhood of thirty million dollars, with, give or take, about five million in gems and jewelry inventory, stocks, bonds, and the ownership of a large apartment overlooking the Hudson, a neighborhood that had emerged from decline and had reached a new phase of gentrification and value.

Their joint calculation also assumed that he had blown about five million on the failed careers of his progeny. He had invested in almost all of Scott's abortive business ventures. Scott, of course, had blamed his failures on luck and timing. Courtney blamed her brother's financial disasters on his easy manipulation and general incompetence as a businessman.

He could, of course, have solved his financial problems immediately by going into his father's business. Courtney had always felt the reason for his refusal was stupid. It was pointless to linger over what they had done years ago. So they had stolen a few diamonds? Their father had never found out, and the money was desperately needed at the time. Long ago, she had closed that case.

She and her brother had helped in the salon during their teen years, mostly learning the intricacies of gemology. For herself, she was appalled at the way her parents bowed and scraped before their rich, pompous, and demanding customers.

Once, after a particularly sickening exhibition of fawning, she confronted her mother and lashed out at such a disgusting display of kowtowing before their wealthy customers.

"Business, darling," her mother had told her without rancor. "It is all about making the sale."

"For them it's all about showing off, using expensive jewelry to validate their self-appointed superiority. It makes me want to puke."

"You puke," her mother had snapped. "I'll take their money."

"It's all part of the strategy," her father had patiently explained, as if he quite understood how his daughter might interpret his sales performance. "There are insecure people who need others to validate their wealth and status. What better way than to hang a jeweled sign out and proclaim one's riches?"

"But you look like such a phony, Dad."

"How I look is only important to the customer. They are hungry for flattery, and what we sell here is not only for vanity but has wonderful esthetic value as well, like any piece of art. Gems are long lasting, immortal, and to many—as well as to me—quite beautiful. To recognize such enduring beauty requires an appreciative eye. People covet beautiful things, especially if they are rare and, as the slogan goes, 'forever.' So there are many components of their desire to possess and display gems on their person. You, my darling daughter, are looking through the wrong end of the telescope."

She had hoped his explanation would be more fatuous and hollow and enhance her reasons for hating their attitude, but he was too crafty and intelligent for that. Selling jewels had, after all, been his final career choice, and she was convinced that he truly believed in the esthetic value of gems and, of course, their financial worth. She couldn't be part of this business, whatever the potential rewards. She knew that was what her father wanted for Scott. Her participation was always optional.

"Not for me," she confided to her mother. "I could never. Besides, I have a different career plan."

"Whatever makes you happy," her mother had told her.

When her father saw her display of talent in her school performances, any suggestion of her getting into the business became moot.

"You're fabulous, Courtney," he told her after watching her as Lady Macbeth in *Macbeth*. "You were beyond fabulous in that famous blood-spot scene. Gave me the chills. You really convinced me, darling, that the lady had gone bonkers for what she had done."

He hugged her hard and kissed her on the cheek. It was, indeed, a happy, unforgettable moment for both of them. See, she assured herself, when such memories surfaced, there was a time when she was softer, truly loving, and really devoted as a daughter, especially when she was the center of attraction. Had she acted a part then? She would never be certain.

"Oh, Daddy, I'm so glad."

"You've got the stuff, darling. I feel it in my bones."

So much for bone feelings, she told herself, heading off to Hollywood after graduating from the New School Actors Studio where Brando went and Walter Matthau and many others who had become famous and celebrated. She did well at the studio, and her teachers told her that her professional destiny was assured. She had gone West with high hopes and the full support, financial and emotional, of her parents. She remembered her optimism and self-confidence as she stepped off the plane at LAX, ready to become an international movie star, a worshipped celebrity.

Despite all that had passed, she was still in the fray, beaten so far, but, as they say, unbowed. Besides, she was long past the point of no return. Becoming a star was the only thought that gave her sustenance. Fuck everything else! She was in thrall to an obsession, and she knew it.

"It's not the time or the place, Courtney," her father told her, when she had raised the issue of money during their moment alone at her mother's funeral after the relatives had gone. Scott, too, as always, escaping from any impending hassle or conflict had paid his respects and hurried away to Seattle where he lived. She had noted that it was as far away as possible from their old homestead in Manhattan—and far enough away from Los Angeles.

Her father's eyes were swollen with mourning tears, and his face was drawn and pale. He smelled of grief and perspiration, unusual for him who was always fastidious. Her parents had been inseparable, working together, their lives inextricably bound up by their business and their children. She could not remember mean words between them, and there was no question that they cared about her and her brother and harbored real aspirations for their happiness and success.

Unfortunately, Scott's situation was far more defined than hers. He would not be let off the hook so easily. As a male, he was the heir apparent to the business, and although he recognized his being groomed for it, he had come to fear and detest it even worse than she did. In the end he had totally rejected it.

For years it had been a bone of contention between them. Often, in the intervening years, during their rare phone contact he would bring it up, always with the same repetitive whine.

"I can't get it out of my mind, Courtney. Doesn't it ever bother you? What we did?"

"Stop dwelling, little brother. It's long over."

"Do you think he ever knew?"

"Done. Over. *Finito*. Give yourself an exorcism."

"You are one tough bitch, Courtney. I wish I had your balls." His weakness exasperated her.

These infrequent conversations always ended badly, abruptly.

It was February and from the window of their high apartment, the Hudson looked like black slate polished by the light of a full moon. A moaning wind filtered through spaces in the old window fittings. A maid had just finished the cleanup of the dining room table and had left the apartment. It was only Courtney and her father now, the perfect moment, she believed, to make her carefully rehearsed pitch.

"Dad, Mom's gone, it's only the three of us now. I need help, real tangible financial help."

"Please, Courtney. Not now. I'm in no mood for this."

"I'm leaving in the morning, Dad."

"Please."

"Dad, if you love me, you'll listen."

"Really, Courtney. If I love you? Of course, I love you. How dare you make such a statement! Please, darling. Please. Spare me this now. We've just buried your mother. I beg of you. Leave it alone now. I am too paralyzed by grief. Perhaps in the morning."

"Now, Dad," she insisted. "We need to talk now. You can't evade this anymore."

She could see him trying to overcome his reluctance to confide, but she pressed on until he yielded.

"You can't shut me out."

"Shut you out? What are you inferring? Please, Courtney. It's time you faced reality. You've been at it for years. It's not happening, darling. I wish it had, believe me, I would have given anything to make it happen for you. I did my part, happily, as any loving father would. Surely, I don't have to remind you...all those years of trying. I understand, believe me, I understand. For your own sake, darling, you must give it up before it destroys you."

"My dream is ageless, Dad," she had countered, feeling agitation rise up inside her.

"I've enabled that dream. No more, Courtney. I honestly feel that I'm contributing to your...your frustration and unhappiness. What kind of a life have you made for yourself? It's no sin to be a failure. You learn from it." His words broke off, and he shook his head and put a hand over his eyes. "Please. Not now."

Between the lines, she was reading his real meaning. She hadn't married. Her relationships had been sporadic, disastrous, and costly. She had problems with alcohol and cocaine but had miraculously escaped total dependence."

"You believed in me once, Dad."

"Of course, I believed in you. I love you, darling. But I can't go on doing this...for your sake. It's not the time, Courtney."

"No matter what," she cried, ignoring his entreaty. "I'm sticking with it," she said firmly, with conviction and finality.

"Please, Courtney," he pressed. "I can't cope with this now." Despite his grief and vulnerable condition, he was holding firm.

"So it's tough love, is it?"

"Call it whatever, Courtney. I just can't handle this now."

"What am I supposed to do?" she persisted. "Become a permanent serving person, more commonly know as a waitress? I'm your daughter, for crying out loud. We're a family."

Roll out the guilt, she thought, spurring herself onward.

"I've done a great deal," he murmured. "It hasn't helped."

"I'm your child."

"That won't work anymore, Courtney." He was obviously growing irritated and impatient. "Honestly, darling," he shook his head and sighed. "If you want, you can still work in the business. Make a real living, have a good prosperous life."

"That again. No way."

He had paused, sucked in a deep breath, sighed again, and shook his head in a gesture of despair. She knew he was weary with grief and unhappiness but pressed on, hoping that his vulnerability would help her gain her goals.

"It's a wonderful business," he said, with what seemed like a sob in his throat, "and it has been very good to us. If you came into it and informed yourself about it, you would love it. I'll start you at a good salary and pay for your education to become a gemologist. You could take mother's role. She was a fabulous helpmate." The sob reached the surface, shook him for a moment, and his eyes watered. "How will I survive without her?"

Show compassion, she urged herself. Be cautious. Guilt him.

"I'm sorry, Dad, you know that the business is not for me." She had heard it all before. "You know my hopes and dreams,

Dad. Acting is my life, my art, my passion, my only ambition—"
She halted her explanation. She was repeating the old worn
argument.

He shrugged and looked at her with tired, watery eyes.

"My poor dear daughter," he sighed. "You're ruining your
life on a dying dream. I'm so sorry. By now it should be obvious
to you."

"What should be obvious? Are you saying I'm a loser with
no hope of ever making it in my chosen profession? What is
life all about anyway? This is what I want, and this is what I will
never stop pursuing. I don't need your goddamned negativity."
She raised her voice. "I need your support, damn it."

Anger was boiling to the surface.

"This is not the time, Courtney."

She felt herself losing focus, stepping out of character. Anger
was becoming rage.

"I know what you're thinking. That I have no talent, that I'm
a fucking failure." Her voice rose further. "Sorry, Dad. I believe
in myself and my talent. I don't care what you think. I know my
destiny, and nothing will keep me from it."

"I know you have talent, darling," he sighed. "You have a
wonderful talent, but it's not enough. To succeed you need luck."

"I know what I need," she exploded. "I need money, you silly
old man. That's what I need. Money to sustain me until I get my
lucky break. It will come. I know it will. I feel it in my bones." She
paused, trying to find her way back to her performance. "You
deserted me, that's what you did." She began to push it. "What
a lousy father you've become! Why are you making me beg?"

"Stop, Courtney." He raised his hands, palms up. "I'll write
a check."

It was working, she thought. He had always responded to guilt, and in his present state, he was fragile and yielding. Her performance was paying off. She immediately switched to a more sympathetic emotion.

"I'm so sorry, Dad, really I am. Please believe me. I hadn't meant to be so…so unfeeling. It's just…well, I am in need." Had she gotten through to him at last?

He thought for a moment, his face grimacing, swallowing hard. She studied his expression.

"What I'm asking for is a regular stipend," she said, calculating. "Something I can depend on. I'm working hard on this, Dad. Believe me. I'm committed. Why go through this? It will be off your shoulders, and I'll never ask you again. I promise. Never again. I love you, Dad. Really I do." She had grown suddenly hopeful. "Cross my heart."

He was silent for a long moment, and she watched his face as he shook his head. Had her performance been over the top? Or had she hit pay dirt?

"I will write a check for ten thousand."

She was stunned by his offer.

"Ten thousand?"

He sighed, shrugged, and turned away from her gaze.

"Shit," she blurted, feeling her rage begin. "What a cheap bastard you've become! You have plenty. Millions."

"Don't count my money, Courtney."

Finally her rage broke through the barrier. A hot flush seemed to erupt in her entire body.

"Ten thousand! That is so fucking stingy. So fucking cheap."

He closed his eyes. His complexion had become chalk white.

"Thank you, darling. What a wonderful thought on the day of your mother's death."

She felt herself out of control now, totally out of the loving-daughter character she had played earlier.

"I'll tell you this," she said, her voice rising, "Mother would not have treated me like this. She was a lot more generous than you were. Only you wouldn't let her be financially independent. You kept her in financial prison. If she had control of it, she would have given me what I needed."

He shook his head again in resignation.

"Suddenly your mother is important. Where were you when she was suffering, my dear daughter? You belonged at her bedside during those last days. You've become hard and indifferent. What happened to the loving little girl I used to know?"

"And what happened to the loving father I grew up with?"

"Why now?" he whispered, his eyes raised to the ceiling.

"It's as good a time as any." He had always been a sucker for what was allegedly the truth. If he knew the real truth, he would blow his cork. "It's time to tell the truth."

Truth had been his mantra. *Never lie, sweetheart*, he had told her repetitively. As long as we tell each other the truth, everything will be all right. She waited for his reaction.

"All right then, Courtney. The truth of it is that, for whatever reason, you're not making it. I'm very sorry about that, sick at heart if you must know. I would have given anything to make it happen. I gave plenty. Now you're getting older. You have no husband, no family. I wish it were different, but it isn't. I tell you this as someone who loves you—"

"Get a life," she snapped. "Is that what you're telling me?"

"Give it up, Courtney. It's destroying you. It may have already. You can't live like this. I am your father, and I love you but…"

"Bullshit," she had shot back, all pretenses gone. "How can you give me that crap? I am your child, your blood. How can you ignore my needs? I need money. I can't make ends meet. What do I have to do to get your attention? I thought parents were to provide for their children. You've deserted me. Hell, you've got it. Why not share it now? Why do we have to wait until you're dead?"

Her voice had reached the edge of hysteria, but she would not avert her eyes from his. His face showed his hurt. His lips trembled, and a nerve palpitated in his jaw. She knew she was inflicting pain. She hoped so, but she was determined to have it out once and for all, to say what was on her mind.

"I don't understand it," she persisted. "Why are you hoarding your wealth? What purpose does it serve? You have two needy children. Why withhold what you have? It's disgusting, controlling."

If she was trying to bait him, it wasn't working. He seemed too exhausted, obviously bruised badly by her mother's death and the long period of her illness. Yet she could not summon up any remorse for her conduct and her words. She wanted to tell him how much she hated him but held back. Stay on the guilt track, she urged herself, calming.

"You wanted the truth," she muttered.

"If you were a parent, Courtney, you would understand. I did give you plenty of money, and it went down a rat hole. You sold your condominium, and I put an enormous sum into that failed—"

"Not that again, Dad," she interrupted, raising her hands. "That's history. It was a business decision, and we all lost. It happens every day."

"A business decision?" he remonstrated. "I know the difference between a business decision and an emotional decision. I supported you. I showed my devotion and my love, yes, my fatherly love, in a most tangible way. I put my money where my heart was."

"That's all you think about. Money. You know how that makes me feel? Like a commodity."

Again he sighed with resignation and ran his fingers through his still-thick, steel grey hair, shaking his head in a gesture of hopeless surrender.

"What's the use? You just don't get it, Courtney."

"I get it all right," she snapped back. "My father is a miserable miser."

"Name calling? Is that what it comes down to?"

Her rage was breaking through his despair, and she sensed that there was nothing she could do to stop it. It was time, she thought, for giving him both barrels of her rage.

"You are a shit, Dad, a fourteen-carat shit. Tell me, are you planning to ever use that money you've squirreled away?"

"You're right about one thing. It is *my* money. Not yours. Your mother and I worked hard for it, and I'm not dead yet."

She had the feeling that he was husbanding his energy for one last gasp.

"Why must you hurt me like this? I am so disappointed in you, Courtney. I used to be so proud. Now what I see before me

is a bitter, angry, desperate human being with not one vestige
of feeling left in her soul. I can't believe you are my daughter.
Your mother would have been appalled and disgusted by your
remarks. She was the greatest advocate for her children. Half for
each. She had insisted that our will give you each equal shares.
Tell you the truth, I've kept that promise. No other behests. I
will honor my pledge to her. And you weren't there when she
needed you in her last hours. She always defended you, and I
am baffled that you could have stayed away during her last days.
Your name was always on her lips. Now I'm glad you were never
there. You spared her the knowledge of what you had become."

"She was your flunky. You used her."

"My God! I don't believe this."

"You will someday," she blurted.

A new thought had emerged. She had bungled her role, but
she was sure he got the message. Perhaps in time, she hoped,
he might find his guilt again.

The echo of that confrontation had never disappeared from
her thoughts since. Spent, frustrated, and angry, she had left him
and gone to bed in her old room redolent with memories, some
of which she dared not dredge up. It was a troubled sleepless
night and in the morning, unable to summon the grace for an
apology, she crept out of the house like a retreating thief.

But any vestige of remorse quickly dissipated, and by the
time she reached Los Angeles and her dingy studio apartment,
her anger had returned. She had, she knew, drawn her line in
the sand. When the check for ten thousand arrived in the mail a
few days later without a note, she was furious. She took it as an
insult, a slap in the face. She cashed it, of course, and in defiance
used some of it to treat some of her fast-track acquaintances to

a bacchanalian orgy of alcohol, sex, and drugs in her apartment, labeling the episode as an act of vengeance against her father.

***

Such memories rumbled through Courtney's mind as they moved upwards along the trail, with Bubba occasionally losing concentration and falling behind, which meant that when he regained his moorings, he would gallop forward to fall in line with the others. This sudden movement had a similar affect on her, and suddenly she, too, regained an interest in her surroundings, and the horses moved forward.

As they ascended, since the trail led ever upward, but never below eight thousand feet, she began to see some of the permanent residents of this alien world. A bull moose looked at them curiously from a stream where he was taking refreshment. A fawn darted away after observing them for a few moments. Harry passed information behind him, pointing out red squirrels and what he called pocket gophers. Lifting his arm, he noted a bald eagle in graceful pursuit of a midmorning meal.

They forded streams and moved through meadows and forest areas where signs of the big fire of 1988 remained. During these passages through blackened spires, Harry offered lectures on how the area was regenerating, pointing out fireweed, spirea, snowbush, and lapine, names that barely penetrated her consciousness.

"Look how high the lodgepoles have grown. Hard to believe this area was burned to a crisp years ago. Nature always wins."

For brief moments, as Courtney's memory of the earlier trip expanded in her mind, warm sentiment began to poke its way through the ice of her rage, and she found herself longing to return to that time when hope and optimism still had strong currency.

Unfortunately such pleasant feelings were transitory, and her thoughts returned to the single-minded focus of her life. Whatever the difficulties, she would submit cheerfully to her father's whimsical attempt at rebonding with his children. Keep your eye on the money, she told herself.

Chapter 3

————⟫◆⟪————

At one point after about three hours on the trail, the first mule on the pack train refused to cross a stream. Tomas dismounted, grabbed the lead, and pulled hard to get the mule to move. Filling the air with angry Spanish invective, he could not get the mule to budge. He pummeled his rump and kicked the animal's legs, all to no avail.

"Pull harder, you idiot," Harry muttered. "Fuckin' dumb Mexican. Pull the sumbitch."

Although he seemed to be making an effort not to be heard by those mounted behind the mules on the other side of the stream, his voice carried.

The more Tomas strained, the more he kicked, the more stubborn the mule became.

"Donno shit," Harry said, cursing under his breath. He jumped down from his horse and roughly pushed the Mexican out of his way. Tomas slipped and landed with both feet into the stream. Recovering, he moved back onto the bank, his pants wet to the knees.

"He 'fraid to move," Tomas said.

"I told you to put him in the rear," Harry muttered. "Stupid ass fuck."

"You tole me put him in front, Señor Harry."

"You calling me a liar, dumb spic?" Harry spit out, between clenched teeth.

"No, Señor Harry," Tomas said.

"Brains in your ass," Harry mumbled. "Bring the others up," he ordered. Tomas stepped into the stream and managed with some effort to get the two mules behind the stubborn one to move forward.

"What's happening?" Temple called from the rear.

"Young mule won't move his ass," Harry shouted. He watched as Tomas led the two mules across the stream, leaving the stationary mule standing in the stream.

"Now what?" Scott asked.

"See if he'll follow the leader," Harry said, pulling on the mule's lead. Tomas attended to the two mules, making sure the burdens they carried were secure. It took the better part of an hour and much frustration on Harry's part to get the mule to finally move. "Dumb as shit," Harry muttered, throwing a glance at Tomas, as if he had been the cause of the situation.

Scott watched, noting that Harry's treatment of the Mexican was both mean and racial, despite his earlier remarks on Tomas's qualities. It struck a sour note and from the expression on his father's face, a predictable reaction of disgust. Repeated instances of such conduct would trigger his father's zealous liberalism and could switch emphasis and derail the prospects of a happy outcome for himself and his sister.

It was bad enough that he was a reluctant participant in this repeat trek through the wilderness, however abridged, but he could do with less extraneous baggage. Yet, despite the loathsome hardship and discomfort that lay ahead, Scott could not deny the ultimate goal, if achieved, would be worth the suffering. All right, he agreed, twenty-odd years ago it had been a blast, but that was then and this was now.

His knees, weakened by basketball and jogging, were killing him. They were not more than three hours into the trek when he had to pop three more ibuprofen. He hadn't realized that his position on the horse would be harder on the knees than the behind. When his sister had called him in Seattle, he had confirmed his participation.

"I hated the idea but I sure as hell said yes," he had told her. "I assume you did as well."

"Of course. He put it on the basis of a family thing. You, me, and him, together in the wilderness."

"How do you read it?"

He was conscious of the old deference surfacing again, the inescapable first response behavior pattern between them. Resist, he warned himself, remembering what had happened when he got too close to the flame.

"He wants his family back, his two little kiddies. He's in reevaluation mode. Who knows? Could be the guilt thing has finally kicked in."

"What the hell does that mean?"

"Impending doom. Acting before it's too late. This is not out of the blue. He must have given it a lot of thought. He wants to recapture something of that earlier time."

"It seems pretty obvious."

"As long as it spurs him to open the old checkbook, I'm all for it," Courtney chuckled. "Despite all the wilderness bullshit."

"Seems a long way to go. Not exactly creature comfort–friendly. But if it does the job, I suppose we should take the medicine."

"That's what I say," she said with a giggle. "It came as a shock, hearing his voice after four years."

"Surprise, surprise. I thought you two were over."

"Blood is never over, brother mine," she said, then began a long pause.

Scott guessed she was giving him review time, offering blanks instead of words. Although they communicated sporadically via e-mail and telephone, he hadn't seen her since his mother's funeral.

Then she spoke again.

"Whatever the reason, I figure he needs this shot of nostalgia to get in touch with his sense of paternity. Maybe make tangible amends."

He knew what she meant.

"Maybe. But then, you've got to admit that both of us have gone to the well too many times. Look at it from his point of view. He's got two losers for kids."

"Same old Scott," she shot back. "Life on the downside. Grow-up time, Scottie. And speak for yourself. I'm still in play, kiddo."

He ignored her rebuttal. He knew better than to argue, knowing her obsession with stardom and celebrity was still very much intact, and her burning ambition was as hot as ever. But then his motives were different, weren't they? Years of therapy hadn't quite worked it out. He had tried for years, by distance and thought control, to extinguish her influence on his life, a futile effort.

"Hell, I thought this last time I was on my way," he continued. "My dot-com was rolling up pretty good numbers, then bingo, the bottom fell out. How do you tell a guy that put up millions that it wasn't my fault?"

"It's never your fault, Scott."

"Shit, look who's talking!"

He hated her in this mode.

"Hell, Scottie. You could have avoided all this crap by just going into the business. Make a bundle. You still can."

"I'd rather cut my wrists."

He had thought often about doing just that.

"Better than the bankruptcy courts," she muttered.

"Do you have to?"

"Sorry."

"I have a talent for bad timing. But I'm not over yet. In fact, I'm noodling a new deal. No more high tech. Restaurants. Food. Basic industry. Everybody has to eat. It's a small chain of Italian restaurants, very viable. I can get in for about a million five and paper."

"I don't want to hear it, Scott. I've been listening to your pipe dreams all my life."

"Don't start, Courtney. No heavy stuff, remember."

"Ditto. No heavy stuff."

She had promised years ago to keep the past between them sealed. He felt a brief nag of memory of their puberty games, then let it pass. It was too precarious.

"Are you in shape for this trek, Courtney?"

"In shape? Story of my life. I work out two hours a day. Hell, got to look good for auditions."

"Not me. I'm showing wear, little sister. Bad habits. Booze, smoking, overeating. Tension and pressure." He sighed and felt himself falling into a pit of self-pity. He tried to visualize her face. Years ago there was an eerie resemblance between them, two peas from one pod.

"It was tough going if I remember. Ten days. For city slickers like us, it was hard but…," she paused, "…unforgettable."

He knew what she meant and quickly changed the focus.

"You think he can hack it? He's really pushing the envelope. Hell, he's nearly eleven years over the guide's age limit for the trip."

"He always kept himself in shape," she said. "Walked a lot. Used the treadmill before it was trendy."

"He takes pills for blood pressure, remember," he interjected. "And the altitude. It's supposed to elevate it."

"His choice. Can't blame us if he…you know."

He knew what she meant.

"I can hear the applause," he smirked.

"That's my heart, Scottie, beating a victory march."

"You haven't got a heart, Courtney."

She let it pass and continued. "Grandma and Grandpa lived until their mid eighties, remember. He's got good genes. With modern medicine he could go into the nineties. Not like Mom. We never knew that side. They all died young. No, expect the old man to go on and on. Maybe even find a new lady."

"Good for him."

"Oh shit, you idiot. That's all we need, another hand in the honey pot."

"I'm sure he'd be smart enough to have a prenup."

"Prenup?" she giggled. "You seem familiar with the nomenclature. Are you considering a union?"

"Not on the agenda, Courtney."

Some of his relationships with women had brought him to the brink. But he could never take the final step. Therapists had provided what seemed like a thousand reasons. He had no desire to discuss them, especially with Courtney, the prime cause of his dysfunction.

"I'm not probing," she said.

"Good," he agreed. Under no circumstances did he want to open that Pandora's box.

"Maybe a new lady is the point of all this," she mused. "Got to be a good reason for his makeover. He's using remembrance of things past to announce his new tack. Tell his kiddies that he's got a Mom replacement. Who knows what guilt goes on in his bleeding heart? Some bitch gets her tentacles into an old dude, there goes the ballgame."

"If there is a ballgame," Scott said. "He might have cut us out."

"You've been in touch with him over the years. No clue?"

"If once every six months means keeping in touch."

"Maybe this is what this so-called adventure is all about," Courtney mused. "If it is a lady, we could be fucked, financially speaking." She added quickly. "But then, as you say, we might have already been cut out of the will or considerably diminished."

"And if we are?"

"There's always lawyers," Courtney said.

"Fuck lawyers. Could drag on for years."

"Of course, if he's got a lady, and she gets her claws into him, say bye-bye to the pot of gold at the end of the rainbow. All that pillow talk after you know what. There's Viagra today. Good sex will do it. Goes a long way."

The comment made his stomach knot. Leave it alone, he begged.

"When did you talk to him last, Scottie? I mean before he called about the trip."

"Couple of months. He never mentioned anything about a new woman. It was not, by the way, a very pleasant conversation. Not at my end. He refused to get involved in my deal, not that I can blame him. But he is, after all, our father, and it wouldn't break him to give me just one more shot. I'm afraid, Courtney, that we've run out the string."

"As long as he's alive ..." She paused for a long moment, cleared her throat, and continued. "Out there in no-man's-land, anything can happen."

"I don't understand...," he began, disturbed by the implication.

Then she continued the thought. "Especially to someone his age."

"Jesus, Courtney."

"It's pretty dangerous out there. And he's not as limber as he was twenty-odd years ago. You know what I mean? He could fall off his horse. And we're going on mountain trails."

"I'm sure he's given it lots of thought. He's been there before."

"So have we. Why choose a trek like that? Your ass on a fucking horse, shitting in a damned hole, cleaning up in water that is colder than a witch's tit in hell, sleeping stiff in a sleeping bag like you were a mummy, coyotes screaming in your ears all night, prowling grizzlies, lousy cowboy food, fucking wild animals everywhere, hungry predators, miles from civilization. Good God."

"He has his reasons, I suppose," Scott said. "Bring us together again. Bonding."

"Well worth it if he shows us the money. Great bonding material, money."

"You've got a one track mind, Courtney."

He had expected the conversation to be at an end. But then his sister began again.

"On the other hand, maybe he's going to tell us that he's been diagnosed with some rare deadly disease, and this is his way to kind of make a statement. A last hurrah kind of thing."

"You seem to be stuck on the subject of his...you know what I mean."

"Wishful thinking maybe," Courtney blurted.

While her remark was chilling, he wondered if he was seriously capable of entertaining such a cold-blooded thought. He was his father, for crying out loud.

"See you on the other side of hell, big bro," she said, hanging up.

Chapter 4

O n the drive to the trailhead, their father had confined his remarks to the glories of the digital camera, which he described as a miracle of technology.

"No more film, and you can instantly check whether you've got the picture right. Takes much better digital than the iPhone."

"I remember last time, Dad," Courtney said, determined to maintain a posture of approval and interest. "You took lots of great pictures."

"Yes, I did," her father acknowledged. "And looking at them always brings back happy memories. I get lots of shots out of this little baby. And if I don't like them, I wipe them out." He held up the camera. "Easy as pie."

"Good, Dad," Scott interjected. "I left my camera home. Old-fashioned kind. Not digital. I'm into happy memories, but I'm not much for the tangible kind. Often they don't tell the real story."

He looked toward Courtney, offering a sarcastic half smile. Despite his vow to avoid assessing her physically, he could not resist inspection. She was, indeed, in remarkably good shape. Her figure, accentuated by her tight jeans and shirt, which pulled tightly against her high breasts, remained youthful and sexy. Her hazel eyes, showing emerald green in the clear sunlight, were as startling as ever, and her high cheekbones and chiseled, straight nose gave her a haughty look, perhaps too haughty for the Hollywood version of female vulnerability. Abruptly, as he contemplated her Cupid's-bow lips, he ceased his assessment, feeling what he had repressed for years begin again.

During the process of matching rider with horse, Harry had checked each person's baggage for weight, noting that they were above his declared weight limit of thirty pounds per person to spare the mules. Scott had brought some heavy cartons of wine, and Courtney had admitted to carrying three bottles of Stoli. Their father declared a bottle of scotch, but after a brief lighthearted debate, they opted to leave other items behind and retain the beverages.

"Booze always wins hands down," Harry laughed, his unusually florid complexion suggesting his own obvious predilection.

As Harry saddled the horses and fiddled with the tack and stirrups, Temple shot a number of pictures, some posed, some candid.

Scott studied his father carefully as they mounted up. He looked reasonably fit, although he had needed help from both Harry and Tomas to climb into the saddle.

Earlier, on first meeting his father that morning, he noted that the man was his usual fatherly self, embracing them, as if nothing had occurred between them that had ruffled the paternal relationship. They were not baffled by his gesture, since he had always exhibited these demonstrative signs of affection, although Scott had noted that it did seem odd after a four-year silence to greet Courtney in a similar manner without comment about their long estrangement.

"You're looking lovely, darling," he told her.

"Thanks, Dad," she had replied. "You're looking very well yourself."

Both siblings exchanged glances, ignoring the obvious change of hair color and whitened, even set of teeth. On closer inspection, he seemed to look slightly different around the eyes, indicating unmistakably that he had had cosmetic surgery.

If their father noted their reaction, he ignored it. Scott was relieved at his affability. There was not a hint of tension or acrimony, and he appeared genuinely and sincerely happy to see them both. Scott admitted to himself that he was pleased to see how well he looked, and it was not without a brief pang of shame that he recalled any unkind thoughts he might have entertained.

It had always amazed him that, despite deep disagreements and heated arguments, his father never wavered from playing the role of the wise and affectionate progenitor. He had always been a doting, concerned, supportive father, and Scott never doubted for a moment that both he and Courtney were loved children. As they grew older, Scott sensed that his father might have thought of them as errant pets that had never been quite housebroken.

Scott had been very disappointed in their last face-to-face confrontation during one of his infrequent visits. He had come to New York specifically for the purpose of getting his father to invest in his new enterprise. The old man had refused.

"I'm sorry, Scott, I've done more than enough, far beyond the call of fatherly duty. Besides, a restaurant business is foolhardy, too labor-intensive and dangerous. Restaurants as a category are the most dangerous businesses in the world."

"And if it wasn't restaurants, Dad, would you back me?"

"That's not a fair question. I have backed you."

"I know, Dad, but that was when technology tanked, this time it's basic. Food. People have to eat."

"I'm sorry, son. It's too risky for you or any investor. Really, Scott, what do you know about the restaurant business? It's hard enough for experts."

His statement had an air of finality. A wall had risen that, Scott knew, would not be easily breached. Besides, his earlier bankruptcies made it impossible to secure credit.

"Are you trying to force me into your business, Dad?"

"No, but it will always be an option. Besides, I'll never understand why you haven't come in. It will be yours and Courtney's some day."

Scott could never reveal the real reasons for his refusal.

"I guess you've lost faith in me."

"You're my son, Scott. I love you, but I'm convinced that going down this new path will only hurt you more, not help."

"I don't agree, Dad. It's a great deal."

"Maybe so. But I won't back it. Believe me, to refuse you is painful for me. But I'm sticking by it."

Before, when Scott had approached him for other investments, he had not even required any pro forma or financial justification. That phase of his support was obviously over. The conclusion of this interview was not very pretty.

"I can't understand it, Dad. I'm your son. You're in good financial shape. Don't say I'm counting your money, just observing the obvious. All I want is a little help. Frankly, I think you're being cheap. What the hell are you going to do with your money? Sure, I'm very, very disappointed in my track record. But hell, who could have predicted the technology meltdown?

Not every deal works. You're a businessman. Someday I'll click. I know I will. Who else would you back if not your own son? You say you love me. I'm not sure. If Mom were alive, she'd be in my corner."

Nothing seemed to move the old man. He stood stubbornly to his conviction. But unlike Courtney, Scott had not closed the door completely. He told himself he was being more practical than his sister, betting that his father's decision would one day be reversed. He hoped that this experiment with bonding might achieve such a reversal.

Seeing his father that morning convinced him that however strained their relationship, the old man had not cut the ties that bind. Nor had his son.

The ties that bind. Scott mulled its meaning. At times, early memories of his childhood, warm happy memories of loving family life would surface. Little vignettes like sound bytes on a television screen would intrude on his mind: clutching Dad's warm hand as they walked through the Central Park Zoo, cuddling in the safety of his parents' bed to dispel the horrors of a sudden nightmare, the sweet pleasant aura of his mother's perfume, parental embraces, words heard around the dining room table, the reassuring timber and tone of his parents' voices, the distinctive taste of his mother's cooking, household smells, the view from the window of his old room, familiar pictures on the wall, his father's proud face when he dumped a basket at a high school game, and echoes of his father's praise, pride, approval, and admiration in his modest childhood achievements.

They were mostly images and memories of life before puberty, when separation and secret treachery began.

He felt transient sensations of a child's love and would often be baffled by their enduring power, no matter how divisive their present differences. When his mind drifted to such memories, he tried gamely to exclude them and perhaps summon up the level of his sister's antagonism to his father. He could not. The memory of his disloyalty and dissimulation was too much of a barrier. His guilt was too overwhelming.

After about five hours on the trail, they stopped in the shade of a stand of poplars near a stream, dismounted, and after their father shot more pictures of everyone including the horses and mules, they sat on a fallen log and ate their lunch. Scott's knees ached, but it did not affect his appetite as he devoured the roast beef sandwiches Tomas had prepared and washed them down with water from his flask. They were also provided with Milky Ways, Snickers bars, and nuts.

During the lunch break, Harry refreshed their memory on the mysteries of the ceramic filter, which was designed to strain the giardia virus from the waters of rivers, lakes, and streams. The virus was spread by animals and could make one permanently subject to cramps and diarrhea, although Harry, who acknowledged drinking directly from the crystal clear water of the mountain streams, had remarked with a chuckle that he found a heavy dose of bourbon could be equally effective, although he was quick to point out that it was definitely not recommended for his clients.

The reek of spirits that clung to the outfitter and his florid complexion were further proof of Harry's frequent use of this remedy. Scott hadn't remembered any suggestion of hard drinking during their last foray but acknowledged that twenty years had made a big difference in all of them.

The mechanical ceramic gizmo took thirty-one hard hand pumps to fill a one-pint flask, but the effort was a necessity since dehydration was an equally serious problem at high altitudes, and the limited water supply carried in by horse and mule would quickly be depleted. The demonstration reminded Scott of the hardships that were still to be endured on the trek, a depressing prospect for someone as out of shape as himself.

"Gorgeous, isn't it?" his father said, his eyes roving the landscape to observe the carpet of wild grasses and the vast forest of evergreens, poplars, and shaking aspens that edged the meadow. Looking upward, he shook his head in admiration of the white cottony puffs of clouds gathering against the background of the cerulean blue sky. He hoped such weather would hold, although the longer-term weather report called for rain.

That first trip through the West had been his father's idea as well. He had characterized it as an obligatory educational trip to see parts of the country radically different from city life in New York. He characterized it then as a broadening experience.

Earlier in Courtney's and Scott's preteen life, their parents had taken them to Europe, Mexico, and the West Coast. Always, they had considered these family trips educational opportunities for the children. Always for the children. Their parents during those early years rarely traveled without their children. Both Scott and Courtney, eager frisky teenagers with exploding hormones, had welcomed the earlier Yellowstone trek with great anticipation. The family had flown to Jackson Hole, hired a car, and proceeded to West Yellowstone.

Their mother, who had never shown any inclination to outdoor adventure, took to it with surprising gusto and good humor. At their last meal around the campfire, she was voted Miss Congeniality by the family, complete with a burst of applause that echoed through the canyons. The recall brought a surprising film of tears to Scott's eyes, and he turned away to hide its effect.

Going over Eagle Pass had been a particular trial for their mother, but she had been a good soldier, making the descent mostly with eyes closed, stiff with fear in the saddle, dismounting with effort as she led her horse along the dangerously narrow switchback trails. When they reached the valley floor, she had thrown up and vowed "never again." But they all acknowledged her as a genuine heroine, offering hugs and kisses of acclaim. The steep climb and equally hazardous descent along narrow switchback trails was often cited as "the worst few hours of her life," and she could always mesmerize guests with a blow-by-blow account, which grew greatly exaggerated by the passage of time.

His father had done considerable research to find the very best outfitter with the finest reputation. This turned out to be Harry McGrath, then the most experienced and expensive in the business. He was determined that the trek give his children a real taste of the hardships of the wilderness and the joys of an adventurous experience. It had easily fulfilled both criteria, although they had experienced it as far more profound than they had bargained for.

More than twenty years had passed since then, and there was no denying that a man in his seventies would have a tougher time than any of them. Chronology was chronology. Their father was indeed putting himself at risk. Courtney was correct in that assessment. Scott pushed her suggestive comments from his mind.

"Beats Central Park, Dad," Scott joked, determined to use banter to keep the atmosphere light and friendly.

His father nodded and smiled. Scott watched his nostrils twitch as he took a deep breath.

"The air is cleansing," his father said.

"And thin," Scott said. "Less oxygen to feed the brain cells."

"Not to worry, Scottie," Courtney chuckled. "Probably not much left for you to feed."

Courtney giggled at her little deprecating joke, and they all laughed. Their general attitude augured well. They were all behaving admirably, Scott observed, a good sign. He exchanged glances with Courtney who, catching the message, nodded agreement.

"Good idea, kids. Wasn't it?" their father said, a reminder of the way they had been addressed growing up.

"So far," Scott commented.

He called to Harry, who was checking one of the mules' legs. "How much longer?"

Harry looked at the sky. "Maybe six hours to camp."

Scott nodded. Six hours seemed like forever. He popped two more ibuprofen tablets.

"Off to the loo," his father said, getting up. Scott watched the old man move behind a stand of trees and then turned to Courtney.

"What do you think?" he asked.

Courtney shrugged.

"He's certainly in a good mood. He's enjoying the whole experience, holding up very well. Very fatherly, I'd say."

"He called us 'kids.'"

"I noticed."

"I don't know how to read it," Scott said.

"Augurs well."

Scott grew silent for a long moment.

"Considering, he doesn't look too bad for over seventy." Scott paused. Perhaps he was putting a better face on his father's physical condition than it deserved. "Probably eliminates the deadly disease theory."

"So much for optimism."

"Jesus, Courtney. That's pretty cold-blooded."

"Nobody lives forever," Courtney muttered.

"You're talking about our father."

"I know. He does have the power to change my attitude. He wants a loving daughter, he knows the price." She winked. "You, too."

"Leave it alone, Courtney. It makes me uncomfortable."

"That's your problem, Scott. Too many things make you uncomfortable."

Harry and Tomas had eaten quickly and were attending to the horses and mules and checking the saddles and horseshoes. Harry paused, lifted his canteen, and took a long drink.

"Booze," Courtney whispered.

"All we need, a drunken guide."

"Now that's something to be uncomfortable about."

Courtney shrugged with indifference. Suddenly she reached into her pocket and brought out her mobile studying its face for messages.

"Shit," she cried. "I forgot. No way to connect out here."

"Too bad," Scott said, chuckling.

"Shit. I don't think I'll be able to handle the withdrawal."
She held up the phone. "This is my connective tissue. How will
I know about auditions?"

"Will it matter?"

"What's that supposed to mean?"

"I mean out here. No auditions out here. Did it sound
sarcastic?"

"Bet your ass it did."

"I didn't mean it that way," he lied.

"Fuck you."

She pouted for a few moments and then sucked in a deep
breath.

"Truce," she said. "We're off on the wrong foot. We need to
portray a common front. No negativity. No sarcasm. Just loving
siblings. For the next few days, consider us in the ingratiation
business. We've got a mission here. Immerse yourself in Daddy
love."

"I'll buy that," he agreed.

They stopped their discussion abruptly when their father
returned. He sat beside them on the log.

"You should both take a pit stop," he said.

"Good advice, Dad," Courtney said, standing, brushing
the crumbs of her sandwich from her lap as she moved to the
privacy of the woods.

"The wilds are for boys," she said when she returned. "Just
whip it out and done. I forgot tissue. We'll smell like rotten fruit
in a few days."

"We can always wash in the streams."

According to the list of things to bring, they had packed
biodegradable soap.

"Freeze our asses off, remember last time," Courtney said. She cut a glance at Scott who shrugged and turned away.

"My turn," Scott said, getting up and moving into the forest, squatting against a tree to defecate, disobeying another of Harry's wilderness caveats: "Dig a hole first, then cover it up. Respect the wildlife."

He could never really understand what that meant. Hell, the wildlife shit in the woods without covering the mess, why couldn't he? He didn't, using leaves for tissue.

When he returned, Harry called on them to remount. Scott led his father's horse to the log, and both he and Tomas helped him up to the saddle, which he accomplished with some effort.

"Sits well," Harry said to them so that Temple could hear.

"Born on a horse," their father replied with a smile from his perch in the saddle.

"Lots of cowboys in Manhattan," Courtney said, laughing.

The mood was lighthearted, friendly. Scott painfully lifted himself into his saddle. Soon they were moving again. But after a few moments, Harry dismounted and moved to one of the mules. Tomas joined him, and they inspected the mule's leg.

"Better dismount," Harry ordered. They obeyed the order and waited beside their horses while Harry and Tomas unloaded the injured mule's burdens and shifted them partially to the other mules. The remainder was wrapped in canvas and raised by ropes to a tree.

"What happens to that?" Scott asked, pointing to the canvas in a tree.

"Mex goes back and gets it. Way it goes. He fucked up."

"How?" Temple asked.

"No problem for you, Temple. Just business. He don't mind. Right, amigo?"

"*Si,* Señor Harry."

Temple looked puzzled.

"Leave it alone, Dad," Scott urged.

"So what happens now?" his father asked, still obviously confused.

"We go to Plan B," Harry muttered. He moved to his horse and from under the cantle bag produced an object wrapped in canvas. It was a rifle. He took it and signaled to Tomas to bring the mule.

Then they led the limping mule further away from where the family waited. At that distance they could see the two men, but their voices couldn't carry, although they did hear occasional shouts and curses.

"What the hell is going on?" Scott said.

"Can't make it out," his father said.

But there was no doubt that an argument was ensuing. At one point, the argument grew physical, with Harry lashing out at Tomas, beating him to the ground.

"The Mexican is catching hell," Courtney said.

"He's mistreating the guy," their father said. "I don't like that. I'm going to talk to him."

"Don't, Dad. It's not our business."

"I still don't like it," their father said. "I don't like the gun either."

"He said he was armed," Scott said. "He told us why."

"Sure is a lot different than last time," their father muttered.

Soon the two men weren't visible. Apparently they had led the limping mule deeper into the forest. Suddenly a shot rang out. After a while Harry came out of the forest holding the gun. Tomas followed, his face expressionless. Scott and his father exchanged glances. His father nodded, silently acknowledging his son's advice. Scott signaled his approval with a returning nod.

"Not to worry, folks," Harry said cheerfully. "Mule's leg was lame. Had no choice. Dumb Mex fucked up on the packing weights. Let's mount up again."

"And the dead mule?" Temple asked. It seemed an extraneous question.

Harry chuckled.

"He'll be scattered bones by morning. Everything gets recycled out here. Now let's mount up."

Harry and the Mexican helped their father mount. Then they all mounted, and Harry rode up to the head of the train and led them forward. Tomas followed, leading the two remaining mules.

"He did say adventure," Courtney said. They looked toward their father who seemed somewhat depressed. Scott moved up and addressed him.

"I'm sure they know what their doing."

"I still hate to see the way he treats the Mexican."

"Come on, Dad. You're not the personnel department. Accept it. Not your call."

"He told me there would be two people to help him."

"For crying out loud, Dad. Leave it alone."

His father nodded.

"You're right, Scott."

Scott brought his horse back into line.

They threaded their way through deep forests, meadows, and ravines as the sun slowly descended. During July, Scott remembered, complete darkness didn't come until late, perhaps ten. The trek seemed endless. Even the horses showed signs of fatigue, stopping more and more frequently to nibble at the grass, despite Harry's cries of "don't let 'em eat."

At one point, Harry stopped the pack train, removed a pair of binoculars from his saddlebag, and held them to his eyes.

"There," he said, lowering the binoculars. "There's your first grizzly sighting. Do I deliver or do I deliver?"

He passed the binoculars to Scott. A grizzly was drinking from a stream. It looked benign, serene. Scott passed the binoculars to Courtney who put them up to her eyes.

"Looks like a teddy bear from here," she said.

"Don't let the big bastard fool you," Harry said. "Just stay the hell out of his way."

"I don't intend to pet him," Courtney said, passing the binoculars to her father.

"You do deliver, Harry," their father said, observing the bear, calmer now.

"That's a male," Harry explained, "the largest carnivore in North America. Always hungry. Cuts a wide swath. Needs lots of range. More and more of them each year. Endangered species, my ass. He's the boss in these parts. Hang the food high otherwise he'll pay us a visit, maybe take a piece of you as a hors d'oeuvre." He chuckled. "Just remember the rules."

"Who can forget?" Courtney muttered.

Chapter 5

After six more hours of what seemed like an endless journey, they arrived at their designated campsite, a flat area surrounded by aspens and evergreens. It overlooked a fast-flowing stream edged by cottonwoods and a trail leading down. The fire pit showed signs of other camping parties. Tomas dismounted, and he and Harry began to unload the mules.

Scott was barely able to take a step after dismounting. The pain in his knees was killing him. Above all, he didn't want to let on that he was suffering, determined to see through this adventure to the end, come what may.

Soon the mobility in his legs returned, and he was able to help both his father and his sister raise their pup tents under Harry's less-than-perfect tutelage. Not only did tents have to be pitched, horses and the two remaining mules had to be turned out and hobbled, gear had to be stowed, a latrine had to be dug—a decidedly primitive affair with a rope stretched tree to tree so that a person could hold on to something and not fall into the pit—and a "meat pole" had to be built so that food could be hung ten feet high so as not to give access to bears. Throughout the process, their father would pause occasionally to shoot pictures.

Scott noted that Harry barked orders to Tomas like a drill sergeant, using language that at times seemed harsh and abusive. Through the setting-up process, Tomas obeyed stoically, his dark face expressionless, unfazed by his bosses impatient orders and cruel taunts.

"Is that really necessary?" his father whispered to Scott.

"Part of their working arrangement, Dad."

"Master and slave."

Tomas, returning from digging the latrine, was quickly instructed by their father in the finer points of using his camera, and the family posed, arms around each other, while Tomas focused and clicked. It was apparent that Tomas had patiently accepted the instruction but had more than a passing knowledge of how the camera worked, probably gleaned from former clients.

After taking the pictures, he set up a grate over the fire now burning brightly in the pit and began to gather his ingredients for dinner, while Scott, Courtney, and their father sat together on a log drinking from metal cups filled from Scott's cache of red wine. Harry, perhaps respecting the privacy of the family, puttered around his own tent, which he had placed at a distance from theirs, crawling inside, possibly for a nap before dinner or some deeper sips on his liquor supply.

"To the Temple clan," their father said, reaching out with his cup. Scott and Courtney clanked their cups to his. They drank in silence, looking about them at the ruggedly beautiful landscape and occasionally observing Tomas at his cooking chores. The wine seemed to work its charms on their father, who grew increasingly mellow.

"I wish your mom was here," he sighed. "I think she would have loved being here again. Remember how good a sport she was, determined to make a go of it? That was your mom. She would never let any of us down."

"I'll buy that," Courtney said, a comment laden with irony.

"She was always there for both of you," Temple said. "Always." He turned toward Scott. "When you were three, you had asthma, Scott. Probably don't remember. She would sit up with you night after night to be sure you were breathing." He turned to Courtney. "When you began to date, Mom would never go to sleep until you got home. If you were late, it drove her wild with anxiety and worry." He shook his head and sighed. "Not easy to be a parent."

The man is reviewing his relationship with his children, Scott thought, reflecting, evaluating. It was a good sign. He looked toward Courtney who, despite her avowed purpose, was behaving herself, pleasantly nodding her understanding.

Scott had only the vaguest memories of his early bout with asthma, but the recall brought it to the surface and set him on a course of deep introspection. He felt the swift, mellowing effect of the alcohol, remembering that it worked faster at high altitudes. That, plus the changing glow of the fading light, seemed to cast his thoughts in an aura of warm sentiment, helping him to revisit pleasant childhood moments before puberty had intervened and created a stark new reality.

All in all that period of his life had been happy. The atmosphere in their spacious apartment was placid. He and his sister had separate rooms, and their parents were, in every respect, traditional and certainly loving. He could not recall anger, animosity, harshness, or conflict. Nor could he ever detect signs of dysfunction or any hint of what would transpire later in the lives of their children. They could be characterized as an ordinary, privileged, upper middle class family. He could recall no financial worries, although his parents did maintain a certain discipline about expenditures.

In retrospect, family life was, up to a point, tranquil, comfortable, hardly unique. He could not remember an argument between his parents nor could his mother be characterized as repressed. By all measures, they lived in a happy home. Scott knew he and his sister were loved children, and he supposed that neither had any doubts that they loved their parents nor seemed uncertain that they returned such emotion. The loving family bond was simply accepted, never questioned, debated, or analyzed. Like the air itself, it was simply there.

Scott studied the man resting on the log drinking wine from a metal cup and tried to imagine him as the father of that early life. Physically, the comparison was barely familiar. The once-jet-black hair had been chemically turned to rust brown. The face had become more rounded, with flesh that drooped around the chin line; the brown eyes seemed highlighted, now that the slack skin around them had been excised, although the shape of his eyes had changed. His skin was partially speckled and ravaged by exposure and chronology, and the back of his hands, the fingers of which could delicately hold the smallest gem, were mottled with liver spots.

Despite the encroachments of age, there was still a jauntiness to his carriage. He could be taken for at least ten years younger than he was. Despite his disappointment with his father's present financial stance, Scott could not deny the old feeling of attachment, the old bond. He was doubtful that this feeling was replicated in his sister, and it pained him.

"Remember what we voted her?" his father asked suddenly, breaking Scott's concentration. He quickly found the memory.

"Miss Congeniality," Scott mumbled, feeling the tug of loss, remembering. His mother had doted on him, and for a long time he had resisted her possessiveness. Upon her death he had grieved briefly, although, at times thereafter, he had been surprised to suddenly feel a sharp pang of loss, far more powerful than he had felt at her funeral.

Sometimes, images of her would surface in his dreams, inducing yearning and often tears. Scott wondered if the same feeling would surface when he remembered his father. Probably more so, one shrink told him, explaining that he had betrayed his father's aspirations far more than his mother's.

They held out their cups for refills, and Scott obliged, warning: "Be careful. It has more punch up here in the high altitudes."

"Hope so," Courtney giggled, already showing the effects.

She turned and watched Tomas cooking their meal. He was making some sort of elaborate concoction using onions, butter, red and green peppers, garlic and oregano, and sliced meat, which he simmered together in a pot.

"What is that?" Scott asked.

"Texicano elk," the Mexican said in accented English, deep in concentration as he stirred, tasted, added salt and pepper, and turned his attention to cutting up lettuce and cucumbers into a large salad bowl. Then he opened up a plastic bag of what looked like cooked beans, put them in a skillet, and covered them with shortening.

"I told you." Harry's whisky scent filled the air, announcing his presence. "Really knows hish cooking shit."

"Smells terrific," Courtney said, her nostrils dilating.

"Texicano elk, he calls it," Scott said.

"Only it ain't elk. It's mountain lion. Tastes better'n elk or beef. Fuckin' mountain lions all over the place. Screwing faster than the wolves. Tough immune systems."

"Good God," Courtney said. "Mountain lion."

"Will it make us roar?" Scott joked.

"Try it." Harry turned to Tomas. "Cut 'em a piece, Tomas." He winked and lowered his voice. "Some say it's better'n Viagra."

The Mexican cut a piece of cooked meat from the uncut portion and handed a sliver to each of them.

"When in Rome…" Courtney said, chewing. "Not bad."

"Shoot 'em, eat 'em. Right, Tomas?"

Tomas nodded, busy with his chores, his face offering little expression of acknowledgement. He doled out the meal, and they ate with relish and washed it down with wine. Tomas spooned out some refried beans and tortillas and carried them yards away to eat, sitting on a log by himself. They ate in silence.

"Am I right about the Mex's chow?" Harry asked.

"Helluva cook," Temple acknowledged.

"We'll sure make music tonight," Scott said.

"At least the performance will be in your own sleeping bag."

"It sure was good going down," their father said.

"What's the program for tomorrow, Harry?" Scott asked.

"Fly-fishing. Got rods and flies. We'll hit the Thorofare River. Cutthroats. Maybe some wandering brook trout if we're lucky." Harry burped, and Scott noted that he hadn't eaten much. Gets his calories elsewhere.

"How far?" Scott asked, thinking of his knees.

"Six and a half miles maybe. Two, three hours."

Harry stood up, slightly unsteady. "She you in the morning," he mumbled, and then moved toward his tent.

"Hope he can handle it," Scott said when he was gone, ignoring Tomas's presence nearby.

"Disintegrated since last time," Courtney observed.

"He was a responsible guide then," their father said.

"People change," Courtney said, looking pointedly at her father.

Tomas served them fruit salad and chocolate chip cookies for dessert and began puttering with the metal plates, which he packed in a net bag and brought to the edge of the stream for washing. They finished their dessert and watched the fire in silence.

"So what's life been like since…?" Courtney asked suddenly, her voice trailing off. She cut a knowing glance toward Scott, who understood. It was, he knew, a light probe.

"Not easy," their father sighed and then smiled. "The loss of your mother never really goes away, no matter what."

"It must be rough, life changing abruptly. It seems like you're coping, Dad," Scott said, struggling for exactly the right note of inquiry. "Any companions of the female variety emerge?"

Their father lowered his eyes for a moment, looked up with uncertainty, and grew silent, his eyes gazing into the still-crackling wood fire as if searching for his answer there. He seemed on the verge of an answer, but after a long pause it never came.

"You're still a good-looking man, Dad," Courtney pressed without subtlety. "Plenty of ladies would like to park their shoes under your bed."

"No one could take your mother's place," he whispered, as if it were a statement meant only for himself.

"Of course not," Courtney said quickly. "We were only thinking of your well-being."

Their father did not react but continued to gaze mesmerized into the still-crackling fire.

Scott looked at his sister with skepticism. Her pose of sincerity seemed too obviously manipulative. He knew she didn't mean it. Four years of shunning, he thought, and suddenly she's interested in his welfare. He doubted if his father was buying it.

"No special friend, Dad?" Courtney pressed, exchanging glances with Scott.

"I haven't exactly been a recluse," their father said, hesitantly.

"I should hope not," Courtney said.

"You have to make the best of what time is left," their father said, lifting his gaze and looking into the darkening distance. It was clear that he was holding something back.

"No one special?" Courtney asked, relentless now.

Their father shrugged, avoiding eye contact. He sipped his wine, then lowered his eyes again, and looked into the fire.

"I do see someone," he admitted.

Courtney shot an I-told-you-so glance at Scott. They waited for their father to continue. Neither he nor Courtney intruded on his reverie. Did he take them all the way to Yellowstone to make that statement, Scott wondered? More here than meets the obvious, he thought. Was this admission the purpose of this wilderness exercise?

In the silence they could hear Tomas washing the metal plates, which apparently interrupted their father's silence and drew his attention to the sound.

"I'm not happy with Harry's treatment of Tomas," he said, deflecting any further explanation of his private life.

"He's right about one thing," Scott observed, becoming a sudden ally to his father's privacy. "He works his ass off."

"Probably scared to death that Harry will turn him in to immigration," their father said. "I'm sure he pays him peanuts."

"Let's not get involved in his labor practices," Courtney said. "Not our business." She waited for a moment and posed the other subject of the conversation. "So tell us about this person you're seeing, Dad?"

"Believe me, children. It wasn't part of the deal with Harry. We did talk about two people. That's what I paid for."

"Don't think about it," Courtney said impatiently, bent on further interrogation.

Their father shook his head in disgust.

"I'd suggest you don't raise that issue again, Dad," Scott interjected. "We're in Harry's hands. No sense getting him pissed off."

"I suppose," their father sighed, again repeating the obvious. "Harry sure has changed since last time."

"Twenty-odd years make a difference," Scott muttered. He shot a glance at Courtney, who nodded her understanding. *He's not ready for revelation yet,* his gaze warned.

"Stinks like a brewery," Courtney said, looking toward Harry's tent. "He's not very sociable either. Not like last time. If I recall, he was gregarious, funny, and full of information."

"Maybe he's bored doing this over and over again. Who knows? He sure is not the same guy."

"He does know his wilderness. We can't dispute that," their father said.

"Maybe he just wants to give us privacy," Scott said, looking for justification of Harry's conduct.

"Or he prefers only the company of John Barleycorn," Courtney snapped.

"Life does bash people around," their father said. "Who knows what this kind of life does to people. He never told us much about himself. And that girlfriend on the first trek…they seemed quite happy together."

"People change, Dad," Scott said, not knowing what else to say.

"Maybe," their father replied. "I incline toward the opposite. I think people deep inside stay the same." He yawned suddenly and covered his mouth.

"Like your new lady?" Courtney asked cautiously, returning to the subject of her chief interest. "Just who is this someone?"

Their father was slow in responding, obviously reluctant to answer. Scott felt a sudden surge of resentment and admonished himself for the feeling. His long association with shrinks suggested an explanation. Poor guy thinks he is betraying his children by choosing a replacement for their mother.

Fucking shrinks, he thought. They overanalyzed with textbook bullshit. He had opted for the talking cure before surrendering to Big Pharma. Still, nothing could erase the old scars. Nothing. The truth is, if they were loving children, they should be happy for the old man.

He stole a glance at his sister. She was clearly pissed off.

"Why be so damned secretive, Dad? You might as well tell us."

They waited through a long pause. Finally, but with obvious reluctance, he spoke.

"A woman with our accounting firm. A widow."

"Great, Dad," Scott said, casting a pained glance at his sister.

"Older, younger?" Courtney snapped, like a lawyer interrogating a witness.

"Late forties."

"Robbing the cradle," Scott said, hoping to put a lighter spin on the conversation.

"Children?" Courtney pressed.

"Two. All grown."

His reluctance to say more was palpable. But Courtney was relentless.

"Is she attractive?"

"I think so."

"Does she have her own place?"

"Lives in Brooklyn."

"Does she stay over?"

"Sometimes."

"What does that mean?"

"Twice, three times. We spend weekends together."

"Nosey little bugger," Scott said, opening another carton of red wine. He refilled their cups.

"Keep this up, we'll run out before the trip is over," their father said.

"So this is serious?" Courtney asked.

"I don't see anyone else," their father said. He was obviously being remarkably patient, letting it happen, doling it out. He seemed uncomfortable and somewhat embarrassed by the revelation, but he did not balk at her questions.

"Are you contemplating a more permanent arrangement?" Courtney asked.

"We've talked about it."

"Is she, you know, independent? Comfortable?"

"She's a working woman. I told you an accountant with the firm I use."

"So she knows your situation?"

"Of course, she does. She handles my books."

"And you've talked about marriage?"

"I just told you. We've talked about it." He grew pensive for a moment. "Does it disturb you?"

Courtney turned to Scott. She seemed suddenly confused about how to reply.

"No...not really...I was just curious," Courtney said, faltering.

"We're happy for you, Dad," Scott said, determining that he had better intervene. "Your happiness is very important to both of us. Isn't that so, Courtney?"

"Of course."

Their father nodded, turned away, and forced a smile.

"It's your life, Dad. Anything that lightens the load. Not fun being lonely."

Scott's thoughts drifted away. It was one subject he could never confront honestly.

"I loved your mother with all my heart. She is not replaceable by anyone. Muriel understands that."

"Muriel. Is that her name?"

"Yes. And she's a lovely woman. And very smart, very intelligent."

"I'm sure," Courtney said. There was no mistaking the sarcasm.

"Nice to have someone that cares about you," Scott said, hoping his father hadn't caught his sister's intent.

"That's what I meant, Dad," Courtney said, shooting a rebuking glance at her brother.

At that moment, their father stood up.

"Got to see a man about a dog," he said, moving beyond the light of the fire into the darkness. They could hear the sound of his stream.

"We got trouble, brother mine," Courtney whispered, showing her anxiety. "Younger wife. Working woman. Grown children."

They heard Tomas returning from his dishwashing chores.

"That was a good meal, Tomas," their father said, returning, zipping up his fly.

"*Gracias,*" Tomas mumbled without emotion.

Temple stretched and yawned.

"Off to dreamland," he said, starting to go then stopping.

"I have a question, Tomas."

"*Sí.*"

"Harry's drinking," he asked. "Could it, you know, be a problem?"

"He be fine, Señor," Tomas muttered, puttering with his equipment.

Their father nodded, then blew kisses, and said goodnight. They blew kisses back, and when he crawled into his tent, they moved into the darkness out of earshot of Tomas, who had begun hauling leftover food up the meat pole.

"We got problems, kiddo," Courtney whispered showing her anger.

"Be happy for him, Courtney. He's entitled to a life."

"At our expense?"

"Above all, he's not stupid. I'm sure he's worked out a prenup."

"Don't be naive. An accountant, yet! You watch. He's vulnerable as shit. And she's got her own kids!"

"You're jumping to conclusions."

"Am I? Think of the pillow talk. Imagine the conversation. 'My kids are a couple of losers, always pushing for money. Pushing, pushing. That's all they think about.' And her reply:… 'They don't give a shit about you. Zip up the moneybag and cut them down.' Meaning save some for me and my kids."

"You sound like you're reading a script from a lousy movie. You don't know the woman, and you don't know the facts."

"True. But that doesn't mean my speculation is wrongheaded."

"You are one mercenary bitch, Courtney," Scott said.

"And you, little bro,…what are you?"

"I know what I am," Scott said, with a sense of sad resignation. His eyes met his sister's. "And I know why."

"Shit. Not that again."

She turned away in disgust.

They remained silent for a long time, listening to the night sounds, the rustle of the nearby quaking aspens, the distant whine of the coyotes, the grunts of the grazing horses and mules.

Above was an incredible canopy of stars, an otherworldly display in the moonless night. He could see the reflection of the stars, like pinpoints of light in his sister's eyes.

"We've got to do something," Courtney said.

He felt a sudden chill run through him as he caught the subtext of her remark. Despite the chill, he began to sweat. Rivulets streamed down his back.

"Whatever is going through your mind," he said, his lips quivering, "I don't want to hear it."

"It's your fucking future, Scott."

She moved away into the darkness. He could hear the patter of her stream. It reminded him of his own need. He did it where he stood.

Then they moved back in the direction of their tents. Suddenly in the near distance, he heard movement, horse sounds. By the light of the moon, they turned toward the path to the meadow where the horses were hobbled. They saw Tomas mounted, moving into the wilderness, a mule in tow.

"I guess he's off to pick up the load left behind in the tree," Scott said.

"Dumb bastard," Courtney said. "Working his ass off for that drunken son of a bitch."

Before she slipped into her tent, she stopped and moved closer to Scott.

"Think about it, Scott."

"Think about what?" It was a knee-jerk reaction.

"Dilution, Scottie baby. Dilution."

Chapter 6

George Temple lay in fetal comfort in the warmth of his sleeping bag, his nostrils tickled by the cool night air. He felt satisfied and proud by the way he had weathered the day. The altitude had not made him dizzy, and he was certain that it indicated his blood pressure remained under control, and he had his trusty pills secure in his toilet kit.

He had been concerned that his aging body might not hold up. He was eleven years beyond the outfitter's age requirements, but he had rigorously prepared himself for the journey with treadmill workouts, and weight lifting and stretching exercises under the tutelage of a trainer. Sure, he needed help to get into the saddle, but others a lot younger probably needed similar assistance. Scott, too, although he had eschewed help, was certainly unsteady mounting. He complained of his knees aching when he rode, and when he dismounted he limped for a while.

Nevertheless, Temple was exhausted from the long trip but oddly content. His mind filled with reminiscences of his early life with Bea and the kids. What they did not realize was that he saw them more in retrospect, as children growing up in their home, than in the present reality.

He could remember each of their tiny faces behind the nursery glass: Courtney bound in her pink blanket, then a couple of years later Scott in his blue one. Beside him was Bea in this mental image, his arm embracing her as they viewed what they had created: miraculous combinations of themselves, representing their mutual hopes and aspirations, their future.

Few events in their lives were more compelling and poignant. Their hearts swelled with love, joy, and wonder. Was it possible to convey to these grown children now what they had felt? Inducing the tiniest smile in their little faces was the greatest reward one could imagine for young parents. No sense of joy was ever comparable.

Wasn't parenthood a gift, the ultimate fulfillment of the married state? Nothing on earth, despite anger, disappointment, and broken dreams could break that natural bond. He had learned that lesson the hard way. His children had not turned out the way he would have liked, the way he and Bea had envisioned their futures.

What had they done wrong? It was sad and heartbreaking. They were—he had to admit the truth to himself—failures. Not only in a monetary sense but also as people. He could not find in them any sense of empathy. Scott had turned out to be weak and fragile. Courtney had become hard, self-centered, and mean-minded. How awful to conclude these things about your own children!

Worse, they had hardened his heart toward them. He had tried valiantly to excise the bond, stamp it out in himself, and this had brought him only debilitating guilt and unhappiness. The hard lesson was that it was utterly impossible for him to break the parent-child bond. He would love them until he died, no matter the circumstances, the betrayals, the disappointments, the disillusions.

His purpose now was to correct an action that had caused him deep personal pain. He had deliberately—perhaps, maliciously—cut them off from his financially supporting their ambitions. He had done this for their own good, he had assured himself, but the aftermath of that decision had tortured his conscience, and he needed to absolve himself from that guilt by restoring his support of Courtney and by providing Scott with the money needed to fund his restaurant deal.

He had maintained his promise to Bea to split his inheritance between both his children. Of course, now that Muriel was going to be a part of his life, he needed to tweak his estate plan. He would, true to his promise, split the estate for his two children up to the time he would marry Muriel. Any wealth acquired during his time with Muriel would be apportioned accordingly with Muriel's entitlement, expanded to include her. He had consulted estate lawyers on this issue, and one of the reasons for this bonding expedition was to explain that to his children.

It wasn't a betrayal of his late wife. By his accountant's and his lawyer's calculation, his children would receive no less than ten million apiece after taxes, a tidy sum by any measure. He wanted them to know this to prevent any undue litigation after his death. He had debated long and hard how he would handle this, soliciting advice from a number of lawyers. Some had objected to his revealing his intentions, but in the end he had made the decision to do so and had picked the moment: this new trek, a kind of repeat performance—although somewhat shortened—of one of the most indelible adventures of their family life.

It was, he knew, in his nature to be fair, ethical, and methodical. By cutting off his children, he had considered it a practical move hopefully to jolt them into reassessing their careers. Between them, they had already cost him in the neighborhood of eight million dollars, and neither had come close to attaining their goals. Okay, he conceded, this was tough love, but it hadn't achieved any result except to make both him and his children unhappy. Courtney had become totally alienated, and Scott had admitted suffering from some mental health issues. It was time to correct the situation and remove this heavy stone from his heart and hopefully from theirs.

Courtney's long silence was especially wounding, since he could have used her daughterly sympathy and attention during Bea's long illness and after her death. Scott, too, was less than solicitous. Neither filled the void of Bea's absence nor made any gesture that might help during his terrible bout of grieving.

As time went on, despite the occasional guilty feelings that visited him at times, his children's increasing alienation tended to add heft to his decision to repair it. He tried not to dwell on it, and he began to slowly come out of his mourner's shell. It was not an easy adjustment.

Friends tried to fix him up with single ladies, but he could not relate to them in any way. Some aggressive females managed to induce a half-hearted sexual response. At times he managed to fulfill their aspirations and on rare occasions his own.

His serious relationship with Muriel was accidental only in the sense that he had known her as one of his accounting firm's fellow associates who had often sat in on meetings in connection with his periodic audits and tax consultations.

Like all mysteries, she crossed that elusive emotional Rubicon purely by chance, her persona entering his consciousness by degrees. She was still in her forties, had experienced widowhood in her thirties, and after devoting herself to raising her two children, had settled in to a life of work and a pursuit of cultural interests in a circle of widows and other single women.

Her face was soft and round, with large brown eyes and a slightly upturned nose, full lips, and she had a large bust, which was her most obvious and sensual feature. She dressed primly in modest business suits that flattened her ample curves and gave no hint of what he later discovered was her erotic nature and of his own reaction to her sexual charms. To make her even more desirable from his point of view, she was standoffish and neutral, meaning she showed little or no interest in him as anything more than a client of the firm.

Since he was the product of a long marriage of over forty years with one woman and had, by then, long ago drained the cup of fervent sexual interest, he found himself surprised by the physical attraction that Muriel triggered in him.

At first, he dismissed any possibility of a mutual attraction. She was more than twenty-five years younger than him, an inhibiting fact of life. He was certain she would think of him as too old, although he was in good physical shape. He was also, by dint of his long marriage, awkward in the ways of dating and mating talk and too shy to make other than a business approach. He approached her as if he might need professional advice and finally managed to offer her a night out as an additional reward for her expertise.

It was quickly clear to both of them that this was more than a professional engagement. He chose dinner at Danielle, a pricey East Side restaurant, where he ordered an expensive wine, a purchase that Bea, with her overwrought prudence, would have rejected.

Muriel seemed to encourage this purchase, perhaps because she had knowledge of his net worth and knew that ordering it would not impact on his pocketbook. She viewed it as a special treat and signaled to him her interest in the so-called better things in life.

"I've always felt sort of deprived," she admitted candidly, explaining that she had been a working woman all her life and that her husband's health had broken early, and as a consequence, she had been forced to be the sole breadwinner. Clever with money, she had amassed a comfortable financial cushion. She lived in a spacious townhouse in Brooklyn Heights that she had purchased at a good price years ago, which in time added much to her net worth. It was clear to him early on that she did not covet Temple's money.

From the beginning, they enjoyed each other's company. His life with Bea was focused more on business than the cultural cornucopia that New York had to offer, although they did have season tickets to the symphony. Muriel broadened his interests, and they regularly attended the opera, Broadway shows, the ballet, and ate in the better restaurants. She liked travel but had not had the time for any long trips overseas or cruises, but she did admit her aspirations to one day fulfill this inclination.

But in a surprise to beat all surprises, she revealed a passion for sex in all its exciting variations, during most of which she was the ringmaster. It was a revelation especially since Bea had submitted more out of duty than pleasure, and he had never experienced any but the most conventional aspects of the act. At first, he thought it was playacting. She assured him that it wasn't.

She turned out to be imaginative and orgasmic, encouraging him to use Viagra on a regular basis, and kept him interested by invention and surprise. She admitted that the sexual flame flickered only briefly in her own marriage, and that she had a vivid fantasy life and various sexual toys that helped satisfy her needs. She had not been sexually active in her widowhood, fearing AIDS, although she had revealed a one-year affair with a married man.

As their own relationship progressed, she became unusually and refreshingly frank, not only on the subject of sex but also on every other issue that concerned her. She was totally open, emptying herself of the personal experiences that made the profoundest impact on her life.

Her openness encouraged him to a transparency that he had never experienced even with Bea. It was a revelation to discover how comforting it was to be open and honest about his feelings, the intimate history of his marriage with Bea, his souring relationship with his children, his concerns, worries, and fears.

For hours on end, they would exchange biographical information and deeply personal matters, conversations that bonded them psychologically and emotionally. The trust between them blossomed and grew. He became convinced that this was a manifestation of mature love and began to explore the idea with her of a more permanent arrangement.

It was not as simple as it sounded. Each brought with them the baggage of a previous life. Muriel's two children, although grown, were still building a future. The boy had followed in his mother's footsteps and had become an accountant. He made a decent living and was recently engaged. The girl was a newlywed who lived in Florida, where she sold time for a radio station, and her husband was a physical trainer.

He was, by far, the wealthier of the two. Muriel knew his multimillion-dollar net worth down to the penny. Each knew that in the event of a marriage—which had been discussed—financial arrangements had to be made, a prenuptial agreement fashioned, and other considerations attended to in terms of property that might be acquired during a marriage.

There was also the problem of age. It was a matter of statistical fact. The odds were that she would certainly outlive him, and he was duty bound to consider her future in the event of his death.

They discussed these issues frankly and specifically. He wanted her to eventually learn the intricacies of his business; take a course in gemology and—as Bea had done—work with him; and, perhaps, after changes in his behests, carry on the business upon his death.

She was reluctant to jump into such a situation, preferring to "test the waters" before full emersion. Even on that score, there was a complication. Despite their constant rejection, he still secretly harbored the possibility that one or another of his children would one day see the light and join him in the business.

More and more such a possibility was fading, although he continued to hold the option open. Would Muriel joining the firm foreclose on such an option? Both he and Muriel hoped not, but it did introduce a further complication.

He remembered his own initial reluctance to join the business and to pursue a vocation in music. But reality had intervened, and he had given in to practicality. Looking back, he had no regrets. He continued to enjoy not only the money the business generated but also the esthetic beauty of the product he sold and did not question at all the desire to display such beautiful adornments, regardless of the motive of the purchaser.

Eventually their range of "issues" centered more and more on the matter of inheritance. As an accountant, she had a great deal of experience with estates and the complex issues between survivors. Also, she knew the value of a dollar, and her long widowhood had made her very conversant with making ends meet.

As the sole support of herself and her children, she had juggled her finances with great success, providing for college tuition and making at least one shrewd real estate investment. If she stayed with the accounting firm, she would earn a decent pension and be financially worry-free when it came time to retire. He was hoping that she would leave the firm when they married. Besides, she would not need the pension because of his ample funds.

As business people, they both knew that such financial considerations had to be resolved before they could enter into marriage.

"I'm sorry, darling," she told him, "but I'm concerned about the aftermath of our marriage. We really need to dot the *i*'s on this to feel truly comfortable."

"I would do anything to make you secure and happy," he responded, as if the three little words would somehow transcend the issue.

"Then we have to put our houses in financial and emotional order."

"Meaning?"

"You've got to make it right with your children. You've got to continue to enable them and support their ambitions. It is tearing you apart."

"That's a switch," he told her.

"Yes, it is. But I want a happy man as a husband, friend, and companion. I don't know if I'll every make it with your children, but I certainly will try. I've learned in life that once you've been an enabler, you can't go back. There is no return road. And you've got to tell them how they'll inherit now that you've got a new wife. Believe me, Temple, in my accounting practice, I've seen families torn apart over money issues."

"It will be costly," he mused.

"You've got plenty, Temple. It's too unnatural," she told him.

"And the other. Telling them that I will make changes after our marriage to consider you…"

"Reveal everything and reconsider your current support. It's made you guilt-ridden. No matter how deep your disappointment in how they've turned out, you've got to provide for them in a manner that reasonably satisfies them, especially if we marry and I am in the picture. However we structure a prenup, I will have a claim on some of your assets upon your death, certainly those we acquire during our marriage. I know all this sounds awful when put into words, but it is an issue that must be addressed. You've got to redo the paperwork, darling, so that your children, however rotten they've been to you, will not cause needless problems. I don't want to spend my dotage in court. Besides, I know how much you love your children and how terribly guilty you would feel if you shortchanged them."

"You sound more like a psychologist than an accountant."

"You cannot go against nature," Muriel had advised him. "Reconcile. Give yourself peace of mind."

"What would you suggest?"

"Continue to finance their dreams, even if they come to naught."

"But for how long?"

"As long as it does not interfere with our future and our lifestyle. Besides, they will get it anyway at some point. Let's hope that is many years away."

"And your children? What is your prognosis on that, Dr. Freud?"

"My kids. I've got a multimillion-dollar insurance policy, and they are the beneficiaries. Besides, my children are doing extremely well. Let's do away with this worry and not let it create problems between us. What you need is peace of mind. If your kids blow it, so be it. Live with it."

"Won't be easy."

"Yes, it will. You will have done all you could for them. Instead of moaning, give yourself a psychic medal." She had dabbed her thumb with her tongue and pressed it to his chest. "I dub thee Father of the Century."

"I accept." He reached out and repeated the gesture with a squeeze of her large firm breast. Of course, he had loved Bea who had small breasts. Muriel's breasts were large and full. For him they were a sexual stimulant, and he lavished his pleasure on them, rejuvenating that urge. She had smiled and winked at the gesture, caressing his groin. Then she winked and got serious again.

"Hell, darling. I've been an accountant all my adult life. I've seen how money can destroy relationships. And don't expect gratitude. Somehow money does not spawn gratitude, and you can't buy love. Just do your Good Dad shtick and expect nothing in return. At least you'll have peace of mind and a guilt-free existence. You can't be responsible for what they do with their lives."

"That's the problem with parenthood. You created them and always feel responsible."

"Let it go, darling. We have our own lives to live." She kissed him then added, "Do they know the original plan? What you and Bea had decided?"

"Bea told them."

"Then they have expectations. Clarify it. Tell them everything. If they feel screwed, they will blame me."

"Why you?"

"They will think that I engineered the deal to get my hands on your money when you pass on to the great beyond. I don't want to live with that. You should resolve all this before we marry."

"What I give them now is sure to go down a rat hole."

"For once, stop being practical. Write it off as the cost of fatherhood. Why make everyone miserable? On the other hand, you may be happily surprised."

"I doubt it," Temple had told her.

"Then figure another few mil going south. I'm your accountant, remember? You can afford it. Besides, I don't want to go into my last chapter worrying about hassles. Besides, judging by how frisky you are in the sack, you may even outlast me."

"Blame Viagra and those big delicious boobs," he had laughed out loud in repetition of that reaction. In the night his voice carried.

"You okay, Dad?" Scottie yelled from his tent.

"Just laughing at an old joke," he replied.

It was Muriel who had suggested the trek as a perfect venue for the financial revelations, the idea being to recall happy times and reunite his family. He had regaled her with this episode numerous times, and there were pictures hung all over his jewelry salon and apartment.

He had fond memories of those halcyon lost days when the children were, well, still children, when they were loving and curious, when a simple grant of permission was eagerly and joyfully accepted as a reward for good conduct or special respect. God, he wished those days had never ended. Then they had morphed into adolescence, adulthood, and now maturity, but the most glorious memories remained locked in the days of their childhood. What he needed most was to break the cycle of parental pain, the scourge of hopes dashed, dreams broken, aspirations aborted.

Realization had been slow in coming but it had arrived finally, forcing him to react in a way that was anathema to his sense of the human aspect of business but not to the cool logic of reality engendered by Muriel's advice. He knew in his gut that throwing more money at his children was a bad gamble, requiring the suspension of his life's experience in the hard world of commerce.

It pained him deeply to acknowledge such an idea, but the facts could not be refuted. Both his children were dreamers, fantasizers. The odds, based on their pasts and their luckless endeavors, were against their attaining their unrealistic goals.

Nevertheless, the money issue became a central point in organizing their future plans and escaping the burdens of family disputes. She was right, of course. Her advice made a great deal of sense.

For weeks, he contemplated her suggestion. In Courtney's case, antagonism had grown deep and ugly. She had rejected any communication. As for Scott, their relationship was strained by Temple's refusal to invest in his new venture, another potential failure.

"Put it all up front, darling. I want a genuine family alliance. Not warring camps."

In the end, after much thought, he took her advice, respecting her wisdom and generosity. Unlike his children, he was lucky in his partner choices.

"Haven't I always taken my accountant's advice?" he told her.

"We're not just number crunchers, darling. We specialize in one of the Seven Deadly Sins."

"Which one?"

"Greed."

Again he laughed out loud, amazed at the clarity of his recall.

***

He booked Harry McGrath, the previous outfitter of their earlier trek, who was still in business. He had been wonderful that first time, and he felt lucky to get him.

Convincing both his children to accompany him had been a challenge, and he was delighted by their consent without too much of a hassle. He was encouraged by their concern for his health. Actually, he was in excellent physical shape. He had just taken a stress test and checked out normal on his blood work. Pills controlled his slightly elevated blood pressure. To bolster his condition, he upped his treadmill sessions and did stretching and weight lifting under the care of a trainer.

More and more as the time drew near, his excitement over the prospect increased. He became totally convinced that Muriel was spot on, that getting together with his children in such a nostalgic and isolated setting could provide just the right atmosphere for reconnecting. It was with some trepidation that he arrived in West Yellowstone, but seeing their faces, embracing them, hearing their voices, and experiencing their warm reception, quickly restoked the fires of fatherhood. He thanked Muriel in his heart and was certain he had made the right choice.

***

Despite the disturbing changes in his old outfitter, he was pleased by the reaction of his children. Both Courtney and Scott had related to him far better than he had expected, and he was careful to avoid any subject that might trigger controversy.

He hadn't planned to reveal his relationship with Muriel at this early stage, but they had pressed him and he was determined not to veer from the truth. He was careful not to gild the lily, making any comparisons that would imply any competition with their mother. He thought he had handled everything, including his revelation about Muriel, extremely well.

Finally he slipped into a dreamless slumber and awoke refreshed to another glorious day, with a rising sun painting the Absaroka Mountain Range in a golden mantle. With a jolt of nostalgia he viewed Colter Peak, which with very little imagination appeared as the image of a man lying on his back serenely watching the sky.

He recalled McGrath on their earlier trek explaining to them that Colter Peak was named for John Colter, a trapper who peeled off from the Lewis and Clark expedition to discover Yellowstone and brought back stories of its thermal springs and vast forests. The explanation, he remembered now, as he viewed the mountain in the morning light, included the mystical suggestion that the contours of the peaks outlining the image of Colter himself had a supernatural connotation. Seeing it again, he felt ready to believe it.

Tomas was already at the grate making the coffee the cowboy way, which meant you threw the coffee grinds on top of the water and proceeded to boil it. The rich aroma was a treat to his nostrils, and he knew the result would be the most delicious coffee he had ever tasted in the last twenty-odd years.

On a skillet Tomas was frying a rasher of bacon and beside him in a bowl was pancake batter ready for use and orange juice in cartons. The delicious aroma of both the coffee and the bacon was mouthwatering. Tomas poured some coffee into a metal cup and handed it to him. It was delicious and triggered in him an air of satisfaction and contentment. The world was a good place, he assured himself. He was happy he had come.

Harry, rubbing the blur from bloodshot eyes, seemed ravaged and sickly as he crawled from the tent. Temple noted that as soon as he was vertical, he upended his canteen and took a deep swig. As he drew closer to the cooking fire, it was quickly apparent by the odor that the contents of the canteen was not water. The sight of Harry changed his mood.

It was particularly troubling to see Harry in this condition, injecting a note of insecurity and danger that Temple hadn't banked on. They were, after all, completely dependent on his judgment and expertise in this wild country.

He debated whether to confront Harry at this point but decided to hold off, mostly out of fear that the outfitter's reaction would be hostile. Nor did he wish to bring the matter up with Courtney and Scott who might become fearful and apprehensive, which could put a damper on the whole experience. Temple did, however, offer hints of his irritation by his expression, although he couldn't be certain that Harry got the message.

Courtney emerged from her tent looking tousled and unhappy and without a morning greeting walked into the woods clutching a roll of toilet paper. It reminded him of her reaction to this lack of dainty creature comforts during their first trip. "Yucky" was they way she had put it, and Bea had seconded the statement but had soldiered on with good humor.

Humor, often self-deprecating and larded with the scatological, was one of the elements that made that first trip so memorable. Temple recalled an incident when his reading glasses had fallen into the latrine and had to be retrieved. When he recounted the anecdote, he had held up his glasses and declared they were "the shittiest glasses in existence."

Laughter, especially in memory, seemed to underline the entire experience. They would laugh at their urban ineptitude and the clumsy way they raised their tents, bitching each morning at the discomfort of the sleeping bags, the pains in the knees and butts, the stops and starts of the horses as they relieved themselves, the so-called whore baths in the icy rivers, the pumping of the ceramic gizmos, their low tolerance of bugs and mosquitoes, the endless griping and longing for creature comforts, and their perpetual whining about the joys of city life and the constant questioning of why they were there.

In memory, though, the griping had the quality of joy. It was celebratory, the source of many a happy anecdote that induced laughter. Where had all this elation and exuberant good cheer and family comradeship gone? This is what he most fervently hoped he would find again.

Scott limped out of his tent, grunting in pain, as he stretched his legs and quickly peed, aiming at the base of the nearest tree.

"Slept like a rolling log," he grunted, slightly hoarse, reaching out his hand for a cup of coffee. Tomas obliged. After a few sips, he appeared conscious of the aroma.

"Man, that smells good."

Tomas poured the batter in large circles, and they watched them turn into flapjacks. Temple marveled at the skill with which Tomas flipped them.

"Looks good, Tomas," he remarked. The Mexican, intent on his work, did not acknowledge the compliment.

"Told you," Harry grunted, taking another sip on his canteen. Tomas handed him a cup of coffee, which Harry brought to his lips with a shaky hand.

Courtney returned from her ablutions with a look of disgust.

"Hanging on a rope to do you know what is not exactly ladylike," she muttered. "I nearly slipped."

Tomas handed her a cup of coffee and began to dole out the flapjacks and pass the syrup. Harry barely nibbled at his and put his cup out for more coffee. Comforted by the coffee and flapjacks, conversation between the three Temples seemed to revive as they recounted their night's experience.

"Did you sleep well, Dad?" Courtney asked.

"Like deadweight," Temple said. "And you?"

"I dreamed I was being chased by a grizzly. Did I scream?"

"If you did," Scott said, "I couldn't hear you. Someone was snoring up a storm."

Scott looked pointedly at Harry, who avoided his glance. He was at that moment indifferent to conversation, nursing his hangover.

"And you, Tomas?" Scott said. He turned to his father. "Spent the night on the road. Right, Tomas?"

"On the road?" Temple asked.

"Brought the load back we took off the dead mule," Harry explained.

Temple shrugged, shook his head, and made no comment.

"Ten hours at least," Scott said, looking at Tomas, who paid little attention. "Without sleep."

"Sleeps on his horse," Harry said chuckling. "Mex talent. Right, Tomas?"

"*Si.* Señor Harry."

"Got the job done," Harry said. "All that matters. We aim to serve."

"I can't imagine..." Temple began, then retreated. Not my business, he thought, dismissing his comment but not his concern. Instead he asked: "What happens to the dead mule?"

Harry laughed.

"Dead meat, Temple. Becomes a restaurant for critters. Nothing dead out here goes uneaten. Everything recycles.

Beauty of nature. Nothing really dies out here. Nothing. It's like a relay race. We pass the baton." He grew silent, lost in thought.

Temple thought about that and looked at his children. Point taken, he thought. Life as a relay. He nodded agreement. The wilderness did indeed suggest a search for deeper meanings.

"So what's on the agenda, Harry?" Temple asked.

Harry nodded and said nothing.

Then Temple repeated his question, remembering with skepticism Tomas's remark of last night, "He be fine." He certainly didn't look fine. It took him a while to acknowledge Temple's question and amplify what he had told them last night about their fly-fishing expedition.

Recovering somewhat after his hair of the dog, he began in a hoarse voice to outline the program. He explained that all the equipment including rods, flies, and waders was packed and ready, and they would ride to the Thorofare River where the trout fishing was best.

He warned of some soft spots that he called "quagmires" both in the stream and along the banks that had the sucking quality of quicksand, but if they each watched each other, they had time to react and pull a person out if they were caught in the muck. As with most of his instructions, he invariably ended with the homily that "we ain't lost anyone yet."

"Make sure you clean up before we get back," he barked to Tomas in an arrogantly commanding tone. Tomas shrugged his consent. While Temple bristled at such treatment of the Mexican, he did not interfere. It wasn't pleasant to witness, and it took considerable discipline to force himself to cast a blind eye.

He was discovering that Harry had turned into a brute. What bothered him more was that he had let nostalgia color his judgment in hiring him. He would have been better served if he had done more research and had chosen a different outfitter, although that would have somehow defeated his purpose.

Leaving Tomas behind to attend to the cleanup and other chores, they moved out of the camp on horseback, following Harry on the lead horse. Occasionally, as if he felt compelled to validate his expertise in the face of his obvious addiction, he would stop to point out wildflowers by name. With obvious expertise, he identified Indian paintbrush, white yarrow, bluebell, wild buckwheat, mountain harebell, Queen Anne's lace, and an array of lilies, mountain orchids. At times, he would dismount and point out patches of wild fruits: raspberry, strawberry, gooseberry, elderberry, silverberry, and thimbleberry.

"Berry good," Scott joked.

At each change in the landscape, Harry would halt the horses and offer more information about the environment. He was encyclopedic when it came to birds, usually recognizing them by their birdsong, and able to point them out as if he possessed superhuman eyesight and hearing. He pointed out an amazing variety of woodpeckers—downy, hairy, white-headed—and insisted he could identify them by their pecking sounds. At times he would get excited and animated when a species surfaced that wasn't supposed to be seen at this time of year.

He would rattle off the names of little critters that crossed their path: Uinta squirrels, chipmunks, yellow-bellied marmots, meadow mice, red squirrels, and white-footed mice. This was his turf, and Temple marveled at Harry's knowledge. He seemed to enjoy imparting the information. Temple understood and listened earnestly.

In a compelling way, this display of knowledge did vindicate his choice, and Temple felt himself willing to overlook his own criticism. This place, after all, seemed on another planet. Different rules applied. Such thoughts made him feel better.

If one discounted the drinking, there was no question that Harry was a man who reveled in the outdoors and was proud of his knowledge. Unfortunately, for whatever reason, probably glimpsing the end to his outfitter's working life and the changing trends in management of the wilderness, he had made his disappointment palpable, numbing himself with booze as he faced the inevitable. He wondered what Harry's life was outside his outfitting career. Had he a family? Children? For some reason, Temple had never asked, as if he had had a secret wish that his outfitter's only real life was in the wilderness.

At one point, as they crossed a meadow, Harry pointed along the tree line.

"There they go," he said. "Wolves."

They followed his gaze. Three wolves had stopped to inspect them then moved on.

"All over the fucking place now," Harry said.

"Is that bad?" Courtney asked.

"There," he pointed to a dead animal. "Elk calves." He looked around and moved to other parts of the meadow. They followed him to more carcasses of young elks. "Sumbitches. Herd went through, and these bastards just killed off the babies."

"Just killed them and left them?" Temple asked. "I thought they killed to eat and survive."

"So they say," Harry sighed.

"You sure about that, Harry?" Courtney asked. It was quickly apparent that she had triggered Harry's ire. "The wolves belong here. Greedy ranchers decimated them. They belong here."

Harry flushed with anger but did not respond.

"Hey, sis," Scott said. "It's Harry's business. I mean, what the hell do you know about it? You live in Hollywood."

"And that explains it?" Courtney snapped.

"Yup," Scott said, chuckling.

The defending voice seemed to placate the outfitter and throw him back into teaching mode. Wisely, Courtney fell silent.

"Good and bad in everything," Harry said. "Wolves have real family solidarity. All for one, one for all. That's the good. Right, Temple?"

"Sounds good to me," Temple said. He certainly could not argue with the concept. Harry had gotten that right. It was, after all, the purpose of this enterprise.

"And the bad?" Courtney asked with obvious skepticism.

"The young ones hone their skills, become sport killers," Harry hissed, shaking his head in disgust. "Must get their jollies this way. Kill off the young. They're supposed to be smart. Bullshit. Soon they'll bring down the whole elk population. There'll be nothing left to hunt. Hunters cull the herd. Wolves decimate them. Moose, too. They'll be gone in a few years. Have to close shop."

"Hunting is so—" Courtney began.

"Enough," Scott said. "You've been in Hollywood too long. Talk about predators. They eat each other."

Courtney sneered.

Temple contemplated the idea as Harry had expressed it. Like Courtney, he didn't really agree with Harry's explanation. It had all the earmarks of self-interest, which he understood.

Besides, he hated guns, which were the choice of weapon in numerous thefts in the jewelry business. Friends in the diamond trade had been murdered and burglarized by hoodlums using guns. He had been lucky never to have been robbed, but security was an enormous expense.

Contrary to Harry's point of view, he was attracted to the wolves' sense of family. He looked at his children.

"Guess all of us creatures are both good and bad."

"You got that right, Temple," Harry sighed, turning his horse back to the trail. The others followed.

They reached the river's edge in a couple of hours and dismounted. Harry unpacked the rods and waders and offered rudimentary lessons on casting, then attached a fly to his own line and demonstrated his skill and prowess by hooking trout after trout, detaching them and throwing them back into the river. He explained that the protocol of fly-fishing was to treat it strictly as a sport, abiding by the rules of catch and release, regardless of the size of the catch.

"Of course," Harry winked, "we'll save the fat old guys for dinner. The Mexican is a wiz at trout."

Temple, as usual, snapped pictures of each of them and prevailed on Harry to take pictures of the three of them in their fishing duds.

Observing Harry as expert instructor, Temple's fear of Harry's excessive drinking abated somewhat. After attaching flies to their lines and letting them practice casting, Harry assigned them different spots along the river, and they moved into the current in their waders and began casting their lines.

Temple took up his position at a spot about fifty yards from where Courtney was stationed and began a clumsy series of casts while Harry went from person to person correcting their mistakes. The process required great concentration, and Temple kept at it for some time without results. Courtney seemed to be having better luck, occasionally screaming her success when she landed a fish and calling for Harry to unhook it and throw it back in the river. Scott, at the furthest point, was apparently having as little success as his father.

About an hour into the activity, Temple managed to get a bite and reel in his catch. He looked around for Harry, who seemed to have disappeared, then called out to Courtney who cried out Harry's name without response and waded back to shore and soon disappeared in an apparent search for him. In the distance, he saw Scott start to move back to shore, assuming he had gone to assist in his sister's search for Harry.

Temple managed to reel in the trout but he was having difficulty reaching out to grab it so that he could disengage it from the hook. He had been standing on some submerged rocks, but in the effort to reach the fish with his hand, he was thrown off balance, and he slipped off the rock and found himself on much softer footing.

With the fish still wriggling on the line, he reached out again and again, not only failing to retrieve the fish but sinking deeper and deeper into the muck. He continued the attempt until he realized that he was now knee-deep and could no longer move his legs. No more clues were needed. He was caught in what Harry had warned was a quagmire.

He tried turning in the direction of where the others had been assigned only to find that he faced in the opposite direction.

He did not panic until he was waist high and, to his horror, still sinking. The more he struggled, the more he sank. Finally, he cried out. He threw the rod into the water, leaving his hands free to create a kind of sound cup. Again and again, he called at the top of his lungs. He heard the echo but was discovering that the sound was being carried in the wrong direction. All thoughts left his mind, except one: survival!

Chapter 7

———

Courtney saw her father downstream casting and Scott upstream looking totally absorbed in the process. After her first two strikes, after which Harry had unhooked the fish and released them back into the stream, her luck seemed to have changed, and for a long time the trout rejected her fly. Then suddenly the rod bent. She had a big one on the line and shouted for Harry.

He did not respond. She called again and again. No response.

She couldn't understand it, although his drinking problem lurked in the back of her mind. Earlier he had been solicitous and instructive, the dutiful guide, dispelling her earlier fear. It now roared back.

Harry had complimented her on her natural casting ability, which greatly increased her interest and concentration. She could barely remember her earlier attempt at the sport on their first trek, but she decided that it was fun and she might, indeed, have some natural aptitude in the process.

The fly-fishing adventure surprised her. Instead of continuing to brood over her relationship with her father and anxieties about her future, she found her mind intensely focused on the predatory nature of the sport. It was predatory in that the hunt required the hunter to goad the hunted into accepting the false premise of the artificial fly and lure it into the trap of its own misperception. She acknowledged that something about the idea must have fascinated her since she took to it with such enthusiasm.

Her first strike caused her to scream with pleasure, attracting Harry's attention. He came splashing in beside her, bringing along his familiar scent, then instructing her on the method required to battle the fish into submission and reel it in. Harry skillfully grabbed the slithering trout, extracted the hook, and sent the fish back on its merry way.

"Seems silly," she told him, as she observed the release and watched the trout slither away, apparently none the worse for wear.

"It's all about the skill and pleasure of the sport," he muttered. "And the rules of the game."

"What about the injured fish?"

"Heals quickly. None the worse for wear. Lives to be hooked again."

"Don't they ever learn?"

"They're like us humans. Never learn nothin'. Always repeat their mistakes."

She supposed there was more than a grain of truth in that observation.

"Spoken like a true cynic," she snickered.

He stayed close, watching her as she bagged another one. "A natural," he muttered, as he repeated the extraction process and threw the trout back into the stream.

"Just holler when you get another strike," he said, moving back to the shore.

She noted that her father and brother were not having much luck, which added to her pleasure. But then she ran into a dry period and for a long time the fish ignored her fly, but she kept up the casting and finally encountered another strike. She caught a glimpse of the trout as it jumped and fought to detach itself from the hook. She called for Harry and continued the fight, remembering his instruction as she let out line and reeled it back cautiously. This was a big one, and she greatly enjoyed what was becoming a fierce encounter, screaming for Harry's attention to help her bring off the final victory.

"Hey, Harry," she cried. "I got a big one on the line."

He did not come, and she stayed with it until the fish finally managed to break the line and with the hook still embedded swam away, destined probably to live with this appendage throughout its lifetime.

Wading out of the river, she cried again for Harry and got no answer. Still calling his name, she moved inland to the flat where they had tied the horses, but Harry was nowhere in sight.

She was surprised to find Scott behind her joining in the search.

"Harry's disappeared," she told him.

"Probably sleeping off a drunk somewhere. He'll turn up."

"He better."

The idea of Harry's disappearance was not lost on her. She hadn't a clue about how to get back to the camp and was certain that her brother and father were equally ignorant.

"Don't panic, little sister. He doesn't want to lose his livelihood."

She took some comfort in his reassurance and tried to put it out of her mind.

"You should've seen what I had on my line," she said, changing the subject. She illustrated the size of the trout. "It broke the line and got away. I needed the son of a bitch to help me bring it in."

"I didn't even get a nibble."

"Dad, too, didn't seem to have any action."

The thought of their father reminded her that he was still out there, and they meandered toward the stream to observe him in action. They had moved some distance away, but he could be seen in the near distance, a dark figure standing a few yards into the stream. At first she thought that the distance and brightness of the sun had distorted her image of him. He looked smaller, and she could not detect any movement, nothing suggestive of active fly-fishing.

They moved toward him but had not gone more than a few steps when they stopped suddenly and looked at each other.

"Are you seeing what I think I'm seeing?" Courtney asked.

Scott swiveled, looking first at his father in the distance then at her.

"Could be an optical illusion," he said, his voice a throaty whisper.

"Or the contour of the riverbed."

"Could be."

Sounds came to them, echoes.

"Maybe the wind," Courtney said, unsure.

She found herself contemplating a course of action, deliberately holding back. Could this be an opportunity? she asked herself.

"We had better see," Scott said, exchanging glances with his sister, stepping forward.

"He's fine."

"Could be my eye's playing tricks," Scott acknowledged. "These sunglasses aren't prescription."

"Could be," she said calmly, remembering Harry's warning.

"We should get closer."

"Let's look for Harry," Courtney said, glancing at her brother, who continued to squint in his father's direction.

"He might be in trouble," Scott said, betraying signs of anxious uncertainty. "He did warn us. We were told to be careful."

"Don't be such a worrywart, Scottie. He's out there fishing is all. Let's find Harry."

She started moving in the direction of where the horses were tethered. Scott held back still squinting.

"Maybe we should go see."

"Stop overreacting."

She stopped moving, looking into the distance. He did seem smaller. She shot a glance at her brother who looked puzzled.

"I'm going," Scott said. "He looks like he's sinking."

"You think so?"

She knew she was stalling now, acknowledging the truth to herself.

"Damn it, Courtney, he's in trouble."

He started to run toward his father. Courtney held her ground, conscious of her motive.

"I'll get a rope," she shouted. "There's one on Harry's horse." She started to move toward the horses again. She saw Harry moving toward them, running.

"Fuck, I warned you," he shouted, moving fast. When he reached Courtney he passed her quickly, and she followed. He caught up to Scott who stood on the bank parallel to his sinking father.

"Hold on, Dad," he shouted through cupped hands.

Their father had turned ashen. He was no longer holding his fly rod.

"Don't fight it," Harry shouted. Courtney noted that he seemed panicked, sobered by the situation. "Hang on, Temple."

Their father nodded, his expression pained. He was clearly frightened.

"We're here, Dad, you'll be fine," Scott cried, his voice trembling.

"We're here, Dad," Courtney echoed.

"Be right back," Harry called. "Just don't fight it."

Harry rushed into the tree line, quickly reemerging with a long branch. He instructed Scott and Courtney to join hands as he cautiously made his way into the stream, stopping at what appeared to be some rock foundation below, which gave him a firm footing. Then he reached out with the branch, ordering their father to grasp it with both hands. Turning toward Scott and Courtney, he cried, "Heave when I say."

They joined hands.

"Heave," Harry shouted.

At first Temple did not budge, but after a number of tries he began to slide forward until his body was free of the muck. They dragged him toward the edge of the stream and rushed over to assist him, Scott holding him under one armpit and Harry the other. At first, he lay supine, trying to catch his breath as the color slowly came back into his complexion.

Courtney and Scott kneeled beside him. Scott massaged one hand and Courtney the other.

"Easy, Dad," she said. "You'll be fine."

Scott shot her a look of reproach.

"Just relax, Dad," Scott said. "You sure had us worried."

Temple nodded, closing his eyes for a moment, obviously exhausted by the experience.

"Easy, Temple," Harry said.

Slowly, their father gained his composure. Then he sat up.

"You had us really scared, Dad," Scott said.

"Powerful stuff, that muck," he said, shaking his head, smiling faintly.

"Take it easy, Dad," Scott said. "Don't rush it."

Their father nodded.

"Was I really in trouble?" he asked.

"Could be," Harry said.

"Now you have something to brag about," Courtney said, deliberately cheerful. "How I confronted danger and—" She stopped abruptly.

Harry finished the thought. "And nearly got my ass in a sling."

Their father chuckled. Courtney noted that the mud on his waders had reached over his waist. If they hadn't come, would he have sunk lower? She quickly repressed the thought. She acknowledged that the near disaster triggered ideas. They were far from civilization. This was wild country. Anything could happen.

"Better get those off," Harry said, as they loosened his waders and, with all three helping, pulled them off.

"For a moment there, I thought it was over," he muttered as the waders were removed.

"No way," Courtney said. "An old tough nut like you."

"You must have hit a real softie," Harry said. "It happens, but it's rare that it swallows you up completely."

"Small comfort," Courtney said, cutting Harry an angry glance. "Where the hell were you?"

She watched him hesitate, certain he was thinking up a good excuse. He appeared dead sober.

"Dropped a spare horseshoe along the trail. Went back to find it."

It seemed implausible, but she let it pass.

"We screamed our lungs out," Scott said in continued admonishment, exchanging a surreptitious glance with Courtney. She wondered what he was thinking.

"We're supposed to be in your care," Courtney said.

"Sorry about that. Hearing is not as good as it used to be," Harry said, shrugging.

"And did you find the missing shoe?" Courtney asked with unmistakable sarcasm.

"Matter of fact, yes. Horse goes lame on you if he loses a shoe. Backup." he explained. Courtney was not inclined to believe him. Shrugging, she turned to her father, who seemed to have fully recovered.

"You had us worried, Dad," Courtney said.

"Would have put a damper on the whole trip," Scott said, chuckling.

Rejecting any further help, their father walked beside them back to the horses, where Harry brought out their lunch: tuna sandwiches and candy bars to be washed down with water from their canteens. Tomas had filled them using the plastic gizmo. They sat in a semicircle, leaning against boulders and viewing the tranquil valley framed by the mountains beyond.

Harry sat with them for a while then stood up.

"Pit-stop time," he muttered, moving out to the edge of the clearing. Soon he was lost among the trees.

"Pit stop, my ass," Courtney said.

"He was there when needed," her father said.

"Bullshit," Courtney cried. She had decided to take a more aggressive stance.

"He should have been watching. That's his job," Scott said, perhaps buying into her latest pose.

"All's well that ends well," their father said.

"We were helpless, Dad. We didn't have a clue what to do. Am I right, Scott?"

"Not a clue."

"We were paralyzed with fear," Courtney continued.

"Scared the shit out of both of us, Dad."

"Can you just imagine what could have happened?" Courtney posed, determined to embellish the point. "Standing by helpless, while you—"

"Never mind, darling," their father said. "Here I am, still kicking."

They rested until Harry returned, bringing with him his usual scent. Obviously, he had imbibed again and got back his buzz. They mounted up with Harry helping their father onto the saddle.

"Feel okay, Temple?" he asked, as their father settled his boots into the stirrups.

"Fit as a fiddle and ready for love," he said cheerfully.

For some reason, his remark made her uncomfortable.

Heading back, they took a different trail, this time along the river. Harry, as if nothing untoward had occurred, again stopped frequently to point out various waterfowl and birds, being once more overly specific, in an obvious attempt to get back his respect as an expert guide.

He pointed out golden-eyed ducks, Swainson's hawks, and the great blue heron among others and called their attention to ospreys and bald and golden eagles. She listened to him, her attention wandering. Despite his earlier extravagant statements, he was not the great guardian of their safety that he had pledged. She mulled the thought. Suppose Harry had not arrived at that moment?

She could not harness her speculation.

A fatal accident. Just what the doctor ordered. It was an optimistic thought, and she let it linger.

Chapter 8

Back at the camp, her father crawled into his tent for a nap, obviously exhausted by his experience. Harry went into his tent. There were signs of preparation for the evening meal but Tomas was nowhere in sight.

"He could have died," Scott said when they were alone. They had walked some distance from the camp, seeking private conversation. Scott leaned against a cottonwood. Beside them was the stream. She saw her brother's face in the diminishing light. She was familiar with his expression, frightened, unsure, vulnerable. My fragile brother, she thought.

"Dad sure was lucky," she murmured.

"Wouldn't have bothered you, would it, Courtney?"

She mulled over the answer, knowing there was truth in it. For both of them, a different outcome would have changed everything.

"I wouldn't put it that way."

"How would you put it?"

"It would have been an unfortunate accident," she replied, cautious, assessing his reaction. "An act of God. Would we have benefited? Hopefully. Provided everything is as originally promised."

"Would you really have given a damn? I mean about him."

"As the politicians say, why deal in hypotheticals?"

Scott remained silent for a long time. She noted a slight tic in his jaw.

"You mean wishful thinking."

His eyes evaded hers.

"It was out of our hands, Scott."

"Was it? You were holding back. I saw it."

"I thought he would be okay. So did you."

"Even when I ran toward him, you stayed back. As if—"

"As if what?"

"You wanted it to happen."

She looked at him and shook her head.

"Murder by wish. Is that it? Don't be ridiculous."

"I was there, Courtney."

"Look," she explained choosing her words carefully. "Why beat around the bush? People die through accidents every day. Heirs benefit, right? We would mourn our loss, and we would probably benefit. Both of us. Are you telling me you wouldn't accept being an heir to a pile of dough and turn back the money?"

"I didn't say that," he snapped, clearly intimidated.

"There you go again, Scottie. Don't be so fucking self-righteous. It's not like we would have caused his demise. Shit happens. Every cloud has a silver lining. It's not like we deliberately lured him to that particular spot. Harry assigned it to him, and Harry had warned us about the danger. We would be blameless, brother mine. Blameless."

"I wouldn't have felt blameless."

"Your problem, Scott. Not mine." She expelled a breath in exasperation. "You're so prone to guilt. Always cooking up some obstacle to acceptance."

"It's an affliction you apparently have escaped."

"I've got a better immune system. Guilt is for idiots."

He grew thoughtful, squinting into the distance as if searching for something beyond his sight. She had seen this pose of worried concentration many times.

"You're right, Courtney. Guilt sucks."

She sensed that it was coming to the surface again, their old story, the secret life. Beyond their silence, she could hear the sounds of the coming wilderness evening. Beside them the current of the stream rushed by. Reaching out, she touched his cheek, caressing.

"Poor baby. If it had happened, the reality is that our troubles might have been over."

"Jesus, Courtney, when you put it that way it sounds...," he paused, obviously searching for the right word, "...horrific."

"How else should I put it? I'm being a cold-eyed realist. Face it. There is a lady in the picture. An ill wind is blowing."

"Leave it alone, Courtney. Gives me the creeps. He's our father."

"Come on, Scott. Focus on the outcome. It will happen someday. It's obvious he wants to reestablish the old bond. Great. He wants to bond, then let's bond. Frankly, I'd be happy with a steady stipend that does the job for me, and I'm sure you'd be happy if he backed your latest folly...sorry...I mean venture. You're making it sound like I'm advocating some drastic action to hasten the result."

"Am I?"

"You're just like him, Scottie baby. Sodden with guilt. Doesn't look like all those years of therapy did you any good."

She searched his face for a reaction. Instead he turned away unable to meet her gaze. She knew she was testing him. The quagmire episode had, indeed, suggested other possibilities, and for this she needed his cooperation and assistance. His suspicions, she knew, were justified. Before signing on to her previous schemes, he had been difficult and wary, but in the end he had joined her.

"I know you, Courtney," he muttered, obviously preparing his defenses.

"Do you really?" she asked gently.

"We have history, remember?"

"Yes, we do," she said, laughing. "What's past is past. Now we have to focus on the future. Hell, that's what Dad is doing. Obviously, he wants to clear the decks for his new journey. Get us all warm and cozy about his new lady. Dear...what was her name? Muriel. An accountant, no less. Speaks volumes. Knows what he's worth. She gets his hooks into him, we're—how shall I put it?—diminished. Perhaps mightily."

"It's his life," Scott pouted.

"Exactly. His life and beyond."

"What are you saying, Courtney?"

"I'm only stating the obvious."

"There's nothing we can do about it."

She grew silent, watching his face.

"We can think about it," she whispered. "This is a big dangerous country.

He swiveled his gaze toward the vast emptiness of the surrounding wilderness.

"I really don't want to hear this, Courtney."

"Maybe not. But you can't deny—"

"Please. I don't want to think about it."

"We are in the middle of nowhere," she pressed. "The possibilities of accident are endless. Drunken, careless guide fucks up."

"Stop it, can't you?" he cried.

"Still the wimpy brother," she said, with some impatience. "We still have lots of life to live, and his is—well let's face it—almost over."

"How can I get you to stop?" he sighed. "It's so…so cold-blooded. This is our father you're talking about. I can't believe this. What's happened to you?"

She could see he was genuinely upset, and she retreated, knowing now it was not over.

"Okay. Okay. I was just—"

"Don't!" he cried.

They were silent for a while. Above all, she did not want to alienate him. He was the first to speak.

"This trip, Courtney. It could resolve those issues between Dad and us. He wants to do right by us. Can't you just feel it?"

"Yes, I can," she admitted. "Could be he brought us here to explain himself. A new plan for us. Who knows exactly what?"

"Are you saying he is setting us up for some revelation?"

"Could be. Something detrimental."

She mulled it over further, but the issue she had raised could not be buried. Not now.

"Of course, if it happened *now*. I mean before this other woman gets her hooks into him."

"Must you?" he whispered.

"Something to chew on, Scott."

"I'd rather not."

"I know how you feel. It's an indelicate subject."

"Indelicate? My God, Courtney! Is that all? It's…it's horrific, macabre. What's going on with you?"

"Yes, Scottie. All of the above."

He nodded, and their eyes met. His reluctance made persuading him more of a challenge. She felt the sudden press of memory, recalling her earlier tactics. Once again, she needed his alliance and was determined to get it. And she knew the way.

"I'd like to forget you raised it."

"Forgotten," she said, crossing her chest with an *x* gesture. "Cross my heart."

He nodded and met her gaze then quickly tried to turn away. Like a deer caught in the headlights, he couldn't. Moving forward, she embraced him, rubbing her body against him. He tried at first to resist then yielded.

"Please, Courtney."

"Is it still there, Scottie?"

"Don't, Courtney."

"A little kiss won't hurt," she said, searching for his lips. He tried to move his face away, but her lips found his and they kissed deeply. Her hand reached down and caressed his erection.

"Remember, Scottie?"

"I never forgot," he whispered, his breath coming in short gasps.

"Let it decide," she whispered.

"Not again, Courtney. Please. Not again. Please."

"Just a little family reunion. Where's the harm?"

"I couldn't go through that again."

But he did not disengage.

"You were always the best, Scottie," she said.

She unzipped him and reached for the bare flesh.

"Jesus, Courtney."

She stopped abruptly.

"You want me to stop?"

He did not answer.

Without another word, she rolled down his pants, got down on her knees, and began to fellate him.

After a few moments, he cried.

"I can't hold."

"Let it happen. Let it go, baby."

He did, and she continued to hold him, swallowing. It took him a while to recover. Miraculously, she too had experienced orgasm, something that hadn't happened in years.

"Same as before, Scottie," she said. "Don't ask why."

"It's crazy, Courtney. It comes with a curse."

"What curse?"

"You know."

"We're mature people taking our pleasure. Who cares?"

Looking at him, she could not deny the power of the old desire. She was sure he felt the same. She removed her slacks and panties and embraced him again. He reacted, ready again.

"The old Scottie," she marveled. "Why fight it?"

"I have been fighting it, Courtney. For years."

He slid to the ground, his back against a tree, and she mounted him.

"We belong like this," she whispered, sucking his earlobe. She began to move in a circular motion. "Remember? It was never the same for me ever again."

"For me either. I love you, Courtney. Always. I knew then. I still know."

His breath came faster.

She felt the urge to scream out her pleasure and did. The effect was multiple waves of sensation.

"Oh God, brother. Fill me up," she cried, feeling his spasms second hers.

Finally, they quieted and remained attached, beyond speech. This was the way, she decided. Suddenly his chest convulsed with sobs.

"Easy, brother."

"No," he sighed. "Not easy at all."

Suddenly she started.

"Holy shit!" she cried.

"What is it?"

"The fucking Mexican."

He turned, following her gaze. In the near distance, they saw Tomas holding a fly rod and a number of trout that he had caught in the stream. He watched them for a few moments, smiled thinly, then moved away out of sight.

Suddenly she giggled.

"So much for deep dark secrets." She said, disengaging. "There's irony for you. We had to come all this way to get outed by some dumb Mexican."

As they disengaged, Scott made no comment.

Chapter 9

—≫•⊂—

It had started out as fun and games, harmless sex games. You show me yours, and I'll show you mine. She was fifteen when it began. He was thirteen. Other brothers and sisters did it. She knew because the girls talked about it. Those of her girlfriends who had brothers were surprisingly open and graphic in their descriptions.

Have you ever seen what happens to your brother's thing? It grows, and sometimes he plays with it like a toy until suddenly something white squirts out. He showed me because he asked me if I wanted to see it, and I said yes.

At first, she had been mildly shocked by their revelations. In her family, modesty was practiced and taught by example. She had never seen her father naked, and it never occurred to her that he and her mother were sexually active. As children, she and her brother were often bathed together, and she had observed their differences with the usual curiosity and casual acceptance. Boys were different from girls.

She and her brother had separate bedrooms from the beginning of memory. Indeed, in many ways, their lives went in different directions. It was a given that all family members were supposed to love each other, which no one ever questioned. There were, of course, brother and sister disputes, but they were always based on possessions, permissions, and alleged equality, which usually resulted in practical compromises engineered by their parents.

At fifteen she viewed herself as an average teenager, thirsty for knowledge and, certainly along with her friends of that age, keenly interested in sexual matters. In her family, sex had of course been alluded to, especially the consequences of pregnancy and disease, but rarely discussed beyond these issues.

Often, she and her girlfriends would talk about boys and their "things." Although somewhat shocking, it was normal adolescent curiosity. Her girlfriends spread their legs to show each other what they had, some with hair and some still bald, and that, too, became an object of exploration.

There was a girl named Harriet who showed her how to masturbate by tickling the tiny thing on top and moving her fingers on her organ. Harriet illustrated how to make oneself feel really good. She called it "coming," which was quite strange. Then she demonstrated something called a dildo, which vibrated inside and could make you reach a climax, the ultimate of feeling good. It had a name called "orgasm."

Soon she had begun doing it to herself—without the vibrator, of course, since she was still a virgin—and discovered she liked it very much indeed. She began to wonder about Scott's "thing," often teasing him about it when she would see a bulge in his pants or pajamas. His reaction was always embarrassment and confusion. She became persistent in her desire for him to show it to her, promising the usual trade-off. You show me yours, and I'll show you mine. At such suggestions Scott continued to be embarrassed and reluctant to take her up on the offer.

It seemed to her so natural. She did not see it in terms of taboo or sin, although she knew that there was obviously something forbidden about a brother and sister playing this kind of sex game. Outwardly, she continued to be modest, making a great show of indignation when her father or brother accidentally walked in on her when she was in the bathroom. But despite her brother's continued reluctance to participate, she was relentless in her pursuit. Then one day, she had acted. He was in his room doing homework. Her parents were out.

She came into his room in panties and bra and sat on his bed.

"You want to see it?" she asked boldly.

He was, as usual, embarrassed, but at that point, for whatever reason, he had turned his swivel chair and looked at her. She was determined and quickly rolled down her panties, kicked them off, and spread her legs.

She remembered watching his Adam's apple slide up and down his throat while his eyes fixated on her exposed genitals, well-coated then with hair, the lips red and aroused.

"Now you," she ordered.

He shook his head.

"I can't. You're my sister."

"Just show me, Scott. Just that. No harm in that."

"No."

"Yes."

Finally, she got up from the bed and opened his belt and pulled down his pants. He made what seemed like token resistance, but in the end she had her way. He was fully aroused, and there was a bead of moisture on top of it.

"Can I touch it?" she asked.

"No."

"Please. Pretty please."

"This is wrong."

"I know. But we're all alone. Who will know?"

He was obviously too stunned to continue to resist and far too aroused to object. She touched his erection, felt it up and down, looked under it, and touched his testicles.

"Gee, it gets big," she said, marveling.

He had blushed beet red, but she detected a note of secret pride.

It reminded her of a funny flower with a long stalk. It was veiny and white and not very pretty. But she liked its satiny touch and continued to caress it. Soon he was eagerly thrusting forward, and as she continued to touch it, he began to make strange throaty sounds, and all of a sudden a jet of white starchy fluid came out of it.

"Look what you made me do," Scott said angrily.

She had been told such a thing would happen but had never seen it firsthand.

"Did it feel good?" she asked.

He blushed a deep scarlet and shrugged while he wiped away the moisture with the edge of his shirttail.

"Well, did it?"

"I won't tell."

"I can make myself feel good, too," she said, spreading her legs and manipulating herself. He watched her bug-eyed as her breath got short, and she closed her eyes and felt her body vibrate with an orgasm.

"God, that was good," she said. "Did you like to watch me?"

He shrugged, but she could tell that he had enjoyed the sight. Seeing him watching her added to the thrill.

"You see? No harm done."

How easily manipulated he was! With the ice broken and believing she had persuaded him there were no consequences, she asked him if he would like to do it again, promising that next time they would do it together, although she wasn't quite sure what that meant.

"It's wrong, Courtney," he said, still protesting but with less and less resistance. He needed continuing persuasion and lots of priming.

"Who said?"

He did not answer, but she could tell that he had surrendered to the idea.

"Isn't it fun?" she asked. "Trust me. Other brothers and sisters do it all the time."

He appeared confused and uncertain.

"I never heard that," he said.

"Well, I have."

"It's wrong."

"So what. It feels good, doesn't it?"

Although they soon graduated to mutual oral sex, they hadn't yet had intercourse. But after a couple of months, Courtney suggested that he "put it in."

He refused. By then they both knew how babies were made.

"I'm afraid," he confessed.

"You can pull it out before you come."

"I can't control it, Courtney. You'll get pregnant."

"I'll get condoms," she promised.

"They could break."

"Boy, are you a scaredy-cat!"

"I'm afraid is all."

They continued their mutual manipulations short of intercourse. She was, she remembered, startled by the depth of pleasure it triggered in her. Scott was perfectly made, with a beautiful body, and his penis had matured with use. He was getting very adept at the process, swiftly recovering his erections. She discovered that she was multiorgasmic and that Scott's appetite for sex, as she learned later from other experiences, was gargantuan and limitless.

They could not get enough of each other. It became, clearly, obsessive and addictive. Soon they went at it, although just short of intercourse, whenever they found safe private moments, which were many, since their parents spent lots of time at their jewelry salon. Not that they were neglectful parents. It was just that raging hormones and proximity made it easier and convenient for them to imbibe, satisfying an appetite that neither of them had ever expected or experienced.

To her it seemed so innocent. Above all, it was convenient and accessible. They were clever in keeping their secret from their parents and were cautious and deft at concealment. Of course, they knew that if their parents found out, they would think that she and her brother were disgusting perverts. Such a revelation was sure to explode their parent's cherished view of a normal, conventional, loving family with good morals and the right values.

They apparently never did find out, which considering the frequency of their activity was a miracle.

It was during that first trek that it happened. They had been at camp one day and had snuck out into the darkness, out of earshot of the others who were sleeping, exhausted by their first day's riding.

"I got pills," she told him. "My girlfriend stole them from her mom."

"Pills?"

"Birth control pills. They don't let the woman make babies."

"Really?"

"I've been taking them," she confessed. "Getting ready. We can fuck now and nothing will happen."

"Are you sure?"

"Trust me, Scott. Come on, let's do it."

She leaned against a tree and bent over.

"Come on, baby. Put it in."

He did. It was fantastic.

"Didn't you love it?" she asked when they were finished.

"You sure nothing will happen?"

"Trust me, baby brother."

During that trek she and Scott would sneak away numerous times, feeling totally secure in the vast wilderness, practicing every sensual delight that filled their imagination. Little did their parents realize what made their wilderness experience truly memorable for them.

Yet while they characterized their actions as simply a form of recreation, they began to sense a need, a longing, a sense of entitlement and possession, which crept into their relationship. They became jealous of other teenagers who expressed interest in one or another of them. What had started out as fun and games was reaching a stage that neither of them could control. They had become lovers, locked in a relationship that they both knew would be looked upon by others as sick and perverted.

Trapped by their own emotions, they came face-to-face with the reality of the taboo. Living such a secret life was draining, the pretense debilitating. Their perceived need to give each other pleasure overwhelmed them. They contemplated running away, disappearing, obliterating their sibling identity, starting a new life somewhere, anywhere.

Scott, who had been reluctant from the beginning, began expressing deep second thoughts. In an odd insight for someone so young, Courtney was noticing things in her brother beyond what she knew was her own obsessive pursuit of pleasure. At the ecstatic moment of his own release, he would burst out with expressions redolent of deep attachment.

"I love you, my sweet sister. I love you with all my heart and soul."

After a while, Courtney discovered that her sensual relationship with her brother was less all encompassing emotionally than how he expressed himself. Soon his outbursts about love began to strike her as over-the-top clichés, the kind of reactions that she had encountered in movies and books. In those teenage years she dismissed them from her mind as merely words expressed in an intense moment. Actually she had no idea what they meant.

"We should stop, Courtney, but I don't know how."

"Why stop? No one knows."

"Besides, I love you. I know it's wrong. But I love you. Not as a sister."

"Don't be silly."

"Really, Courtney. I swear. I don't even know how to explain it."

"Okay, then. I love you, too."

"Not just, you know, being together like this. More. I swear it. I hate it when I'm not with you."

"We're having so much fun, Scottie," she told him. "Aren't we?"

At the time that seemed to be the only definition she could muster.

"Don't you just love doing this? The feelings you get. Don't you just love when it happens?"

"That especially," he had admitted, but even then she could tell he was confused by what was happening inside him. At that point she had no idea how deeply it was affecting him, and how the experience and its consequences would impact so profoundly on his later life.

Then Courtney found herself pregnant. She was sixteen years old.

Chapter 10

⟫⟪

They had taken too many risks, been carried away by the intensity of their emotions. She was sure she was impregnated on their trek through Yellowstone. Perhaps she had not followed the directions she had been given about the use of the birth control pills. She would never be certain.

The condition complicated their dilemma. They pondered running away, having the child, their love child. When they learned brother-and-sister children could be born retarded, they quickly rejected that option.

Their only solution was to abort the child. That took money. They didn't have any. Not enough. They had found a place in New Jersey where the doctor would do the abortion and make sure there were no records. Above all, they did not want any record of the procedure, and they wanted to be sure there were no complications. The cost was a thousand dollars.

At that point in time, both she and Scott worked after school at their parents' jewelry salon doing odd jobs, tidying up the premises, arranging and bringing out trays of gems for customers, and generally being helpful.

Their parents normally locked all their valuable stock in their big safe in a room off the main display area. There were many trays in the safe, all carefully arranged and containing row upon row of precious stones that would find their way into rings, bracelets, broaches, and necklaces, according to the customer's wishes, as well as many finished jewelry designs.

They knew that their parents had very accurate inventory controls, and occasionally she and Scott were called upon to count the gems as a double check. It was before computers were in common use. All of their parent's recordkeeping was done by hand.

Desperation moved them to commit a theft that would never have occurred to them if Courtney had not become pregnant.

"A couple of diamonds would solve the financial problem," Courtney suggested.

"Some of these trays are rarely shown. Besides, most of the time we do the counting."

"Steal from our parents?"

Scott's reaction was outrage.

"They might never find out. We could fake the double checks. And if they did find out, they would think that they were careless in their inventory. Even if they thought the diamonds were stolen, they're insured."

"I can't do this, Courtney," Scott protested. She was used to his timidity and amazed how his sexual prowess was astonishingly so much more powerful and assured.

"Okay, then what's your suggestion?" she goaded. "We need the money for this procedure. Hell, I'm the one that has to go through with it. Or should I tell the folks that I screwed some stranger and got careless?"

She observed him as he grappled with this new dilemma. Even then she was well aware of his fragility and prone to guilt and knew all the flash points of manipulating him. But the one emotional underpinning of his character that had always baffled her was his self-defined idea of eternal love and his constant iteration of his feelings for her. He seemed to dwell on it, obsess over it, as if she were some strange creature created in her brother's mind.

For her on the other hand, Scott had become merely the means to, the instrument of, overpowering pleasure that could cause an inner sexual eruption so thrilling and ecstatic that it was beyond any rational explanation. It was, then and in retrospect throughout her life, a unique once-in-a-lifetime happening that had never occurred to her again. As for any connection beyond that, she could never understand the obsessive power it held for her brother.

"I hate this, Courtney," he had whined when their argument grew heated.

"You sure as hell liked the fucking part," she rebuked. "You liked that a lot, didn't you? Felt good, right? You enjoyed that part."

"You said you were taking pills, that it wouldn't happen."

"Well, it did and your stuff did the trick."

He had called it "love juice" which amused her.

"You can't run away from that, brother mine. Or maybe you should confront dear old Mom and Dad with a confession. Go tell them, Scott. I screwed my sister, and I made her pregnant."

She was deliberately relentless, goading him. He had to be part of it. Her principal worry was that he would in the end crack and confess to their parents.

"I can't do this."

"You're such a pussy, Scott."

He started to cry, which required much soothing sexual activity on the table in the back room of the salon where the safe was kept. Nothing was more persuasive.

"Do you really love me, Scott?" she would whisper repeatedly.

"With my whole heart forever."

"Then we must do this, Scott."

She waited until his body tensed at the ecstatic moment. She would freeze her movement.

"Do you love me?"

"Yes."

"Then you must prove it."

"I love you, my sister. I love you."

"Show me then."

"I will. I will. I promise. Oh God, I promise."

At that her movement had commenced.

"They'll never find out, Scottie," she assured him. "We'll get the money and it will be over. Besides, I'm the one at risk, and you need to help me. It's something we have to do together. It will be our secret. Another solemn secret. I'm the one to go through the pain. If you really love me, you will. "

"Of course, I love you. I will love you forever."

As she knew he would from the beginning, he went along.

They picked two pear-shaped diamonds from the least-used tray and fenced them with a jeweler in New Jersey, who bought them for far less than their worth. It gave them enough for the abortion. The physical experience of the procedure was so traumatic, it left her with what she later would realize was a kind of fractured libido.

The event ended their physical affair, but it did not put an end to his obsessive "love" feeling for her.

"That part is over," she told him, leaving it deliberately open-ended. "For now."

Of course, he agreed, obviously fearful of the risks, although she sensed that what he felt would not disappear with maturity. Apparently, as she suspected, it never had gone away.

The experience left her with a diminished interest in the sex act, which never ever reached the sexual power of her relationship with her brother. She was well aware of how it had distorted her relationships with men, none of which were ever satisfying. Nor was any relationship with a man ever a priority. As her passion for her acting career grew more intense, she was able to put her energy into the obsession that forever would dominate her life.

As for her brother, although they never referred to it openly, she was convinced that his experience, like hers, had a profoundly negative effect on his relationship with women.

Nor did she dwell on it. Like her, he had to cope with his demons on his own. When the memory would pop up in her thoughts, she ruthlessly edited them and willed them to disappear from her consciousness.

Chapter 11

⟫•⟪

Throughout the preparation for dinner, Scott observed the Mexican. What they had done was risky and stupid. He forced himself not to dwell on the whys and wherefores. Hundreds of hours with shrinks hadn't reached the root of his vulnerability. There are two things at work here, the shrinks would tell him: love and sex. But it was only the sex part that they could explain. Not the love part. It was beyond their analysis, beyond their definitions, beyond their conclusions. And his.

Worse, it had all come back in a flash, revising the fire in long-smoldering embers.

Reimagining their early encounters had been a powerful aphrodisiac. Such fantasies were unstoppable, despite keeping his physical distance, and a massive effort at self-discipline. He was well aware that it had always been the prime obsession of his life. He knew, too, the power of its consequences.

All efforts at normality in his relationships with women had gone awry. Even the shrinks had observed that the obsession might be the root cause of his other failures, suggesting that he felt so unworthy and guilt-stricken that he deliberately evaded success. He had resisted such an explanation as psychobabble. He had given up all shrinks more than five years ago.

There is no such thing as eternal love, he concluded, especially an obsession complicated by incest. It had taken years for him to say the word to himself. The struggle to excise the idea of it, beyond the taboo, had been the central battle of his life.

It was, he had finally concluded, a form of madness, a built-in dysfunction that could only be handled by isolating it from his thoughts and emotions. Indeed, he had tried mightily to suppress it, but there was no twelve-step program for a love addiction. He could understand pure sexual addiction, the need for the perpetual high of sensual stimulation. This was different. Like a fatal disease, it could go into remission but never be cured. As he had just found out, it was still raging beneath the surface.

And here he was again, an easy mark for Courtney's swift seduction, a sexual pushover. His surrender had been eager and explosive. Nevertheless, the Mexican's observation of them was a warning. He bore watching.

If the Mexican knew he was being watched, he showed no reaction as he concentrated on the details of cooking. He was frying trout along with onions and garlic in a big skillet and was making what appeared to be a tomato and rice concoction in a separate skillet. Beside him was a bowl in which he was mixing a salad. Apparently while they were away, he had made biscuits and on the grate was the cowboy coffee.

The three of them sat on logs around the fire watching the process and the efficiency with which he operated under what were clearly primitive conditions.

Harry was in his tent incommunicado. Their father, looking rested now after his ordeal, sat on the log sipping wine, while he and Courtney sat quietly beside him looking into the fire in deep contemplation.

In this atmosphere, seeing his father alive and well, he dismissed Courtney's earlier remarks. They were, when all was said and done, sick speculation on her part. Desperation had made her irrational. Her suggestion was both cynical and bloodthirsty. Even for Courtney, such a level of evil was unthinkable. Thankfully, contemplation was not action.

Scott looked toward his father. He was a good man, decent, compassionate, fair-minded, and quite obviously searching to make peace with his children before entering a new chapter in his life. Scott supposed, too, that he needed to overcome his disappointment in them. They had not, after all, fulfilled his aspirations and their own dreams.

The sun had dipped behind the highest Douglas firs, the light throwing orange flickers as it filtered through the breeze-brushed, pine-needled branches. An outward sense of serenity pervaded the scene, softening somewhat the turmoil of his interior life.

It was too late for regrets or remorse. The cat was out of the bag. Scott's thoughts now centered on the Mexican and what he might be thinking. Of course, he must know they were brother and sister. Did it matter to him? Still, the exposure of their secret, albeit to a complete stranger, seemed a ridiculous irony. Was he making too much of the exposure? In a few days the Mexican would disappear from their lives.

Surely in the course of these treks, Tomas had observed bizarre conduct on the part of Harry's clients. Wasn't he outside the orbit of their lives, a mere facilitator of the wilderness adventure, with absolutely no interest in making social contact? Then why the angst? Perhaps it was the idea that someone knew, that they had been outed finally, their guilt exposed.

Courtney seemed far less concerned than he.

"That wasn't very smart," he had commented on their way back to camp.

"Depends on your perspective. So he saw us. So what?"

"He knows. That's what."

"So he knows."

"It means, Courtney, that we have a witness to our—"

"What does it matter? He's just a flunky doing his job. He has no investment in what Harry's clients do. So he saw two people screwing. What does our relationship mean to him? So what? You've always been a nervous Nelly, Scott, and you're getting worse. Where's the downside here? Threaten to tell Dad? Such an idea would be far beyond his radar range. He wouldn't understand it."

"Who does?" Scott mused.

"Let's be honest. We turn each other on. Always have. Call it an aberration, call it a taboo, call it a perversion, call it whatever you like. When we do it, the pleasure comes from somewhere real deep inside, deep, real deep. Don't ask why, and don't take it so seriously. And stop all this love crap. It doesn't mean squat. Just leave it alone."

"Leave it alone? Simple for you."

"Come on, Scottie. Older is supposed to make you smarter."

"I've heard that before."

"I know. Besides, after this so-called adventure, providing all goes well, we'll go our separate ways again. Meanwhile get it while it's hot. Fifty years from now, who'll give a rat's ass about who fucked whom?"

"So that's all it was about."

"Get real, Scott. Time to stop making a molehill into a mountain."

He shrugged. Any discussion was pointless. Life had certainly toughened her. More so than him. Constant rejection, frustration, and failure had made her more ruthless, more determined, more cunning than ever. She had armored herself with harder stuff than he had. Perhaps it was time to learn from her example.

"Go with the flow," she went on. "Who cares? Worry about that little Mexican prick? You've got to be kidding. Let him jerk off on it. Besides, we've got more important fish to fry."

They had walked back to camp mostly in silence. It continued to bother him. Someone else knew. He could not dismiss it as trivial. As for the other matter discussed, he put it aside. It was too appalling to contemplate.

They sat around the fire, sipping their wine. He forced himself to disregard any further thought of Tomas and what he had seen.

"What's on for tomorrow?" Courtney asked.

"Harry mentioned a ride around Bridger Lake," their father said. "I think I remember that. It was like a mirror if I recall, lots of trumpeter swans, gulls, great blue herons. Good picture material."

"And the largest trout you'll every encounter."

It was Harry who had come up behind him, in the familiar aura of an alcoholic haze.

"I'm game," their father said, laughing.

"Maybe get some rainbows or brook trout," Harry said. "They get fat in the lake. Good hiking, too. There's a trail around the lake. Besides, it's a great ride about five miles from here, a lovely trail ride. We'll see lots of game. Maybe fucking wolves again. Or a grizzly."

They drank more wine until Tomas served their dinner. Handing him his metal plate, Scott was suddenly aware of his eye contact, and the quick flash of a thin knowing smile. Oddly, he expected a wink, which thankfully never came.

"So, Dad," Courtney began cautiously, as if she were merely making idle conversation. "Tell me about this lady you're involved with."

"You mean Muriel," her father answered.

"It's comforting to know you have someone," Courtney said.

"She's a wonderful woman."

"Is she?" Courtney asked.

"Very much so. And sincere."

"Did you say you were contemplating a more binding relationship?"

"We've discussed it."

"Despite the age difference?"

"It is a consideration."

"And all its implications?" Courtney asked. Scott remained silent, wondering if she was getting too close to the bone.

"Yes, we have."

He noted his father's reluctance. He seemed to be holding back.

"Are you sure she's right for you, Dad?" Courtney asked, probing carefully.

"Yes. I believe so." He nodded as if it needed such a gesture of reassurance. "She's very wise, very practical, very sensible. I told you that she could never take your mother's place. She knows that. She wants us to be one happy family, all of us. Her children and mine." He paused and smiled. "As a matter of fact, this trek is mostly her idea."

"Her idea! That's curious, Dad," Courtney said. "Why would it be her idea? She wasn't here before."

"As I said, she wants us to be one happy family. Let's face it, we've had some difficulties. No, no, let's not go there. I promised myself. Muriel thought it would be a good thing if we went someplace, you know, the three of us alone, where we could sort of reconnect, know each other again. Resolve all matters between us. What better place than here? We were a real family here."

"Smart woman," Scott said, with obvious sincerity. He noted that Courtney had cocked her head and narrowed her eyes. The gesture struck him as ominous.

"You mean you've confided in her?" she asked, unable to hide her discomfort.

"Of course."

"A stranger?"

"Not to me, Courtney. She has confided in me as well. We think that's appropriate. We need to know what baggage each is carrying. We have a wonderful open relationship."

"How nice," Courtney said, barely audible. The remark did not hide the edge of sarcasm.

Scott became agitated at her attitude.

"She sounds great, Dad," he intervened quickly. "I mean her suggestion to resolve differences."

"What about her children, Dad?" Courtney persisted. "Are there differences with them as well that have to be resolved?"

Temple offered a genial smile, obviously ignoring any signs of "attitude" in his daughter.

"Believe it or not, they don't seem to have any issues between them or with Muriel. She was a working single mother. A widow. She raised them by herself. Seems to have done a very good job. They are extremely devoted to her."

"I'm glad to hear that," Courtney said, with some annoyance. "Are they devoted to you as well?"

"They want their mother to be happy. And they do approve of our relationship."

"Who wouldn't?" Courtney muttered under her breath. Her sarcasm was making Scott nervous.

"I suppose she plans to keep her job with your accounting firm?" Courtney asked.

"Depends." He paused, his eyes shifting between his children. He seemed suddenly hesitant. "I told her she was welcome to come in with me."

"Like Mom?" Courtney said.

Scott gave his sister yet another admonishing look. Cool it, sis, he tried to tell her with his eyes.

"I told you nothing could ever replace Mom. Muriel would work with me, help me." He looked again at his children in turn. "Look guys, how many times have I offered each of you to come in with me? That offer still stands. Frankly I am baffled by your refusal, both of you. I have a going business that is interesting and profitable. You can make an extraordinary living. I guess I haven't been persuasive enough."

"We don't want to, Dad," Courtney said. "Don't you understand that? We have our own lives, our own destinies." She turned to Scott. "Isn't that right, Scott?"

Scott nodded. His own motives had little to do with personal destiny.

"I'm sorry, Dad," Courtney explained. "I wish I had the passion for it. I'm an actor. It's my calling. I hate the jewelry business. All that butt kissing. Besides, we've been through that so many times. I'm sorry about that, but I just don't want it."

"And you, Scott?" Temple said, turning to his son. "Still no interest?" He paused. "Considering."

Scott knew his father's shorthand. It meant "considering your many failures." He did not reply.

"So this woman would be your partner?" Courtney pressed.

"Muriel, darling. Her name is Muriel."

Scott noted his father's effort at patience and tolerance.

"Yes. Muriel. I had forgotten for the moment," Courtney acknowledged.

"We haven't discussed that part," their father said. "She would have to leave her job, of course. But she seems eager to help. And she does know the business aspect and the numbers."

"Of course. The numbers," Courtney muttered.

"Be nice to have someone who knows so much about the business," Scott said, determined to keep the tension down.

"So she will be a partner?" Courtney asked.

"If we marry, we're automatic partners, aren't we?"

"You'd better be sure about this, Dad," Courtney said. "I've heard lots of horror stories."

"Actually I am sure. Why would I consent otherwise?"

Scott could see that he was beginning to get somewhat uncomfortable under her interrogation.

"Father knows best," Scott interjected, hoping to lighten the atmosphere.

Thankfully, Harry joined them, and they aborted any further conversation on the subject of Muriel. Their father seemed relieved.

Tomas collected their plates and poured coffee into metal cups.

"Nishe night," Harry said, his slurred speech and the usual alcoholic mist that surrounded him a telling barometer of his condition.

Tomas handed him a full plate, and he made a pretense of eating, but it was obvious that solid food was not his principal interest.

"Not hungry," Harry said, emptying his plate in the fire. Tomas shrugged and took the empty plate from him. Scott noted an unmistakable sneer of disgust in the Mexican's face. No love lost there, he thought. Neither man enlisted his sympathy, although, he feared the Mexican far more than he tolerated the outfitter.

Like many drunks, Harry seemed to believe that he was in control, and he again announced in a rambling slurred way that tomorrow they would go to Bridger Lake and have lunch on its banks. Worse, he did not realize that he was being repetitive. They looked at each other with some confusion. This man was obviously not operating on all cylinders.

Speaking slowly as if to disguise his state, Harry repeated his description of the area. They listened with forced tolerance, exchanging nervous glances. After his brief and badly articulated description, Harry rose and staggered back to his tent.

"Good God," Scott murmured.

"He's a menace," Courtney said.

"Is he like that often?" their father asked Tomas.

"Sometime," Tomas replied, without expression, addressing the cooking fire.

"He wasn't that way the last time," his father said. "If I had known…" His words trailed off.

"Does shake one's confidence," Courtney muttered. "People change."

"Maybe we should talk to him," Scott said. "Let's face it, we're his dependents out here."

"Not a very secure feeling, is it, Tomas?" their father said.

"He okay," Tomas said, obviously determined to shield his employer, showing his dependency. "He know if rangers come, he be in big trouble."

"Trouble?" Temple asked.

The Mexican turned away, perhaps thinking that he had talked too much. But Temple continued to prod him.

"What exactly do you mean, Tomas?" he pressed.

Tomas turned again and lowered his voice. Despite his mostly expressionless face, his cunning and intelligence showed in his eyes. While his command of English seemed adequate, his understanding of the language seemed acute. He's not fooling me, Scott thought.

"Lose license to guide. People give bad report, he got trouble." He cast a surprisingly revealing contemptuous look in the direction of Harry's tent.

"Why would he take the chance of losing his livelihood?" Temple pressed. "It sounds stupid."

Tomas nodded and shrugged, feigning ignorance, but their father still wouldn't let the matter drop. Scott worried about his persistence for other reasons.

"Do they pull inspections? You know, a surprise visit? They see him in this condition, they've got to blow the whistle. Surely, they must look around. Not a very good image for the park service. He must have a pretty hefty supply of booze."

Tomas did not answer, but there was a sense that he was holding something back.

"Leave it alone, Dad," Scott said.

"And the booze. Smells sweetish, like bourbon." Temple pressed, ignoring Scott's appeal. "And the weight. He did make a big deal about weight. How many bottles could he possibly bring in?"

Posed as a question, Tomas exchanged glances with their father. His only reply was a shrug as he continued to fuss at the cooking fire.

Scott listened to this conversation with increasing impatience.

"What's the point, Dad?" Scott muttered, looking at Courtney.

"It's a legitimate concern…" Temple muttered.

"He be fine," Tomas blurted suddenly with some show of impatience, looking up. "Be okay. You no worry."

"Let's hope so," Scott said, looking at his father.

"But what happens," Temple said, his concern accelerating, "if he can't do his job?"

"Dad!" Scott said sharply. "What do you want from him?"

"Listen to Scott, Dad," Courtney seconded.

Tomas glanced at Scott then at Courtney, a thin smile forming on his lips. He seemed to be mocking them.

"Suppose he gets, you know, really smashed?" Temple posed, ignoring his children's rebuke. "Unable to function?"

"Tole you. He be okay," Tomas said, getting more and more defensive under Temple's interrogation.

Courtney spoke up. She seemed genuinely frightened.

"There's always a first time. Addictive people think they can handle anything. Unfortunately, they crash. It could happen out here. Not a very comforting possibility. What the hell happens if he can't function? Do you take over, Tomas? Hell, I hope you know the way around here."

"I know," Tomas said, looking at her archly, his expression clearly brazen. "I tole you. He okay. No worry too much about notheeng. He like booze. Four years I be with him. Everybody go home happy."

"Hope you're right, Tomas," Temple said.

"Not worry," Tomas said, as if repeating a mantra. "He okay."

He shrugged, mumbling something in Spanish, then turned away, concentrating on the cleanup chores, leaving the three of them to their conversation as they sipped their coffee and munched on Twinkies. They were silent until Tomas picked up the plates and headed for the stream for washing.

"I think I better talk to Harry," Temple said, when Tomas was out of earshot. "Could be dangerous. A drunken guide . . ."

"Better be diplomatic, Dad," Courtney interjected. "An addict gets insulted when you tell him you think he's addicted."

"I don't think we should worry about his being insulted," her father said with annoyance. "He's getting paid well for this trip. Hell, I thought he was in big demand as he had been years ago. He made it sound like people were out there bidding for his services. We're the clients for crying out loud. This keeps up, I'm going to report him. Why would he want to endanger his livelihood?" He was growing increasingly agitated.

"Just tread easy," Scott cautioned. "We're out here alone."

"Something about Tomas also bothers me," Temple said.

"Bothers me, too," Scott muttered, cutting a glance at Courtney.

"I think he's playacting, a lot smarter than he appears. He wants us to think he's just a lackey," Temple said.

"Not our business," Scott said, suddenly fearful of involving the Mexican.

"Harry sure treats him like shit," Courtney said.

"That's his problem. Not ours," Scott said, hoping that would end it.

Their conversation hinted at a diminished authority on their part, as if what Tomas had witnessed had made them lesser in his eyes, not worthy of even that special respect reserved for clients. Scott forced himself to deflect his thoughts.

The three of them sat in silence for a long time. Scott wanted them to put the issue of Harry's drunkenness behind them and pick up the strings of their earlier conversation.

He was also wary of any conversation involving Tomas. Besides, they were veering away from the main issue between them. He needed to force them back on track.

It was obvious that their father was begging for a reconciliation, his mind and heart open to a change in the way he dealt with his children. They mustn't, under any circumstances, deflect his purpose. He had come all this way to make things right. Nothing must interfere with that process.

"All we want is for you to be happy, Dad," Scott said, looking at his sister. "Isn't that right, Courtney?"

"Of course, Dad. That's our wish."

Her sincerity was suspect, but Scott was gratified that she was, at the very least, playing the part of the devoted daughter.

"I'm glad," their father said. "And I want you both to be happy."

They were quiet again for a long time. The air became chilled, and Scott threw another log on the fire. They watched the flames catch and flare. Scott sensed they were heading back on track now, the worries about Harry put on hold.

For the moment.

Chapter 12

—◆—

"God, I miss your mother," Temple said, his eyes moistening, reflecting the flickering light. "I loved that time when you guys were young and we were a family. They were good times, weren't they?"

Scott and his sister looked at each other. Looking back, Scott had mixed feelings about what could be defined as good times. His incestuous relationship with his sister had distorted memories of his upbringing. The shrinks said his failures might be attributed to his need for punishment.

"Yes," Courtney said suddenly, perhaps unable to bear letting the question hang between them. "They were good times, Dad. Yes, they were great times."

"Mom and I loved watching you on the stage, Courtney. You were terrific, and we were proud as punch. Your Shakespeare parts were extraordinary. Moving. Nothing, but nothing, could beat your Lady Macbeth. Gave your mom and me the chills."

"Thanks, Dad. I loved that part."

"And you, Scottie," their father mused. "I remember the first time I saw you in that basket at Mount Sinai, a little bundle of blue, roaring your lungs out. Mom and I standing by the window, wondering if you were in pain or something. Courtney had been a quieter baby. Maybe more contented. It amazed us to see your little body. We both kept counting your fingers and toes. You just can't convey what it meant to us young kids ourselves seeing your little body. And here's the funny part. We took you home and Mom laid you on the bassinette, and we removed the little piece of gauze you had around your penis from the circumcision. Must have triggered an urge or something and by God you peed right in your mother's eye. I'll never forget that. I'll never forget any of it. God, we worried about you."

He turned to Courtney. "Both of you. We worried ourselves sick over each of you. The slightest little cough. If you didn't burp. Hell, even your bowel movements were carefully inspected for who knows what. Courtney, you were colicky and I spent the first few months of your life walking you across the apartment, trying to get you to sleep. You were one hell of a howler. Funny, how you remember those things. So long ago…After all, you were the most creative achievement, brother and sister. One of each, how lucky to have conceived one of each!" His eyes moistened as he wiped them with the back of his hand and cleared his throat. "You can't imagine the initial feeling of parenthood. It never leaves you, no matter what. It becomes part of you and can never be obliterated by subsequent events. It is beyond simple sentiment. It is a lifelong attachment and can only end with…death."

His father's comment recalled his sister's remarks earlier and sent a cold chill through Scott.

Despite the fact that he had not fathered a child, he could understand the depth of his father's feelings. He might have been easier on himself if his father had been more indifferent to his children, less loving, less devoted.

In the silence that followed his father's words, Scott could hear only the crackling of the fire fed by a new log piled on by Tomas and, beyond, the wind rustling through the top branches of the trees.

"Funny how the memories roar back in a foreign environment, especially in the wilderness," their father said, breaking the quiet. "Do you guys remember what we talked about around the fire that first time? I do. Did I ever tell you how I met your mother?"

Many times, Scott wanted to say, but held back. It was important to let his father continue without interruption. He was moving back in time, getting in touch with their past. Scott glanced toward Courtney who had raised her eyes in a gesture of exasperation.

"Actually I picked her up on Jones Beach," their father said, needing no permission. "She was this lovely, slender, dark-haired girl lying there sunning herself at the edge of the ocean. It was a hot day, and she had brought her blanket to the water's edge. I stood watching her for a long time. The water kept edging up as I watched her, and just as a foamy wave threatened to roll over her, I woke her up. And she opened her beautiful brown eyes, and that was that. I was hooked. Hooked for a lifetime. Her lifetime."

He shook his head. "Damn. Damn. Why did she have to go first? It just wasn't fair." He stopped for a moment as if holding back a sob. He did not seem interested in a dialogue but only in the monologue of his life, as if he was compelled to tell this story and had deliberately chosen this most basic unspoiled spot where only nature reigned, raw and pure.

He went through the events of his courtship with their mother, how they had gone down to city hall to get married because she had not wanted to embarrass her parents, who could hardly afford even the most modest of weddings and would not accept any stipend from the better-fixed Temples.

As his father talked, Scott glanced periodically toward Courtney, certain that her reaction to their father's monologue was nothing more than patient toleration. Of course, they had heard it all before.

At the same time, he felt his own childhood feelings toward his father reasserting themselves, opening again, the firewall of adult indifference crumbling. He was a child again, before life and all its mysteries and complications intervened. His gaze met Courtney's, opening up yet again all the old wounds of chronic, despairing, unrequited love.

"I guess I'm boring you both with all this memory stuff," their father said abruptly.

"We're still your kids, Dad," Courtney said.

Scott was certain the words did not reflect her sincerity.

"And you'll always be our loving father," Courtney added, pausing for a moment. "No matter what our differences."

He knew she was acting, plying her trade. She reached out and took her father's hand, bringing it up to her lips. "We love you, Dad. Don't we, Scott?"

"Of course, we do." From his vantage it was an honest acknowledgement.

"We must never forget we're a family," she continued. "A loving family. Connected by blood and history. Right, Dad?"

"Blood and history," their father mused. "I like that."

"There is something I'd like to say, Dad," Scott began, searching for the clear outlines of his father's face, difficult to discern now in the growing darkness. He felt compelled to articulate his genuine feelings. It had been many years since such sentiment had surfaced.

"You've been wonderful, Dad. Nobody could ever fault you for your decency and generosity." He looked toward Courtney, knowing that he was speaking only for himself, but that circumstances meant he would think he was speaking for his sister as well.

"We are a family, Dad. We could never ever forget that. Granted, we haven't lived up to the promise, but we're still out there trying, Dad. Who else can we turn to for help? I know we're not kids anymore, and sometimes we do appear...well... too materialistic. I've had nothing but lousy luck, and Courtney, well, sometimes it takes a long time to weather the bumps in her business. The point is, Dad, we're still trying to make something of ourselves on our own. Sure, we'd love to have your continuing support financially, but I just wanted you to know that whatever you decide won't change the fact that you're our father."

He felt a well of emotion inhibit his speech and grew silent, berating himself for expressing himself badly. Yet he was conscious of having made the point.

"The whole concept of family is one for all and all for one. That's what family means, Dad," Courtney interjected, obviously taking her cue from him. Instantly, Scott knew she was summoning up everything she had ever learned about drama. "I've been awful. I know it. I should never have done what I did at Mom's funeral. It was wrong. Unfeeling. I've been so terribly embarrassed about my conduct and how it must have hurt you. How can I make amends, Dad? "

She paused, wiping away tears that had suddenly appeared.

"I can make it, Dad. I can. Sure I've made mistakes, and God knows I've wasted a lot of your money. I know that. But I believe in my talents. I can make it, Dad. Just give me the opportunity to focus exclusively on my art, my talent."

Listening to her confession, Scott felt carried away on the tide of emotion, even knowing it was false. She was really, really good at her craft. She had convinced him, but then she had always convinced him.

"Sometimes life takes you on a journey you didn't expect," Scott said. "Here I am. Call it whatever you want. My timing is impeccably bad, but I think I've learned a great deal about business, basic industry is where it's at. No wild speculations in technology. Hell, it's not my forte. I know this is my moment, Dad. I can make it big in the food business."

"Yes, he can, Dad."

"And so can she. Your little girl is one talented woman. We just need that little bit of help to make the difference."

Their father remained silent.

"Look, Dad, all we're asking you is just to think about it. That's all we can ask. Mull it over. Don't make any commitments now."

He felt strange. They were both working the same ploy but at different sides of the street, each soliciting him with a different pitch. Above all, despite all his misgivings, he felt his own sincerity. Apparently they had both picked the time of his deepest vulnerability, out here in the isolation of the wilderness, where human beings were strangers.

Their attention was diverted suddenly by Tomas, who had returned from the stream and was fussing with the details of securing the campsite for the night. The fire had died down, and a deep chill began to permeate the air.

"Guess we've talked enough for one night," their father said. They all rose in tandem, and he embraced them both.

"You've both been wonderful. God, how I love you both."

"And we love you, Dad," Courtney said, as they hugged. Scott too returned his father's embrace.

"You're the best, Dad," he said.

"'Night, kids," he said, as he moved to his tent and crawled inside.

Courtney and Scott sat watching the dying embers of the fire as Tomas continued his work. Finally without a word of goodnight, Tomas went to his tent, which was pitched farthest away from theirs, and disappeared inside.

"I just don't trust that man," Scott said, his attention diverted suddenly by imagined consequences.

"What can he do?"

"I don't know, but he knows something he shouldn't."

He felt the sudden pressure of wild speculation. Tomas could tell their father what he saw. Would he be believed? And if he did believe it, what then? Was Tomas smart enough to understand the implications for blackmail? Paranoia! He rebuked himself for the absurdity of the ideas.

"Looks like the old man is primed and ready," Courtney whispered.

Her remark filled him with disgust, and he did not comment. They grew silent again, lost in their own thoughts.

"I don't like this business with that woman," Courtney said, revealing her concerns.

"It's his life. Mom is dead."

"She's got her hooks into him. In time, she'll take over. Hell, he's going to put her in the business."

Her vehemence was undisguised, the words emerging as a hiss.

"She has kids. She'll have his ear. Pillow talk. Our drill is to persuade him to cough up now. I think he might be ready for that."

She grew silent, nodding as if she were debating with herself.

"We're on the verge of being fucked," she persisted.

"Dark thoughts," Scott mused. "Leading to someplace I don't wish to go."

"You're being squeamish," she said.

"And you, Courtney, are being malignant."

"Don't you get it? We need to save ourselves, protect our interests. Self-interest is no sin. Hell, you did pretty good tonight yourself."

"I meant every word."

Reaching out, she caressed his thigh. His reaction was instant.

"You were great tonight, brother. You deserve an award."

She started to unzip him, but he pushed her away.

"No, Courtney. Never again."

He looked toward Tomas's tent. She stood up and looked down at him and shook her head.

"Nighty night," she said. She stretched and went into her tent.

For a few moments, Scott watched the still glowing ashes of the fire, then moved into his tent, and without undressing slipped into his sleeping bag. But the events of the day crowded into his thoughts. His mind churned with anxious and terrible scenarios. Sleep would not come.

At some point, he heard movement, reached over to the tent flap, and peered out through a crack. Logic told him it could be an animal foraging around the camp, maybe a grizzly.

He saw a human figure skulking in the darkness. Curious, he crawled out of the tent and crept stealthily in the direction of the moving figure.

At the edge of the clearing, he stopped and saw Tomas clearly. He was digging with a small shovel at the base of a tree. Lying supine on the ground, Scott watched. After a while, Tomas stopped the process and removed something from the hole he had made. It had the shape of a bottle.

He lay there for a long time watching Tomas cover the hole. Through the trees he saw him open the flap of Harry's tent, put in the bottle, then move back into his own tent. When Scott was certain the camp was quiet again, he crawled back to his tent and slipped back into his sleeping bag.

How clever and resourceful they were: Tomas, the trapped retainer, Harry, the cagey alcoholic and martinet. Slave and master. After a while, admiration turned to fear, and Scott shivered but not from the cold.

Chapter 13

⟶‧⟨⟩‧⟵

They moved along the trail in the crisp morning air. Temple's horse was the last in the line, following Courtney. Ahead of him was Scott, and leading the group was Harry, his complexion pasty, his eyes bloodshot, obviously nursing a profound hangover. He was slumped in his saddle. From time to time, he unscrewed his canteen and took deep sips.

Temple was discomfited but not yet panicked. He'd given Tomas the benefit of the doubt. Perhaps he had been right, and Harry could handle things. He hoped so. At some point, despite Courtney's warning about angering an addict who didn't believe he was addicted, he promised himself that he would talk to him, approach him diplomatically.

Temple had felt great after a good night's sleep, and he was determined not to let the anxiety he felt last night disturb his thoughts. He was bonding with his children, and this seemed more important than worrying about Harry's drinking problem.

He greeted Courtney with a kiss, and they eagerly attacked Tomas's breakfast of bacon and eggs, hot cowboy coffee, and fresh biscuits and jam. The eggs were made to order, and Tomas fixed them with perfect efficiency, handing them their metal plates as each order was completed.

Soon Scott joined them, looking slightly rumpled and bleary-eyed. Temple noted patches of grey in his son's sprouting beard, yet another sign of his family's aging. The burst of nostalgia he had articulated the night before had comforted

168

him, helping to vent any residual hostility and disappointment he might have harbored about his children.

Perhaps, he acknowledged, he was wrong to withhold his largesse from his children, despite his belief that they were dogged by failure and false hopes. Maybe he was the one at fault, going from generous and supportive to what they perceived as an unyielding and stubborn miser.

It was too late for any attempt at behavior modification. He had to accept reality. So what if they continued to fail and waste more money? They were his kids for God's sake, his progeny; and he loved them.

Besides, who was he to judge? They both might make it after all. Some people were late bloomers. Some people had to take hard knocks early in life to give them the strength to find their path. After all, he had taken the easy road, scuttling his early aspirations in music for the safe bet of his father's business. So what if they didn't want to go into his business? They had a right to their own life, their own ambitions.

It would hardly break him financially to accede to his children's wishes. Hell, even if he wrote it off, there would still be enough left for the good life with Muriel. As for their inheritance, he would honor Bea's promise, with the proviso that such valuation would consider anything earned after he married Muriel. He was determined to be fair-minded and ethical.

He felt relieved to have unburdened himself to his children about his relationship with Muriel, and he was deeply moved by their wishes for his happiness.

Muriel had been very wise and understanding to suggest this trip. It was giving him a chance to reunite with his children and bridge the divide between them. Suddenly he missed Muriel.

The line of horses followed trails that circled upward then down again. The terrain was a series of small hills. Ahead of him, Courtney's horse seemed distracted, stopping occasionally to munch grasses along the trail. He had to halt his horse to wait for hers to finish its snack.

When the gap between horses ahead lengthened, Courtney's horse bounced forward in a canter to catch up. Temple's horse did the same. It was not a smooth ride.

Not far from camp as they rounded a bend, Harry raised his hand to stop the train and pointed in the direction of a small waterfall in the distance. He could make out the outline of a large animal.

"Grizzly," Harry said. "There by the fall. Big sumbitch, isn't he?" He handed Temple his binoculars. "Big bastards are always hungry."

"He's gorgeous," Temple commented, passing the binoculars to Courtney.

"Looks lie a teddy bear from here," Courtney commented, handing the glasses to Scott.

"Wouldn't want to meet him on a dark night," Scott said.

They watched the grizzly until he caught a fish in his big paw and put it in his mouth.

"He was poking around the camp last night," Harry said. "Could smell him."

"Now you tell us," Courtney said.

"Didn't want to scare you," Harry laughed. "Don't think he's not watching us. He'd love to have that meat we got strung up on the pole."

"That's a happy thought, Harry," Courtney muttered.

"Long as it's not us he's after," Scott said.

"Bet you'd make one tasty munch, Scottie," Courtney said, giggling.

"Better we watch him from here," Temple said.

"You got that right," Harry chuckled.

When the grizzly had finally passed out of view, they moved forward on the trail. Occasionally, Harry pulled his lead horse to a stop and pointed to various sights along the way: an elk cow and her calf lazily drinking from a stream, a moose grazing on low-hanging aspen branches, an osprey circling in the sky looking for prey.

His knowledge assuaged Temple's earlier fears. Perhaps Tomas was right. Harry could handle the situation.

Through the trees Temple could see the slate grey, mirrored surface of what he had been told was Bridger Lake glistening in the rising morning sun. They moved through forests of aspens and evergreens, following the trail. Ahead of him Courtney was still having trouble with her recalcitrant horse, which continued to stall and munch the grasses that edged the trail.

Periodically, she pulled on the horse's reins with shouts of impatience when it wouldn't obey. At one point, all the pulling and cursing got her so frustrated and angry that the reins dropped from her grip.

Her horse, now free from the tension of the reins, moved suddenly off the trail. Instead of softly trying to talk the horse back on the trail, she panicked and screamed. The horse, equally panicked, started to move forward in fear, threading its way through the forest at an accelerating speed.

The sound seemed to wake Harry into instant alertness, and he turned his horse in pursuit, shouting for Courtney to stop screaming. Miraculously, she grew silent, and found the presence of mind to embrace the horse's neck and avoid the low-lying branches. The horse slowed, but the danger to her did not abate until she managed to extract her boots from the stirrups and slip to the ground.

Scott and his father followed Harry, who had dismounted near Courtney. She sat on the ground, exhibiting both anger and humiliation, but she appeared, except for her dignity, to be uninjured.

"Damn it, woman!" Harry rebuked. "Didn't I tell you? Never leave go of the reins."

"Fucking horse," she fumed. "It nearly killed me."

Harry, shaking his head, helped her to her feet. She brushed off her pants and shook her head.

"I guess the Temples are accident-prone," she said, in self-deprecation.

"You scared the hell out of us," Scott said, with a glance at his father.

"All's well that ends well," Temple said, greatly relieved.

"Not ended yet, Dad," Courtney said, looking pointedly at her brother.

Harry had remounted quickly and caught up with Courtney's horse, which had stopped to graze. He led it back to where they stood. Apparently, his anger had accelerated.

"Don't you people understand?" he said, his expression taut with anger, his face florid. "I warned you about this. Please pay attention. You can't be dumb about this. Read my lips, for chrissake."

"Hey, Harry," Courtney said. "It was an accident."

"All I ask is you pay attention. I haven't got eyes in back of my head."

His remark had an edge of nastiness.

"Hey, Harry, we're the clients, remember," Temple said. He was tempted to bring up the high cost of the trek but demurred.

"You're paying for an adventure, Temple, and I'm trying to give you your money's worth. But I can't do squat unless you pay attention."

"Cool it," Scott interjected. "We're paying attention. And there's no call to browbeat us."

"Fair enough. I apologize. Just don't do dumb-ass things. I'm a guide not a babysitter."

Courtney exchanged glances with her father then turned to the guide.

"You got your fucking nerve," she said.

"Easy, Courtney," Temple said. A bad hangover he assumed was giving Harry a nasty edge.

"Don't tell me what I got, woman!" Harry shot back, his face growing to beet red. "Out here I'm the boss, and I'm responsible for your safety, which means you listen to me. I know this turf, you don't. You'd all be dead in a few days if I weren't here. So don't tell me my business."

"God damn it!" Courtney shot back. "You're our fucking employee."

Temple could tell that worse was coming.

"Hold on. Hold on, Courtney. This is getting out of hand."

"Yes, it is, Dad. We don't have to take this shit from him."

"Easy, Courtney," Scott cautioned.

Temple turned to Harry, desperately trying to assume the role of peacemaker. The reality was that they were indeed completely at Harry's mercy. Temple searched his mind for some way to defuse the situation.

"Come on, Courtney," he told his daughter. "No sense making more out of this than it deserves. You're fine. No harm done. I'm fine after yesterday's problem. Let's leave it at that."

Obviously trying to control her anger, Courtney kicked at the dirt and grew silent.

"Scott," Temple said. "Take Courtney for a walk. I want to talk to Harry alone."

Reluctantly, offering a mad parting look at Harry, Scott moved her away.

"That daughter of yours better watch her tongue," Harry said. His anger had not abated.

"It was an accident, Harry," Temple said. "Let's not blow it out of proportion."

"All I ask is that you people follow instructions. Is that so much to ask, Temple?"

"No it isn't, Harry. We'll try to keep out of trouble."

"Better believe it."

"Let's clear the air. We know you're a great guide and all that. So let's all calm down."

They exchanged glances while Temple tried to summon up the courage to discuss the man's obvious drinking problem.

"There is one thing, Harry," Temple began, clearing his throat. "Believe me, I don't want to start more trouble, and I'd like to discuss this in a nice way."

"What are you talking about, Temple?"

"It's just that we don't feel comfortable..." Hesitating, he sucked in a deep breath.

"Well, go ahead," Harry pressed.

"In a nutshell, it's...well,...your drinking."

Harry's eyes narrowed, and a nerve had begun to palpitate in his jaw. He cocked an ear in Temple's direction.

"What are you saying?"

"I'm calling it to your attention is all. You seem to be drinking more than I remember, and it has us concerned."

Nostrils twitching, Harry looked away. He kicked at the ground.

"You trying to make trouble for me, Temple?"

"Not at all," Temple said, trying desperately to keep his voice level and show a calm demeanor. "I just thought…well, it makes us uncomfortable. I'm not being accusatory. Our last experience with you was wonderful, Harry. That's why we thought it would be great to hire you again. It's just that…" He could tell by Harry's expression that he was in deep denial, which was exactly Courtney's point last night.

"I say we drop this, Temple," Harry muttered. "You're way off base."

"Well, Harry," Temple sighed. "I just thought—"

"Stop thinking, Temple. For your information, it's bullshit. Besides, there's a weight limit to what we bring in here. Like you and your children, I brought a modest supply, and I don't, despite what you think, abuse it." He seemed to have worked through his anger, and his tone grew more conciliatory as he spoke.

"Listen, Harry. As you say, I could be way off base. If so, I apologize. No need for us to have any differences at all. I mention it only because it's our perception."

"Fuck your perception."

Temple was stunned by the outburst and again forced himself to remain calm. It occurred to him suddenly that in a fit of rage Harry could leave them stranded here. At the thought, he felt his stomach tighten.

"You're taking it the wrong way, Harry."

"Am I?"

His belligerence was palpable.

"Look, if I've offended you—"

"Just bug off, Temple. I know my job."

"I know that, Harry."

Harry shrugged, muttering under his breath, and started to move the horses to the trail as Temple followed beside him.

"So let the matter drop, Harry. Okay?"

"God damn citified, spoiled, soft-assed, fucking shits," he muttered.

"I told you, I'm sorry."

"Just don't tell me how to run my outfit."

"Let's just drop it, Harry. Okay?"

Harry nodded, spat, and grew silent. He moved the horse back to the path. Temple followed. He had made his point, but it gave him little comfort.

When they reached the trail again, Temple noted that Courtney and Scott huddled a few yards off. They were deep in animated conversation. Harry looked toward Temple.

"Just get her to cool down," Harry said in a more conciliatory and businesslike tone without the slightest hint of apology. "We don't need any contention out here. Counterproductive for the experience."

"I'll talk to her."

Harry tied Courtney's horse to a tree, mounted his horse again, and set off to gather the other horses, which had moved off the trail.

Temple joined his children.

"You talk to him about his drinking?" Scott asked.

"Yes, I did. He was madder than hell."

"What did I tell you?" Courtney said.

"I hope he got the message."

"You think so, Dad? They never get the message until something bad happens."

"Like what?"

"Delirium tremens, maybe. Or he does something stupid, endangers himself and others. You expect him to have an epiphany out here and take the pledge. The son of a bitch is a shit-faced drunk, and we're stuck with him out here..." Her eyes scanned the horizon. "...in the middle of fucking nowhere."

"Say what you want, he has been helpful to us when we got into trouble." Temple, despite his own misgivings, was trying to put the best face on the issue. "The important thing is that we're all right." He looked around him and swept the area with his arm. "Besides, nothing can spoil this. And...," he paused, his eyes searching his children's faces. "We're getting to reconnect out here. That's worth its weight in gold to me. So please, kids, let's cool it. We don't have much choice."

He watched them digest his plea, exchange glances, and shrug their understanding.

"Sorry, Dad," Courtney said. "You do have a point."

"Look, as long as he can function well," Scott pointed out, "no need to look for trouble. Let's try to smooth things over."

"You mean apologize?" Courtney asked, snickering.

"Just try to hold down your temper," Temple said. "No matter what, he's got the upper hand."

"What do you think, Scott?" she asked.

"He owes us the apology, Dad," Scott said. "Not the other way around."

"Let's not complicate things," Courtney said. "I'll apologize."

"Good girl. Anyway, he says that he could not have brought lots of booze in anyhow because of the weight problem."

"And you believed him?" Courtney chortled.

"It sounded credible enough," Temple said. "Remember the fuss at the trailhead?"

"Sure, Dad, I remember," Courtney replied, shrugging and looking away. "Tell him, Scott."

"I was waiting for a chance when we were alone. He's got booze stashed away," Scott said. "Buried." He recounted what he had seen Tomas dig up the night before.

"Buried?" Temple was aghast.

"Maybe in case the rangers visit," Scott added. "Or because of the weight. He's probably got booze buried everywhere. Clever bastard. And his Mexican sidekick is his willing accomplice."

"Do you think we can blow his license?" Courtney asked.

"Let's not blow anything," Temple snapped. "Let's just try to keep things calm. At this stage, he's functioning and apparently doing his job. No sense stirring the pot. Besides, things seem to be going well and—let's face it—we can't blame Harry for our missteps. Let's just pay more attention to his warnings."

He was worried, but he didn't want them to see it and add to their own anxiety. They grew silent, watching Harry as he led the horses back to the trail.

"I agree, Dad," Courtney said. "No point in getting him all riled up."

Harry came closer. He looked much calmer, less tense. Temple speculated he had had a few nips. As he came forward, the familiar aura of booze was unmistakable.

"Hey, Harry," Courtney said. "Forgive me. I went bananas. I guess the whole episode pissed me off. My fault entirely, I didn't use my head. Bygones, okay?"

Harry nodded, appearing as eager as the others for the apology.

"I forgot it happened," he said, forcing a smile. "Now let's mount up. And hold on to the reins."

They went through the process and all were up on their horses, except their father, who had to be led to a fallen tree to give him the height he needed to mount.

Harry changed the order of the riders, putting Courtney directly behind him and Scott and in front of Temple.

"As old Duke Wayne would put it," Harry said, lifting his arm with a flourish, "move 'em out."

Trouble averted for the moment, Temple thought, trying without success to erase any anxiety from his mind.

Chapter 14

⟫⟫⟫◆⟪⟪⟪

During lunch, Courtney and Scott listened to their father recall memories from their earlier trip. They sat in the shade of a cottonwood tree, munching canned tuna fish sandwiches and candy bars, washing them down with water. Harry had disappeared with his usual explanation to "see about the horses," which were tied to trees out of sight. By now they knew he would be "out of sight" for hours, sipping on his booze.

"Off to the gin mill in the wilderness," Courtney said. "Guy needs twelve steps."

"Sorry about this, kids," Temple said.

"Not your fault, Dad," Scott said.

They watched white, scudding, cottony clouds throw their reflection on the mirrored lake. The light breeze rustling the leaves and branches of the embracing wilderness sounded like soft background music. By then, Courtney was fully recovered from her anger and managed to put it aside and observe the spectacular natural surroundings. Despite all the angst and emotion that punctuated her life, she felt herself begin to relax and soak up the wonders of this unspoiled scene.

Her father had been right about one thing. To disengage from the terrible reality of everyday life with all its frustrations and thwarted dreams and to immerse oneself in the embracing majesty of nature did, indeed, have a positive affect on one's attitude. She found herself enjoying her father's anecdotes of their early family experiences. His enthusiastic recounting and astonishing memory of their early days emphasized how much he enjoyed and cherished those past moments.

It surprised her to note that she had deliberately locked away her most pleasant memories, as if focusing on them would render her too nostalgic and sentimental for the task ahead. Stay focused, she urged herself.

"You were two of the cutest kids on the planet," their father told them as they sat on a flat stone outcrop eating their lunch. "Do you remember when you were little and frightened by nightmares or some imaginary enemy, how you would crawl into bed with your mother and me?" He turned to Scott. "Both of you did that, sometimes at the same time. It could go on for weeks. At times, the four of us would share one king-size bed. Tell you the truth, kids, we both loved it, your mother and me. You were everything to us. Everything."

He grew silent again, undoubtedly savoring the old memories. When he spoke, it was to recall yet another memory of their childhood. Listening, Courtney found herself reflecting on what others might call a gap in her life, the lack of progeny. Was it really a gap? Children would inhibit the pursuit of her dream. For her father, their childhood had been the highlight of his life. Good, she thought, let him revel in the memories, prime himself.

"And when you got sick," Temple continued, "with the flu or measles or chicken pox—you had them all, both of you— your mother and I would go crazy with worry and sit by your bedside all night until you were out of danger. We were both worrywarts when it came to you guys. And you, Scott, you scared the daylights out of us. Remember how you fell and sliced your head just above the eye, and your mother and I rushed you to the emergency ward of Columbia Presbyterian? Hell, we thought you'd lost an eye."

She watched as her father searched Scott's face for any sign of a scar. It had faded but was still visible, and he touched it with his finger.

"Living memories," he said, shaking his head. "Powerful stuff."

She hadn't realized how overly sentimental he had become and was unable to reconcile it with his cutting off financial help. Okay, Daddy, she thought, cheering him on. He was moving in the right direction. A profound change was taking place. He was definitely softening.

Finishing their lunch, her father took out his digital camera and shot more pictures of both her and her brother and the landscape. She felt a sudden wave of resentment grip her when it crossed her mind that the pictures would also be shown to Muriel the Wise, as she began to characterize her in her mind.

Later, after Courtney and Scott had left their father to nap under a tree and had begun a hike along the lakeshore, they reflected on what appeared to be his changing attitude.

"He wants to do the right thing, Scottie," she told him. "He is in thaw mode."

"Would be nice," Scott muttered. "He sure as hell got a bang out of bringing us up."

"Let's hope the memories work their magic." She paused and grew reflective. "Of course, we need him to come across now. But looking ahead worries me. Muriel won't be idle. She's sure to cut into our take when the old man checks out."

"Seems a crude way to put it."

"Never mind crude. I'm talking logic. She'll water us down. That's a given."

"Jesus, I hate this subject," Scott said.

"You may hate it, Scottie, but the implications are pretty clear."

"So what? So we're watered down. Who cares?"

"I care," she snickered. "Maybe we can get him to gift us for heavy bread now. Why wait until D-day? It's the perfect opportunity."

"Here we go again," Scott sighed.

"I'm serious. You heard him rave on about us little kiddies. It's as good a time as we'll ever have to…get us out of the Muriel loop."

"What do you suggest?"

She thought for a long moment.

"Maybe gift us now. Let the shysters figure out a way. Don't tell me you'd object, big brother. It would buy him a lot of conscience, get rid of any residual guilt." She laughed. "One way to get at it. I'd settle at this stage for a generous continuing stipend. And you, brother dear, a nice big investment in your deals."

"God, Courtney. Is that all you think about?"

"Not all," she winked.

"Be nice thought. He gets back, makes the changes, and can move ahead to wedded bliss with a clear conscience."

She shook her head. Another thought had popped into her mind.

"What the fuck does he want to marry her for? You don't have to do that today. He's nuts! Nobody gets married until it's absolutely necessary," she said, giggling. "Look at us."

"You know him. Wants to do the right thing. Man is probably in love."

"Ain't love grand?" Courtney sighed, with obvious sarcasm.

Scott grew thoughtful. His complexion seemed to have paled. "But it does change the landscape." He spat on the ground. "Love! When it strikes, you lose control." He resisted meeting her gaze.

Not *that* again, she thought. It was a condition she acknowledged she had never really experienced.

"Ring around the finger. That's her game. Love shmove. Prenup or not, marriage is a binder. He has her down as the wisest lady in the land. And she gets all the brownie points for her marvelous advice. How sweet and noble! How thoughtful! Bringing the family together again." She felt a wave of antagonism washing over her. "Believe me, I know her strategy. A woman knows. She thinks she's found a patsy. I don't trust her. I don't trust her one bit."

"You don't even know her, Courtney."

"Believe me. I know her. I know the type."

They had stopped walking and moved to a spot with an extraordinary view of the lake and mountains beyond. The sun hung high in the sky, and the temperature was comfortably warm. Her mind still swarmed with ideas regarding her financial future.

"What we've got to do, Scottie, is stop hinting and start laying it on the line, talking in practical terms. He's a shrewd negotiator as well as a father. What we want is a real commitment. Get close and personal. Have it out."

"What's does that mean?"

"Before he gets in deeper with Muriel, let's try to hammer out a solution for us. Hell, we're the first family. There's a certain entitlement in being, well, being first in line. We've got to protect our turf."

"I hate talking about this, Courtney. It's so…so calculating. Can't we change the subject?"

She snickered, then moved away from him into the tree line beyond the shore, and stretched out on a patch of grass, putting her hands behind her head.

"Feels good," she said, smiling, watching him, knowing her pose was seductive. He got the message and chuckled.

"Why not?" she purred, swinging her hips from side to side.

"It's trouble," he sighed.

"Just fun, Scottie. Why not?"

"It's hard to live with, Courtney."

"Not for me, Scottie. Hell, take a peek at the Internet for chrissake. It's a fucking orgy. Brothers and sisters. That's only the tiny part of it. You'll see mothers and sons, mothers and daughters, fathers and daughters, fathers and sons, girls and boys with sheep and dogs, fucking horses and mules, pissing, fisting, every fucking so-called aberration on the planet. And that's just the Internet. It's mainstream, buddy boy. Just don't be so self-righteous and scared, brother mine. If it feels good, do it. So come on in and stop this guilt trip. It'll drive you crazy. It *has* been driving you crazy."

"It's still wrong."

"Screw wrong. Who says?" She started to open her blouse. "Besides, I can't help it, Scottie. Nobody ever made me horny like you. No one. Not ever."

She felt him watching her as she took off her blouse and began to open her jeans. "Come on in, baby, the water's fine."

"You're impossible," Scott sighed, but he did not move away. She reached out, and he stepped away, but she saw his reactive bulge.

"Come on. I know you want it."

"I guess I'm like Pavlov's dog. Always have been." He cleared his throat. "With you."

"Good. Let's put that bullshit away. I'm your addiction, Scottie," she said, pulling off her jeans. "And you're mine."

"Wrong, you're my substance abuse."

"I like that, baby. So abuse me."

She rolled down her panties, kicked them off, and spread her legs.

"See what I got for you, Scottie."

He could not take his eyes off her. She remembered the look, the hunger, and lust. Her reaction was the same. She was being shameless and loved it. Besides, she was testing herself, proving her ability to control him. The sex had always been her most powerful persuader. She waved him forward.

"Come on, Scottie. Fuck your big sister."

He moved a few steps closer.

"It was always best with you, Scottie," she said, reaching out and caressing his erection.

"We're playing with fire," he shrugged. She struggled with his jeans, and soon he was exposed.

"Yum, yum," she whispered, moving closer, beginning to fellate him.

"I always loved to do this," she whispered, stopping abruptly. Then she pulled him down and into her.

"Jesus, Scottie," she cried out, unable to stop the sudden deep orgasm. "Oh God." She felt the trembling pleasure run through her. Then she felt his spasm and heard his gasp.

"As good as it gets, Scottie."

"Story of my life."

It took them both a while to calm down. She lay in the crook of his arm, and they looked upward through the branches at the sky.

"When it's this right, it can't be wrong," she whispered.

"Let it go, Courtney. I can't deal with serious reflection."

"Just plain old recreational sex."

She started to caress him, and again he was aroused.

"It always saluted for you, Courtney," Scott said, reaching for her.

"And it was always ready for you, Scottie."

She insinuated herself under him, and he mounted her, and she rested her thighs on his shoulders.

"Are you...you know?" Scott asked.

"I've been on the pill for years, Scottie."

She felt him inside her, thrusting.

"Deep, baby, as deep as it goes," she called out.

She felt a sense of surrender, of giving way, of letting go, a feeling that she could remember was part of that earlier time. She heard her voice calling out in the wilderness, the cry of a female animal in heat.

"Fuck me hard, baby. Hard." She started to shiver. "Come with me, Scottie darling. Now, now. Let it go."

She felt his spasm and the bottomless pleasure of her own orgasm, long lasting, infinite. They lay locked together, lost in an unknown time zone, cooling down.

"Crazy," she whispered. "Some kind of fever. The intensity..."
Her voice trailed off.

"Madness," he said.

"I'm addicted to brotherly love."

He put a finger on her lips.

"Not the L word. Let's not confront that ever again," he said firmly. "Never. Don't think. Don't analyze. Don't interpret." He seemed to be talking himself into a mindset.

"Go with the flow. Reject all the bullshit," she said, giggling. "Surrender to the pleasure. Don't put your head into it."

"Easier said than done," he mumbled.

"No man ever did this for me, baby brother. You want the truth? I never got off on anyone else. Not once. Only when I remember and think of you all alone."

"Ditto," he said.

They lay intertwined, embracing, attached, and after a while, she felt it happening again.

"Can you believe this?" she said.

She moved her torso in a circular motion.

"Jesus. Again," she cried, as she gripped him, and he responded, thrusting. She caressed his buttocks, gripped them, drew him in, felt explosive ecstatic spasms.

Then, like a wave had washed over them, its energy spent, they found themselves becalmed. She disengaged and slipped into her clothes, and he did the same.

"Call it the wilderness experience," she said, reaching for humor, her refuge now. "The birds do it, the bees do it," she trilled, briefly singing a fragment of the Cole Porter tune. He chuckled.

"How I spent my summer vacation," he mused.

"Fucking your big sister," she said laughing, excising any moral considerations.

He shook his head in mock disapproval, reached for her hand, squeezed it affectionately then let it go again.

"Better than chopped liver," he chuckled, then grew serious. "As long as Dad doesn't know. He hasn't heard your lecture on the Internet. Different generation. Different moral code. He'll think we're pigs, and you can kiss his largesse goodbye."

"We're also thieves, brother mine. He didn't find that out and, if we use our brains, he won't know about the other. Not unless you have the urge to confess."

"No way. I'd die first."

She opened her arms with her palms up in a gesture of "so be it."

"Not on my agenda either, Scottie."

"That Mexican better keep his mouth shut."

"Fuck him. He's too stupid."

He shook his head in silent agreement, and they moved out of the tree line onto the path that ringed the lake. He was right, she decided, to keep what was happening at this mostly mute level, ignoring anything judgmental or reflective. Feeling was all. Pleasure, extreme pleasure was the only criteria of judgment. Fuck the whys and wherefores.

In a few days it would be over, without complications. They would go their separate ways, pursue their separate dreams, perhaps employ the images for private lust, and leave it at that. If all went well, and they played their cards right, they might solve their economic problems at last.

They walked farther around the lake for another hour, then turned back, and headed to where they had made camp. As they came closer, they saw their father sitting on a rise. He held a paperback in his hand, and shielding his eyes from the sun, he waved, and they waved back.

"Is now a good time?" Courtney asked.

"You mean for the big pitch, the closer?"

"What else?"

"Just be kind."

"Kind?"

She wasn't sure what he meant. Of course, she would be kind if that's what it took to gain their objective. Sweetly aggressive was the way she might put it.

"Just follow my lead, Scottie."

"Don't I always?" he sighed.

Chapter 15

⟫◆⟪

"How was it?" their father said, as they got close enough to hear him. He was sitting on a boulder, watching them come forward. She calculated that they had been gone nearly three hours.

"Pretty, Dad. This is a beautiful place," Courtney said. "What have you been doing?"

"Taking pictures. Endless opportunities." He brought out his camera, held it up so that they could see each photo clearly through the viewer.

"Good stuff, Dad," Courtney said.

"Hard to make a mistake with these digitals." He picked up the camera and reviewed for them the last few pictures he had taken. "Fantastic, isn't it? You print the pick of the litter and download to your computer. I'll send you both a set to jog your memory."

"Great, Dad," Scott said.

"Be fun to reminisce," Courtney acknowledged.

"Meaningful fun," Temple said. "I hope it gives you great pleasure."

"It will, Dad. It surely will," Scott said.

Courtney winked at her brother, who nodded. They sat down on either side of their father.

"This was one helluvan idea, Dad," Courtney said, a deliberate opening ploy. "It does bring back the old memories. You were right to get us together in this place."

"I agree, Dad," Scott said. "It would have been great if Mom could be here. Like last time."

"I hope it brings us closer, Dad," Courtney said. She shook her head. "The fact is I haven't been a very good girl. I've been awful." She thought it wise to make that point again, show contrition. He loved contrition, Courtney decided.

"Please, Courtney, none of that. This is a new start for all of us. Right, Scott?"

"I'll buy that, Dad."

"It's really hard to give up a dream, Dad," she said. "It is too powerful, especially when you believe in yourself. I am a realist, Dad. I know I can't make it as an ingénue anymore, but for an actress as she ages, character parts start coming up. I know I can do it. You once believed in me. Remember my Lady Macbeth, how proud you were. All I ask is your support, your loving support. Time is my enemy, Dad. Especially if I have to take all these grunt jobs just to survive. It's exhausting, debilitating. I need your help, Dad. Really. You know what I mean? Permanent, steady financial help."

Their father nodded, obviously reflecting seriously on her request. It wasn't like last time. No lectures. No tough love. Numbers, Dad, she begged him in her mind. Think numbers. Two, three hundred thou a year would do wonders, she thought, maybe a lump sum. She summoned the figure and said it aloud.

"I understand, Courtney," he said without protest. "I really do and, yes, I am reevaluating my decision. Perhaps I was wrong to take such a hard line."

She felt a sense of rising optimism bordering on elation. Was he really in the process of changing his mind?

"I agree with Courtney, Dad," Scott interjected, obviously following her suggestion.

Good boy, brother, she thought as he continued.

"She's got the stuff. Okay, she had a tough time when she was younger. The competition is deadly, and most people, probably ninety-nine percent, lose out in that business. A lot of the breaks are based on pure luck. Give her credit for tenacity, Dad. She's still out there in the fray, and she's right about character parts. But if she's breaking her ass trying to support herself, well, it's a drag. She needs your help, Dad. She really does."

She exchanged glances with him and smiled. They were together again, allies.

"We're not losers, Dad," Courtney explained, sensing the necessity to take up her brother's cause now and to reinforce their sibling solidarity. "Scott has had some bad breaks. It was just bad timing. You can't blame it all on him. Besides, people learn by their mistakes. Scott is a winner, Dad. All he needs is the backing and breaks." She turned toward her brother and their eyes met. "I love my brother, Dad, and I'd really like to see you get behind him again. He'll make you proud. I know he will."

Their father nodded in agreement. He had always believed in sibling solidarity, family loyalty. They were hitting exactly the right notes. Apparently, they had estimated correctly about his net worth. The figures in question would hardly make a dent.

"Children," their father began, when they had respectfully paused to give him a chance to respond. "I will admit that I've made mistakes in the way I have handled the situation with both of you. I never felt good about having to turn you down, although you've got to admit that I had been a very supportive dad. Hell, I love you guys, and I'd like nothing better than to see you succeed in any endeavor you choose. And you both know that you are always welcome to join me in business." He smiled and lifted his hands. "I know. I know. It's not your cup of tea, and I haven't been able to persuade you. I understand. Believe me, I do. Maybe I have been too harsh recently, and I fully intend to make amends. I don't want us to be estranged ever again. Not ever. And I intend to do what it takes to bond us as a family again."

He cleared his throat. It sounded like a statement that he had rehearsed and turned over and over again in his mind. She could see, too, that he was genuinely bothered by their estrangement. It was happening. It needed a gesture, and she obliged, throwing her arms around her father.

"Oh, Daddy. That was so wonderful. Oh, Daddy, I love you so."

She hugged and kissed him, and he returned the gesture. She could see her brother's eyes well up with tears as he patted his father's arm. After an appropriate length of time, she disengaged. It was obvious that their father wanted to make a further comment.

"You both will be very well provided for on my demise, children. I promise you."

"And we sincerely hope that such a time will be far away down the road," Scott said. "Isn't that right, Courtney?"

"Of course, Dad. The longer the better."

"What I want to happen as I start...you know what I mean...what I have to call a new life." He paused, sucked in a deep breath, and looked down at his hands. "God, I loved your mother. She was everything to me." He lifted his head and looked at both of them in turn. "Of course, you both know that. I was lost when she died, totally lost. It was the worst experience of my life. To lose a loving mate of long-standing is just about the most horrible thing that can happen to a person, perhaps as terrible as the loss of the child. I think I've found someone who—although she could never take your mother's place—could be good for me, good for all of us. She wants us to be one happy family, and I want that as well. Believe me, children, I want that more than anything. Of course, I will have to amend the estate plan to take into account my new wife. I promise you that it won't affect your own inheritance prospects. I want to be fair to everyone."

He was on the verge of tears and had to look away to get control over his emotions. Courtney turned to Scott and lifted her eyes.

"Amend—" she began, but just at that moment Harry came out of the trees, leading the horses. As he came forward, his condition was unmistakable. He was very drunk.

"Shit," Courtney murmured, aborting her statement.

"How the hell do we handle this?" Scott asked, observing Harry staggering forward.

He came closer, bringing with him his special scent stronger than ever.

"Got to go, folksh," he blubbered. Courtney wondered if he really thought he was hiding his condition.

"Here we go again," their father said, in a whispered aside.

"Don't get him riled," Courtney warned.

"Let'sh roll," Harry croaked.

"Just do as he says, Dad," Scott whispered. "He's got us by the short hairs."

Scott helped his father onto his horse. Then Courtney mounted, and Scott did the same. All eyes were on Harry as he attempted to get into his saddle.

Harry lifted his left foot into the stirrup, then slipped, and fell backward on the grass.

"Sombitch," he cried. "Am gonna beat the shit outa thish fuckin' horsh."

"Wasn't his fault," Scott muttered.

"Easy," Courtney warned.

Harry rose, giggled drunkenly, and looked at them with a bleary stare. He lifted his left foot into the stirrup again. In his state, his boot found no traction and slipped out. He averted a fall by grasping the pommel.

"Damned pea-brained sumbitch," Harry grunted, lifting his foot into the stirrup once again. This time it held, and he managed to lift himself onto the saddle, listing to the left once his butt settled in the saddle.

"Fuck outtahere," he cried, lifting his arm and waving them forward. His perch on the horse was precarious, but apparently the horse knew the way or Harry managed to guide it by rote through the trail.

They moved up the low hills and down again through the trees and meadows. Courtney's horse was between Scott's and her father's, which brought up the rear. Turning, she exchanged worried looks with each of them as they moved forward.

There was complete silence among them. Like her, they were too fearful to comment. Frustrated by his interruption at such a critical moment, her paramount concern now was to get back to camp in one piece. Then what? She was genuinely frightened.

She did not recognize any of the terrain, but then she had no real knowledge of the landmarks. The immensity of the terrain was daunting. She could not conceive of them being able to find their way out of such vastness without expert guidance.

At a turn in the trail, Harry nearly fell over but managed to stay put by holding fast to the pommel. As they progressed, Harry's head dropped onto his chest, but his horse continued along the path. The path to where?

She tried to take comfort in the notion that the horse did know the way, but in this place, there was no way of being certain. This new threat of danger had quickly rearranged her priorities. They were in the middle of nowhere in the hands of a drunken guide. Dire speculation ran rampant in her mind. Were they moving toward camp or going in circles?

Harry had informed them during their first meeting that they were heading deep into territory where few people normally went, the furthest point from a road in the lower forty-eight. She cursed Harry for putting them in this predicament. He was ruining the trip. Worse, he was interfering in their reaching their goals. His sudden appearance had been galling. Her father mentioned "amendment." What did that mean? The idea of dilution that she had expressed earlier came to mind.

At one point, Harry's horse stopped dead in its tracks and began to graze. Scott immediately caught up with the horse and slapped him on the rump, a good hard reminder to get going. Harry shook himself into semialertness and, for a brief period, kept the horse moving forward. He was mounted precariously, listing from side to side. At any moment she expected him to fall off, perhaps sustain a life-threatening or incapacitating injury.

The horses moved more slowly than they had in the morning, which raised yet another fear in Courtney's mind, namely that darkness would descend before they made camp—if they made camp—and then where would they be? She pulled up on the reins, and her horse stopped moving. Scott turned his horse, and they waited for their father to catch up. Harry's horse moved slowly forward, with Harry oblivious to what was happening behind him.

"What the hell do we do?" she asked her brother and father.

"What can we do?" Scott said. "Just follow along and hope for the best. Sooner or later he has to sober up."

"Unless he's got more booze with him," Courtney said.

"I'm sorry, kids," their father said. It had become a mantra. "I had no idea."

"Not your fault, Dad," Scott said, looking ahead at Harry's horse still moving. "Better catch up. We have no choice."

He moved his horse forward, and it cantered ahead. He looked back at them and waved them on. Courtney kicked her horse, and it moved forward to catch up with Scott's. Their father's horse followed. Scott was right: they had no choice.

After an hour or so of steady progress, Courtney noted that Harry's head was no longer on his chest. Apparently the alcoholic haze was lifting. He turned in his saddle and looked back, squinted, and made a limp hand signal for them to keep moving. His action was encouraging but could not erase the atmosphere of danger.

After a while, they caught the scent of the cooking fire and soon after were back in camp. Harry dismounted clumsily and, still unsteady, headed straight to his tent. Tomas had come up to take charge of the horses.

"He was drunk as a skunk," Scott said.

Tomas shrugged but said nothing.

"Not exactly a secure feeling," Courtney said.

"He be okay," Tomas muttered.

"Broken record, Tomas," Courtney said.

"Okay?" Scott said. "He's *not* okay. The man's a menace."

"Got any suggestions, Tomas?" their father asked, repeating himself when he did not get any answer. "He can't continue like that. He's not in control. He's putting us in danger."

"He be okay," Tomas muttered yet again, not looking at them, gathering the reins of the four horses.

"You keep saying that," Courtney snapped, her voice rising. "He's not okay. He's a goddamned drunk. My father is right. We're in the hands of someone…unreliable. Damn it, Tomas. We got problems here."

Tomas said nothing, his expression cryptic, as if he were wearing a mask.

"Jesus, Tomas," Courtney blurted. "He treats you like shit, and you keep defending him."

Tomas shrugged and turned away.

"I take care of the horses, and we have dinner."

"I don't believe this," Scott said, as Tomas led the horses away toward the meadow to be hobbled.

"He be okay," Courtney mimicked. "He's not okay."

"I'm really sorry about this," their father said.

"Never mind that, Dad," Courtney said. "No more apologies please, enough of that. You didn't know. Don't blame yourself. The truth is we're in a pickle."

"I'll promise you this," Scott said. "He's got to be reported. He can't do this work anymore. As soon as we get back, I'm gonna turn him in. The man's a menace."

"*If* we get back, Scott," Courtney said.

"Let's not panic, kids," their father interjected. She remembered him always as the voice of reason. "Let's think about this. I'm sure he doesn't want to ruin his livelihood."

"He's doing a great job of it," Courtney snapped.

They watched the Mexican return. He looked at them briefly, then moved to the fire, and began making preparations for their dinner. His face was expressionless.

"Let's not overreact," their father said. "Despite everything, we did get back in one piece." He looked pale and tired.

"Why not rest a while before dinner, then we'll decide how to handle things."

He embraced them both and crawled into his tent.

"What a bummer," Courtney said. "Just when things were going great."

"He has a point," Scott said.

"He mentioned 'amendment,'" Courtney said. "I know what he meant. He was going to make changes in his will to protect his beloved Muriel, that's what he meant, to screw us out of what is rightfully ours."

"Weren't you listening?" Scott admonished her. "He is going to reevaluate his situation. We're going to get what we need for your maintenance and investment money for me. Trust him, Courtney. He is doing exactly what we wanted of him. Let's just leave it at that."

"I want to know what he means by 'amendment.'"

"Damn it, Courtney. Leave it alone. We got what we want, both of us. You've got to trust him. He loves us. He won't screw us."

"That woman," she replied, her anger rising. "She'll control. That always happens. She'll work her wiles. In the end we'll get screwed. We mustn't let that happen."

"You've got to trust him, Courtney."

"I've seen it happen over and over again."

"You have?" He offered a forced smile, shaking his head. "You've read too many movie scripts and seen too many movies."

Her eyes narrowed and her attention began to drift.

"You know what I want now?" Courtney said.

"What?

"I want to get the fuck out of here."

Chapter 16

Tomas, looking unperturbed, concentrated on serving their dinner. He ladled out a thick vegetable soup and had prepared spaghetti and meatballs and biscuits. Harry stayed in his tent. They ate in silence, without appetite. After he collected their plates, Tomas carried a plate to Harry's tent and returned to clean up.

"How's he doing?" Scott asked.

"I tole you. He be okay."

Tomas scraped the leftovers into the fire then headed to the stream to wash the plates. They sat around the fire and sipped coffee.

"Johnny one note," Scott said, mimicking. "He be okay."

"Too bad," their father sighed. "I hadn't expected this."

"Enough, Dad," Courtney said, petulantly.

"We'll get through it, Dad," Scott murmured.

"Sure we will," Courtney said, obviously determined to get their earlier conversation back on track.

"I really fantasized about this, kids," their father shrugged. He appeared gray-faced and tired. "Sitting around the fire. Like last time. That was the best part of it, remember?"

"Sweet memories, Dad," Courtney said, obviously bored with the nostalgia.

"I loved that part. Hell, you can't really recapture the past. Besides, it's never really accurate in memory, not really."

"It was a great moment in our lives, Dad," Scott said.

"Let's hope we have this to remember as well, despite the unpleasantness," their father said.

At that moment, they heard movement in the guide's tent. The flap opened, and Harry crawled out and then stood up, shaking himself like an old dog. Carrying his half-eaten dinner on the metal plate, he came toward them. Moving into the circle of light thrown by the fire, he looked haggard but reasonably sober. He squatted next to them and spat on the ground.

"I'm really sorry, folks," he said, his eyes looking down. "I made a damned fool of myself."

They exchanged surprised glances.

"Yes, you did," Courtney said. "You had us really worried. You were looped."

"I don't know what got into me." He shook his head and looked at them. He did actually appear contrite. "It won't happen again."

As he put the plate on a rock, his hand shook, and the metal clattered. This close, his alcoholic aura was nauseating. He looked toward their father.

"I really let you down, Temple. Maybe our little discussion earlier set me off. I guess when you get older, your tolerance for a lot of things goes down. I did give you a great experience years ago, and in the few days we have left, I'd like to replicate that. Once again, folks, forgive me."

His contrition seemed sincere, but Scott was still not convinced, remembering the stash of booze buried just outside their camp.

"You scared the hell out of us, Harry," their father said.

It struck Scott as too gentle a remonstrance. He decided to offer his own.

"Think about it, Harry. We're out here under your care and guidance. It's a violation of your responsibility." He hoped Harry would see it as a barbed threat.

Harry looked down at the ground again and shrugged.

"Believe me, I understand, and I apologize sincerely. This is definitely not what you signed on for. Hell, I've been doing this for more than thirty years. I've always been steady and responsible. You know that, Temple. I admit my conduct was unforgivable, and I hope you'll cut me some slack."

Scott looked toward Courtney, who raised her eyebrows and turned away. He knew she was unconvinced.

"Thing is," Harry said. "Been carrying around a lot of problems lately." He shook his head and spat into the ground. "Lots of changes happening in my business. Not like it was. The hunting part is going down the tubes. Fucking wolves." He pursed his lips and shook his head regretfully. "Maybe I'm just getting old is all." He shrugged, looking pitiful.

Wallowing in self-pity, Scott thought. He felt no sympathy for the man.

"I'm willing to let bygones be bygones," their father said. "I'm sure my children feel the same way." He turned toward them.

"Whatever you say, Dad," Courtney said, obviously unconvinced.

"All we ask, Harry, is that you attend to business," Scott said. There seemed no point in antagonizing him at this stage.

"It won't happen again," Harry said. "Bear with me."

"We will, Harry," their father said, obviously determined to show sympathy, probably truly convinced of Harry's promise. "Life does have its ups and downs. Nobody really escapes.

People cope in different ways. We accept your apologies, don't we, kids?"

Each offered what could be taken as a gesture of consent and understanding. Scott was wary. One glance at Courtney assured him that she was not convinced.

"Thanks for the vote of confidence, folks," Harry said, obviously relieved. He stood up and rubbed his chin, looking very much like someone who needed a drink.

Again Scott thought of the stash of booze buried not far from where they sat.

"Let's drop it, Harry," their father said, with a sense of authority. "We accept your apology and leave it at that. We're here for...well...the experience and reliving old memories. Right, kids?"

The repetition was beginning to grate.

"Sure, Dad," Scott said, nodding. He winked at Courtney who shrugged with resignation.

Their father looked up at the star-studded sky. "In the face of that magnificence, how can anything on this planet be more important? Makes you feel...well, insignificant...and all the petty problems of us humans irrelevant."

"You got that right, Temple," Harry said. He looked up at the sky and started to point out the constellations.

The man knew his stuff, Scott mused. He knew about the wilderness, wildflowers, animals, trees, the sky. It was his turf, and he had spent his life at it and did not want to throw it away.

On the other hand, he might be feeling trapped in the repetitive cycle of trek after trek with strangers over much the same terrain. Obviously, he had gotten frightened as he sobered

and saw the possibilities of a terrible and humiliating ending
to what had become a lifelong career. Although Scott could
understand the man's fear, he did not quite trust his ability to
make good on his promise.

As he listened to Harry point out the constellations with
expert knowledge, Scott found his glance drawn to the area of
the buried stash. An idea was growing in his mind.

"Just like the planetarium at the Rose Center," their father
joked.

"Nothing like the real thing," Courtney said.

Harry chuckled, obviously relieved that the crisis had
passed. Tomas came back with the plates and went about his
business of cleanup and hoisting the remaining food supplies
up a log crossbar, the so-called meat pole, that he had erected
to discourage the bears.

"Maybe tomorrow we can ride to the Table Mountain
trailhead. Nice easy ride. And if you feel up to it, maybe a climb.
Great views."

"I'll take the ride," their father said. "But no climbing. These
bones are too old for that."

Scott remembered the climb, smiling at the memory. He
and Courtney had stopped along the way up and made love
half standing, leaning against recesses in the rock. They were
young and supple with boundless energy, far outstripping their
parents who had climbed as well, but much slower.

They were so self-absorbed then that they had no fear of
consequences. He noted that apparently that trek had been
a kind of demarcation point between fun and games and
obsession. When they returned to New York, somehow the

relationship had changed. They had become more than mere carefree siblings. They were lovers, and it was likely that their child had been conceived in the wilderness, perhaps on the way up the mountain trail.

For years, he had attempted to dismiss it from his mind, excise the memory. Now he found himself drawn toward it like a moth to the flame. It was, he sensed, all coming back, the old obsession, the angst, the guilt, and the excruciating pleasure. He cursed his inability to resist.

After a while, Harry moved back to the tent, and the three of them were alone again, talking in whispers.

"Do you believe him?" Scott asked.

"I believe he believes himself," Courtney replied.

"Meaning he wouldn't be able to keep his word."

"He'll try, but I think he's reached the stage where he'd have trouble quitting cold turkey. The guy needs AA."

"Let's not presuppose," their father said. "I say we give him the benefit of the doubt."

Scott started to argue the point, but Courtney poked him in the thigh, an obvious signal to desist.

They sat in silence for a long time listening to the night sounds of the wilderness. In the distance Coyotes bayed, showing themselves masters of the night sounds.

"On that other matter, Dad," Courtney began. She exchanged a brief glance with Scott.

"Other matter?" their father said, recalling. "Yes. I remember."

"You said, well, that you were reevaluating," Courtney said, pausing. "You said something about amendments."

"We were discussing, you know, helping us out again."

"I said I was certainly open to it."

"In the end it comes down to numbers, Dad," Courtney said, with obvious hesitation. "I know its sounds crass, and this may be the wrong place and time."

"I don't know, kids," Temple said. "This is not the place for numbers."

"We're all together, Dad. It's as good a time as any."

Scott felt somewhat shocked. He had not expected them to get down to brass tacks so soon. Nevertheless he felt obliged to follow her lead. Resisting her was his Achilles heel.

"Please don't think badly about us for bringing up the matter," Scott said. "This is one great deal I have, Dad. I've checked out everything. I get control for eight hundred thou. That and a cushion could give me a chance to rock and roll. People still have to eat. It's basic. No big-deal technology required, just the software to keep track of inventory, sales, and expenses. I've done the due diligence. It's the greatest opportunity that's ever crossed my path. It'll come back to you, Dad. I'll pay back every cent—in spades. I've never had such a positive feeling. I know, Dad, that I've had my hard knocks, but I've learned from my mistakes, and I think I can really hack this. It's not pie in the sky, Dad. All I ask is for you to help me take this shot. If this goes down, I promise no more asking for loans. I make this a solemn promise."

"Give him a break on this, Dad," Courtney interjected. Their father looked into the fire as if in deep contemplation. Scott watched and waited nervously.

"If you need to see the figures again, Dad..." Scott began.

Temple nodded, but the gesture seemed ambiguous, the sale not yet made. Scott decided to retreat for the moment, change direction.

"And, Dad, consider Courtney's career. She is going to make it. She has the talent, but she needs the leisure to focus." He looked toward his sister. "I know she can do it. Faith goes a long way, Dad. We both need your encouragement and support."

"I'm not against it, kids. Believe me. I'm not. Muriel, too, would welcome the idea. We've discussed it. She's no dummy when it comes to numbers. That's her business. Dealt with them all her life. Believe me, I know what you're saying. I want to do the right thing by both of you. I do."

"We won't blow it, Dad," Scott said. "We'll try like hell not to disappoint you, Dad. No way."

"You'll see, Dad," Courtney pressed. "I promise you on Mom's memory. We won't let you down."

They watched their father's face, his eyes reflecting the fire's last gasp. His eyes were clearly moist. He looked up at them.

"All I ask is your love and respect. That's all I want in return."

Scott felt an odd sense of both elation and sympathy. For years he had always believed that he had betrayed his father, had been an evil ungrateful son. The weight of his betrayal hung heavy in his mind. The affair with his sister, the theft of the diamonds would never be excised. He did not really believe he was worthy of his father's largesse and confidence.

"You've always had our respect, Dad," Scott said, a lump welling in his chest. It occurred to him suddenly that he was begging for something for which he was not entitled. His deception gnawed at him. It could never disappear.

"Okay, son," their father said, obviously deeply moved. "I'm the father here. I gave you life. I will not let you down. Not ever. Win or lose. Actually, Muriel and I have gone over the figures."

"Muriel…" Courtney began, cutting her brother a knowing look that said: Told you so.

"She'll be a fantastic help to me. You'll see. You'll adore her. She's wise and understanding and respects my feeling for my kids."

Scott embraced his father, and his father held him closely. For the first time in years, he felt connected, a loving son. He was genuinely grateful, although he would always question his worthiness. Then he remembered Courtney's plea.

"And Courtney's request, Dad?"

"Muriel is all for it."

"Sounds like she's very influential," Courtney said. Although the sarcasm seemed obvious, Scott noted that it sailed right over his father's head.

"Yes, she is."

"Is it possible to be more specific, Dad?" Courtney asked, her tone too obviously businesslike. It seemed to Scott that she was adopting a negotiating stance. An old hand at business, his father appeared to note the fact.

"Hardly in this place. But just as soon as I get home," their father said. "That is my commitment to you both."

Scott had no doubt about his conviction and intent. Courtney's expression had turned sour.

"I suppose you'll need to talk with Muriel."

"Of course," Temple said.

"Remember though, kids, it's not about the money. It's about family. It's always been about family. Why shouldn't I share with my children?"

"For me as well," Scott said. Courtney remained silent.

"Oh God, how much I miss your mother," Temple whispered. "I wish she was here beside us now."

"I'm sure she is, Dad," Scott said, looking into the darkness. "Somewhere."

"I feel that," their father said. "I do."

"But now you have Muriel," Courtney said.

"A stroke of luck, kids. I'm sure your mother would approve. She would hate to see me lonely and unhappy."

"You think so?" Courtney asked.

"Of course, she would," Scott said, hoping to forestall any more sarcasm from his sister. In the diminished light of the fire, he was thankful he could not see his sister's expression. He got up from the log and patted the seat of his pants. "Now let's hope we can enjoy the rest of the trip."

"If we can," Courtney said. "Frankly, I don't trust Harry. He's a fucking drunk. Maybe we should force him to take us back as soon as possible."

Scott cut a quick glance at his sister. He understood her machinations. Staying now would be redundant, and she was right about not trusting Harry. Besides, from his point of view, their mission had been accomplished.

"Let's give him the benefit of the doubt, kids."

"I told you, Dad," Courtney said. "You can't reason with an addict. His apology may have been sincere, but he can't beat his addiction. No way. Not out here. The man needs help."

"She's got a point, Dad."

"Let's ask him to stop the trek," Courtney said.

"We'll see how it goes," their father said.

"I mean it, Dad. He's dangerous. Out of control. Let him keep the money and bring us the hell out of here."

"Let's not panic," their father said. "He did promise."

"The man is a chronic drunk. He could get us all killed."

"Let's put it on hold, see how it goes tomorrow," Temple said. "Sometimes you have to take the good with the bad. Look how wonderful we've gotten along."

"Dad's right," Scott said, throwing Courtney an admonishing glance.

Throughout this conversation, Scott had assumed that Tomas was out of earshot, busy with his usual closing-day camp chores. But a sudden sound very near them reminded him that he had not heard any movement during this brief conversation. Had the Mexican overheard them or was this merely an extension of his earlier fear? Once again, he dismissed the idea that any of what Tomas had seen or heard had any relevance or presented any danger.

"Off to dreamland," their father said, rising. After more paternal hugs and kisses, he proceeded to his tent, leaving Courtney and Scott alone. Tomas suddenly materialized near their fire. He looked briefly at Courtney who had also risen.

"Maybe you're right, Tomas," Scott said, acknowledging his presence. "Harry came out of his tent and apologized for his conduct. He seemed fine."

"He be okay," Courtney blurted, mimicking Tomas.

Scott observed a flicker of anger in the Mexican's expression, as if he had taken Courtney's mimicry as an insult. He could not shake the feeling that there was something sinister percolating in the man.

"I guess you were right, Tomas," Scott said, feeling a sudden need to mollify him. Tomas nodded and shrugged with an air of indifference.

"He drinking man but not a fool," Tomas said. "He don' wan' no trouble." Then he added for emphasis. "Don' make no trouble."

Was it a threat? Scott waited for more to be said, but suddenly the Mexican was silent.

"We're cool now, Tomas. No problem," Scott said, looking at Courtney.

Tomas seemed to be studying his face. Shrugging, he moved away toward his tent.

"He makes me uneasy," Scott said when he had gone. "I hate him knowing."

"Forget it."

"Do you think he heard what we were saying?"

"So what? He sees things. He hears things. Why should it matter to him? Why should anything we do or say be on his agenda? Forget it."

Courtney rose and embraced her brother. She whispered in his ear.

"I'd call it a good start."

"Good start?"

He was puzzled.

"There's still Muriel," she said.

"What are you thinking?"

"Nothing." She laughed and patted his arm. "Why think, when we can do?"

He knew what she meant.

"Come on, Scottie. Don't be coy. A little pleasure won't hurt."

"Not here," he whispered.

She giggled, and they moved stealthily beyond the camp to the edge of the meadow where Tomas had hobbled the horses.

"Just don't scream," he whispered, putting a hand over her mouth as they made love.

"As good as it gets," she said, her mouth close to his ear.

"Better."

"Time to crash," Scott said, when they disengaged.

"Me, too," Courtney said. She lifted her face, and Scott kissed her. Again he recalled their earlier problems. He knew it could happen again, the compulsive attachment. Love! Maybe that part would never be over for him.

"Let's not push it, Courtney. Let's call this trek the swan song. No more. Once and for all," he said. "Besides, if Dad comes across, we'll both be pretty busy. Why look for trouble?"

"Poor Scottie," she said. "Always worried. Hell, it's been two decades. Consider it pure recreation. Nothing more."

"Once out of here. Over. Agreed?"

She nodded and squeezed his crotch.

"Bye, bye, Birdie," she sang in a whisper.

They made their way back to camp and with a brief wave to each other crawled into their tents.

After a while the camp grew quiet, except for the sound of snoring coming from Harry's tent. Scott must have slept, but some inner sense of alertness awoke him, as if he had been waiting for the sound. Scott struggled out of his sleeping bag and peeked through the flap. He saw Tomas quietly digging at the edge of the campsite where Scott had observed him the night before, and he watched as the Mexican lifted a bottle from the hole then covered it up again. Moving stealthily, Tomas placed the bottle through the flap in Harry's tent then went back to his own.

Keeping his breathing shallow, Scott waited and watched. The camp grew quiet again. He needed to think. Courtney was right. Despite his promises, Harry was not going to stop. His little speech of contrition was contrived.

Scott turned a number of scenarios over in his mind. All of them spelled danger. Then an idea struck him.

He left his own tent and crawled into Courtney's and gently awakened her, putting a hand over her mouth. He bent over and whispered in her ear.

"Don't make a sound."

"Really, Scott. Talk about risk. We could wake Dad."

"Not that. Tomas just delivered another bottle from Harry's stash. Get dressed. We have to talk."

She nodded, asking for no explanation.

He waited outside the tent as she dressed. When she appeared, he put a finger to his lips, and they moved silently outside the perimeter of the camp out of earshot.

"I got an idea," he whispered.

"Don't try to take away the booze. He'll go bananas. Get nasty. Make things worse."

"I'm talking dilution not deprivation. He won't be completely sober but maybe not drunk enough to get us the fuck out of here in one piece. Unfortunately he's got his fifth for tomorrow."

"So let's not stray tomorrow. Stick to camp. Take a little hike. No danger of getting lost. It's the home trek that worries me."

"Next day he gets half his quota. Lesser evil."

"We'd have to break the seals," Scott said, as the thought crossed his mind. "He might catch on."

"Maybe. Maybe not."

"Let's hope he doesn't. That's our risk."

Scott, followed by Courtney, moved in the direction of where he had seen Tomas uncover the stash. He reached the spot, behind a shrub, well hidden. He felt around with his hands and dug his nails into the soft dirt.

They dug with their fingers, piling handfuls of dirt beside the hole. The bottles were well covered but close to the surface. Scott felt around, counting four bottles.

"Probably has a stash at every camp," Scott said.

"As he says, he knows the turf. Resourceful son of a bitch."

Scott carefully removed the four bottles, gave two to Courtney, and moved toward the stream. It wasn't far, and the path was well trod. They kneeled next to the stream, carefully broke the seals, and poured out more than half the contents of each bottle.

"Wild Turkey," Scott noted.

"Think we'll make drunks out of the goddamned trout?"

"They'll have to dip the flies in booze to get a strike."

"It'll piss off the tree huggers."

"Let's just hope we don't piss off old Harry."

They filled the bottles from the stream, tightened the tops, and tried their best to make the seals look as if they hadn't been broken. Then they silently retraced their steps, put the bottles in the hole the way they were found, and carefully covered them with dirt, patting it down.

They made their way carefully back to their tents.

"A couple more days, and we're home free," Courtney said, squeezing Scott's hand.

"I think we got what we came for," Scott said.

She put her mouth close to his ear. "There's still Muriel."

"He says this was all her idea."

"That's the problem. Seems like everything from now on will be her idea."

They headed back to their tents.

Chapter 17

They hiked for a mile or so along the bank downstream until they found a spot where the stream widened, and it struck Courtney as a good place to wash. The sun was rising orange through the tree line.

They had informed Tomas, who had served them eggs, bacon, toast, and coffee, to tell Harry whenever he awoke that they preferred that today be a down day. Their father had told them that he would be spending most of the day taking pictures around the camp, and they had all agreed that they would meet for dinner. Tomas had packed them a lunch of cheese sandwiches, apples, and cokes.

They both carried a towel, a change of underwear, and socks and fresh shirts. Before attempting to wash in the icy stream, they sat on the bank and waited until the sun warmed the cold air.

Courtney had stayed awake after their return from diluting Harry's bourbon, contemplating their financial future. Something had begun to nag at her concerning her father's generosity. Other implications began to surface. Danger signals had emerged. She put it directly to Scott.

"You realize, of course, that Dad's apparent generosity could all be a ploy to placate us, while Muriel gains the bulk of his estate when he dies."

"Not that again," Scott said.

Courtney paused, ignoring his comment.

"Considering that his current will probably names us as principal heirs, he's sure to make changes when dear Muriel gets her hand on the tiller. We might be selling ourselves short."

"For crying out loud, Courtney, we can't stop him from making changes."

"Just thinking out loud."

She was fully aware where her thoughts were taking her. Was he getting the point? She looked at her brother, who turned away.

"Let's clean up," Scott said, obviously avoiding the subject.

They undressed and moved cautiously into the cold water.

"Colder than a witch's tit in hell," he said, soaping himself. She did the same.

"Let me do you," she said, laughing, splashing him with water, soaping his body, particularly his genitals. He did the same to her. They splashed water on each other like children, giggling and screeching.

Blue with cold, they ran out of the stream and toweled each other dry, but their teeth still chattered from the icy water.

"It looks lifeless," she laughed, caressing him. "Needs a warm-up."

Soon they were both aroused and making love in whatever postures they could devise. Naked, they enjoyed the sensation of doing it in the wilderness, which heightened their enjoyment. She screamed out the intensity of her pleasure.

"You'll scare the grizzlies," he said.

"Bring 'em on. I feel as if I could fuck a bear."

He doubled up with laughter. They found a grassy knoll nearby and warmed themselves in the sun.

"I love this freedom," she said. "Don't you feel like an animal?"

He roared and beat his chest.

"We are animals," he said.

"They have no taboos, no distinctions. Everybody screws everybody."

She turned and got on her hands and knees.

"Let's do it their way," she said. He got down behind her, and she drew him into her.

He obeyed, and they were locked together in an animal sexual pose.

"Bark for the audience," he cried.

"Woof. Woof."

Finally it was over, and they disengaged and lay down while the sun warmed them.

"*Lady Chatterley's Lover*," she said, laughing, nestling in the crook of his arm. "Remember?"

"The book?"

"She was fucking the gardener. Fancy lady of the manor. Having a ball in the garden. Just like us."

"Life outside the box," he whispered. She knew what he meant, and it added to the thrill of it.

"Abandonment," she said, conscious of the purity of its definition.

He embraced her. They were like two fitted spoons now.

"I'll never forget this day," she said, sure of its endurance in her memory. "It's like stepping into another dimension. Letting go. Getting down to the nitty-gritty. Shrugging off all so-called civilized behavior. I feel like…," she paused, "pure flesh and spirit." She turned and looked into his eyes. "And you?"

"Different," he said. "Weird, but as you say…pure flesh and spirit. One with nature."

"That's it. Yes, Scottie. One with nature. How could this be wrong? This is as right as it gets. We're…well, Adam and Eve. Can you imagine what she must have thought, seeing that damned thing rise, stiff and hard?" She looked at him. "Like now."

This time she rose and mounted him, making strange sounds like talking in tongues as she rotated on his body. Again, they felt extreme pleasure together, and she screamed out her ecstasy. When the spasm was over, they lay together in an embrace and, without speaking, dozed. When they awoke, they dressed and started back to camp.

"No one would believe this," she said to her brother.

"Who would we tell?" Scott asked.

"Maybe," she said, "we could meet somewhere, say once a year, and be together like this. Our secret life, our deliriously wonderful secret life."

"Over when it's over, sis," Scott replied. "Let's keep it as an idea."

"You're right," she said, remembering the angst of years ago. "Let's not get carried away. Keep it in your memory bank."

They dozed then copulated yet again. It was getting late, near lunchtime.

They dried themselves and dressed, then headed back toward the camp. She felt energized and alert, calm and confident. A sense of well-being filled her with optimism. Walking beside her, Scott looked at her, winked, and nodded as if he had read her mind.

They walked for an hour in silence, and when they arrived in the camp, they saw only Tomas working the fire, obviously preparing lunch. Neither their father nor Harry was anywhere in sight.

"Dad," Courtney called. She inspected her father's tent. It was empty. Then she turned to Tomas who shrugged.

"Went riding," he answered, in an indifferent noncommittal voice.

"Where?"

Tomas shrugged and continued to work preparing the food. He was making some kind of bean concoction, probably chili, and toasting leftover bread. A pot of coffee was beginning to boil. For some reason it struck her as somewhat late for making lunch, long past noon. She let the idea pass. Her concern was for her father, who had planned taking pictures around the camp in the morning.

"He go with boss," Tomas informed them.

"Without us?" Scott asked.

Scott beckoned Courtney, whispering.

"Guy gives me the creeps," he said.

"They say when they would be back?" Courtney asked.

Tomas shrugged.

"No say."

"That's unusual, isn't it, Tomas?" Scott pressed.

Tomas didn't answer but continued preparing the food, mixing the chili with a ladle.

"You eat now?" he asked.

"We'll wait for them," Courtney said, moving with her brother to the edge of the camp to a spot overlooking the stream.

She felt a rising sensation of anxiety but fought it off. It was not a logical feeling at that point. But after an hour had gone by, both she and Scott became more concerned. Tomas squatted near the fire. From time to time he mixed the chili, looking toward them.

"I'm really concerned, Tomas," Courtney said approaching the Mexican. "Shouldn't we go and look for them?"

"They be fine."

"Hey, don't start that routine," Scott said angrily. She knew, of course, to look for them on horseback could not be a course of action. They would lose their way quickly.

"I'm getting really worried," Courtney said, when another hour passed. The sun had fallen behind the highest treetops. But beneath her anxiety was yet another thought. What if something did happen to their father? What then? No Muriel to spoil their inheritance prospects. The thought was strangely comforting.

"Do you think he's all right, Scott?" she asked, conscious of the rehearsal aspect of the remark, as if an air of innocence would be appropriate at some point in the near future. Scott looked at her archly but did not comment. Had he read her thoughts?

They sat on a log, and Tomas brought them their dinner, for which they had little appetite. Tomas cleared away their metal plates, not commenting on their leftovers.

The sun had dropped behind the tree line when they heard approaching horses. This spared her any further reflection on such issues. Harry and their father rode into camp.

Their expressions told the story of their absence. Harry's complexion was florid and his anger palpable. He was quite obviously drunk. Temple's complexion, on the other hand, was ashen, and he looked exhausted. Harry seemed shaken by rage and frustration. They watched him as he dismounted clumsily, shaking his head, fuming, barely able to stand. They ran toward their father and helped him down from the horse.

"Fuckin' pain in the ash," Harry fulminated, looking toward their father with anger and contempt.

"Mean drunk," their father muttered with disgust. "Look at him."

"Fuckin' stupid jackass prick," Harry cried. "Can't even take care of your own shit."

"What the hell is he bitching and moaning about?" Scott asked.

"Lost hish fuckin' camera," Harry said, pointing a finger at their father. "Had to go all the way back there to the goddamned lake to look for hish fuckin' camera."

"Lost your camera, Dad?" Courtney asked.

"At first I thought maybe you guys had taken it with you, but then neither of you knew how to work it. Besides, you would have told me. I must have lost it yesterday on the trail or where we stopped at the lake. All the pictures were in it, everything I took out here. You know how important those images are to me. I can't imagine how I could have lost it."

"Five fuckin' hours we looked for that fuckin' camera," Harry ranted drunkenly. "Can't even take care of your fuckin' camera. You people are nothing but trouble. Fuckin' trouble. I don't know why the fuck I took you on. Worse mistake I ever made. God damned shtupid…" He upended his canteen, discovered it was empty, then threw it at Tomas. It missed.

"And where the fuck were you, you dumbass spic prick?" He shook his head. "Nowhere around when you need him. Where the fuck were you?"

Tomas shrugged and pointed with his chin toward the stream.

"I got hoarse calling you. Gone deaf suddenly?"

"I no hear," Tomas said defensively.

"You could've gone with this *stupido* damn spic idiot."

His accusation made little sense to Courtney. None of it made much sense. Yet he continued to roar out insults to their father and Tomas. Then he turned his drunken ire on Courtney.

"And you, you stupid bitch. Did I tell you about dropping the reins?" He looked at Scott. "Did I tell her?" Then to their father: "Did I tell you about the fuckin' quagmire in the stream bed? What am I, your fucking nursemaid?"

He was obviously beyond reason, a man in a drunken rage and probably dangerous. Besides, as they had learned from his killing of the mule, he had firearms. They speculated that he had emptied a half-full bottle and was frustrated and angry that it had shortchanged his intoxication.

"Why don't you calm down, Harry," their father said, forcing himself to be the gentle voice of reason. "Go sleep it off."

"Fuck you."

"I'm grateful, really grateful for your helping me look for the camera," Temple said, with both condescension and caution. "I appreciate it. I really do, but it's the booze talking now, Harry. Really, don't ruin things for yourself..."

"What did you say, Temple?" Harry cried, charging menacingly toward their father. Scott moved quickly between them. "You threatening me?"

"Don't be dumb, Harry," Scott said. The outfitter stopped abruptly, his eyes moving to the faces watching him. He fixed his gaze on the Mexican.

"Bring me more," he said, turning suddenly and staggering back to his tent.

Tomas looked at them, said nothing, and did not move. Something in his expression seemed strange. There was a thin smile on his lips, and his eyes reflected a bold assertiveness that Courtney hadn't seen before. It puzzled her. She looked toward Scott and motioned with her eyes toward Tomas. Suddenly, she sensed that the three of them were communicating in a weird way, with Tomas projecting something ominous that both she and Scott understood, although they could not articulate what it meant.

Suddenly their father broke the circuit, beckoning them to his tent. Courtney and Scott crawled in after him. They sat cross-legged in the tight space and spoke in whispers.

"I'm really sorry, kids," Temple said.

"No point, Dad," Scott said. "We drew ourselves a hopeless drunk. We've got to persuade him to take us the hell out of here. And fast."

Tomas kneeled at the tent's entrance and handed over their father's dinner then withdrew. Temple picked at it with little appetite.

"It was scary out there," Temple said. "The more he drank, the more belligerent he became. It was awful." He shook his head. "All for naught. We never did find the camera."

"Are you sure you lost it?" Scott asked, starting to look around the tent, looking under the sleeping bag and feeling around the duffle bag that held his father's possessions.

"I've looked everywhere," their father said. "I must have dropped it somewhere. It's a real bummer, kids. I was hoping to make a record like last time."

"It's okay, Dad," Courtney said. "Unfortunately, the issue at hand is how do we get out of here unscathed? I feel as if we're held hostage by a madman."

"He's okay and perfectly rational when he's reasonably sober," Temple said, reaching for logic to ease their obvious anxiety.

"I don't think we can count on that, Dad," Scott said.

"And I wouldn't trust him to take us out of here."

"Would you trust Tomas?" Scott asked.

"I don't know," Courtney mumbled, giving Scott a quick glance.

"It's like being caught between a rock and a hard place."

They were silent for a while. Courtney looked out through a gap in the flap. Tomas was busy cleaning up around the fire, his face impassive.

"We've watered his liquor supply, Dad," Scott said, explaining their action during the night.

"Is that good?" Temple asked.

"Never can tell with an addict," Courtney sighed. "Maybe it made things worse. Maybe it wasn't too smart."

"Let's think this out," Temple said. "Maybe try getting out of here on our own."

"Bad idea, Dad," Scott said, shaking his head. "We're city-folk tenderfoots."

"We might make a deal with the Mexican," Courtney said. "Probably knows the way out."

"You mean buy him?" Temple asked.

They exchanged glances.

"How much cash do we have between us?" Scott asked. "I have a couple a hundred."

"About the same," Courtney said. "And I doubt if he'll take credit cards."

Her attempt at humor fell flat.

"I have about five hundred dollars. Obviously there is no need for cash out here," Temple said.

"Might be enough for the Mexican," Courtney said.

"Okay, so he takes it and then what? Harry sobers up and comes after us. Or the Mexican has second thoughts and leaves us stranded," Temple reasoned.

"And remember Harry has a firearm," Scott said.

"Let's not jump from the frying pan into the fire," their father said, now in thoughtful mode. Courtney had often seen him this way, reasoned, practical, logical. Sometimes this attitude infuriated her, resulting often in more rumination than action.

"Our most important consideration is safety," Temple said. "Let's hope we can talk to Harry when he sobers up."

"We've been there," Scott said, with a worried glance at Courtney, who nodded.

"And what happens when he finds out his booze has been watered?" Courtney asked.

"He blames Tomas," Temple said, quick to understand the implications.

"Less booze, less effect," Scott muttered. "Which was our motive in the first place. I guess lacking the full dose freaked him out."

"We'll have to see how it plays out," Temple said. "The way I see it, we've got to negotiate a way out of here."

"From his attitude, one would think he'd be happy to take us out," Scott said. "He thinks we're shit."

"Or he may come on contrite again, full of remorse and willing to make amends," Temple said. "Frankly it has me baffled. I've never come up against this in my life."

"Spend some time in Hollywood. You'll see all kinds of irrational conduct, some by people addicted by substances and some by people addicted to meanness." Courtney looked at her father.

"I just want us to get out of here safely," Temple said.

"You meant well, Dad," Scott said. "And hell, we did bond and get some family business out of the way."

"Some family business," Courtney said, with an edge of sarcasm.

Scott threw her a glance of rebuke. Their father smiled and nodded.

"I just wanted it to be perfect."

"Not your fault, Dad." Scott cut a glance at Courtney who remained silent. "It will be okay. You'll see. Probably sober up and realize he's made a perfect ass of himself. All we need is for him to be reasonably clearheaded until we get the hell out of here. In the meantime, let's just stay cool and not tempt the devil. Our objective is to blow this place in one piece. Right, Dad?"

"You betcha," Temple said, shrugging. "Now let me take a nap. I'm really done in."

Courtney and Scott crawled out the tent. Outside, they noted that Tomas appeared to be observing them with unusual interest, something rare for him. In the light of the dying fire, they noted that he gestured with his arm, motioning them forward as he started walking toward where the horses were hobbled. He turned and beckoned them to follow.

Courtney was puzzled by his sudden interest.

"What the hell does he want?" Scott asked. He looked none too happy.

"We'll know soon enough."

Chapter 18

————⟆•⟅————

They followed him across the meadow to a grove of aspens, out of sight and earshot of the camp. They could hear the quiet neighing of the horses and the metal of their hobbled movement. Tomas stopped and waited for them, leaning against a tree. As soon as she saw his expression and pose up close, Courtney noted that he seemed transformed, no longer the abused lackey, more like someone in charge.

"I get you out," he said, his eyes narrowing.

He waited for his words to penetrate.

"You heard?" Courtney said in the form of a question.

The Mexican's eyes narrowed, and he suddenly opened his lips in a broad smile. He pointed to his eyes then his ears.

"I see. I hear. You think Tomas is dumb wetback." He made a sound that seemed a cross between a sneer and laugh.

"Shit," Courtney said. "The little turd has a brain."

"Cool it, Courtney," Scott warned. His voice betrayed his nervousness.

"What about Harry?" Courtney asked.

"No mind Harry. He too drunk. I take you out of this place."

"What happened to all that 'He be fine' talk, Tomas?" Scott pressed.

Courtney's insides had tightened. She was certain that there was more to this rebellion than Tomas was revealing and could barely control her inner panic.

"He not be fine, hombre."

"You know the way?" Courtney asked, exchanging troubled glances with Scott.

"I know. I know this place good."

"And when do you propose to go?" Courtney asked, puzzled and wary by Tomas's new incarnation.

"Tomorrow early." He looked toward the mountain range. "Over Eagle Pass."

"Eagle Pass!" Courtney hissed. "You can't be serious. I don't know if I can handle that." She remembered how precarious it had been on the previous trek and her mother's reaction.

"Shit," Scott squealed, as if he were in physical pain.

"Best way back. We go easy."

"Just leave Harry here? Just like that?" Scott asked. He turned toward his sister. "There's more to this, Courtney."

Tomas shrugged and grunted.

"Why you worry about Harry?"

"That's not the point," Scott said. "He could come after us. He has a gun. Aren't you afraid of repercussions, Tomas?"

"He no got gun. I got gun now. We leave him horses and mules. He got plenty food. We be back in at trailhead in say one day."

"Can't he make trouble later?" Courtney interjected, frightened, tamping down a sense of hysteria."

"I tole you. You no worry about Señor Harry. He been paid. Bastard no make trouble, lose his license."

"Why this sudden interest in our welfare?" Courtney asked, beginning to harbor dire suspicions about his answer.

"I don't understand," Scott said, his words barely audible.

"Here is plan," Tomas said, surprisingly commanding in his tone. He lifted a finger. "You listen."

"Shouldn't Dad hear this?" Courtney said, looking toward her father's tent. Her fright was palpable.

"You pay me hundred thousand American dollars, you understand what I say?"

Courtney was stunned.

"What the hell are you talking about?" Scott said, raising his voice.

"You listen. You pay me one hundred thousand American dollars. I hear how much money your *padre* got. I take you out of here. You get me money. You understand what I say?"

"You can't be serious," Courtney said. She looked at her brother. "Where the hell is he coming from?"

"No argue. You brother and sister, right? "

"Oh, Jesus," Scott sighed.

"You think your father like brother and sister fucking together?"

Courtney felt her knees go weak. Scott's expression clearly showed his reaction.

Tomas's smile broadened. He turned to Scott.

"You fuck your little sister, gringo. Me sure your *padre* no like. Big sin. Very bad."

His smile became laughter, which turned into a mocking guffaw.

Courtney felt her heartbeat accelerate and bang inside her chest.

"You lousy son of a bitch," Scott said, starting to move forward. Courtney held him back.

"Don't make it worse, Scott," Courtney snapped. Her first reaction had been disbelief.

"Could it be worse?" he said, retreating. "We're being blackmailed."

Her mind was reeling. Internally, she felt physically sickened, fighting nausea.

"His word against ours," Courtney said, barely managing to find her voice.

"You expect my father to believe what you saw?" Scott pressed.

"I no expect that." He smiled, showing his gold teeth glinting in the sun. "I got pictures. Mucho pictures. This morning. You fucked good."

Courtney could barely contain a dry retch.

"Son of a bitch!" Scott cried. "You took Dad's camera."

He moved forward again. This time he grabbed the Mexican by the shirt. "You show those pictures to anyone—you hear me?—*anyone*, I'll kill you. I promise. I'll kill you."

"Scott, please," Courtney cried, trying to get him to disengage. The Mexican looked at him languidly, unafraid, continuing to smile. She felt herself calming. Face the facts, she urged herself. Think!

"Slimy bastard," Scott mumbled.

"Enough, Scott, please," Courtney said sharply. Slowly, Scott reluctantly released his hold on the Mexican.

"Remember my words," Scott said, pausing. "Hombre."

Courtney felt herself calming, her mind groping for a way to handle this. Dad would know how, she thought suddenly. The irony felt bitter. There was no Daddy solution available here. She and Scott were on their own. We're in deep shit, she cried to herself, repressing a hysterical giggle.

"If you really listened to our discussion, Tomas," she said, finding her voice again, "then you know we're both broke and won't be getting any money from our father until he makes arrangements."

"*Si*. I listen. I understand. You think I dumb Mexican?"

"It might take time. I can't tell you how long."

Tomas did not respond for a moment, obviously turning over all possibilities. Their father had said he would make the arrangements as soon as he got home. Tomas had heard.

"I figure deal this way. You got cash now. I take. Then after, you find way to get me one hundred thousand from *padre*." He tapped his ear. "I hear."

"This is crazy," Scott said. "We can't guarantee that."

"I patient wetback," the Mexican said, smiling.

"Scott's right," Courtney said.

"Your problem," the Mexican muttered. "You find way. I got pictures. You give me lump sum or in pieces. You no pay, I show *padre*."

Courtney had read enough movie scripts to know that she and her brother were clearly in a "double bind" plot device. The Mexican held the whip hand. He had stumbled over his main chance. Exposure was likely to shock their father into banishing any idea of coming across with his promised largesse, despite his professed love for his children. For him what they had done was beyond the pale.

On the other hand, they might confess and opt for his forgiveness. They would be betting on his sense of fatherhood and sentimental nostalgia—a long shot. Other scenarios crossed her mind. He would have the camera in his possession, and they were still in the wilderness about to traverse the most dangerous mountain trail in Yellowstone. She shot a glance at Scott. Was he having the same thoughts?

She had met many people like Tomas in her lifetime, cunning, street-smart, living on the edge. He had already proven his ingenuity. She felt seriously challenged by the danger Tomas posed.

"Suppose our father changes his mind about the money?" Courtney asked.

"He could do that," Scott chimed in, as if his sister's question was a hopeful sign.

"Then there is the question of time. It will take time for him to provide the money."

"Amigos," Tomas chuckled. "I Mexican. *Cuándo* you give me money, I give you camera."

He makes it sound so reasonable, so easy, Courtney thought. Their father had indicated he was going to make provisions, but they had not talked amounts or frequency. Only when he died could they expect the kind of money that Tomas was asking.

"I don't think we can deliver," Courtney said. "I think you misunderstand, Tomas. Getting our hands on that kind of money in a lump sum would be near impossible."

"She's right, Tomas."

"Your problem children," Tomas said, mimicking their father.

"It's impossible," Scott mumbled.

Tomas spat into the ground.

"Fuck you both," Tomas said chuckling, showing the glint of gold teeth. "We leave tomorrow before light. You tell *padre*."

"He might not agree," Courtney said. "It would certainly bother him to leave Harry alone and drunk in the wilderness."

"You make him, Señorita. He your *padre*."

"We can't make him do anything against his will," Scott said.

"He's right, Tomas. He could say no."

"He say no, I show him pictures."

It was, of course, a viable threat, although Tomas would gain nothing by such a revelation. Of course, she was certain that she and Scott would lose everything as well. Their father would be appalled, of course, certainly shocked and stunned by the evidence.

An incestuous relationship on the part of his children would be too difficult for him to accept. Any largesse on his part, she speculated, would be over. Such conduct would be unacceptable to him, offensive, and forever mark them as evil, bad seeds. She had no doubt that they would be written out of the will, forever alienated.

It was clear that she was dealing with someone shrewd and calculating, hardly a stereotype of the dumb, exploited Mexican. This was one sinister and canny bastard. Worse, he had nothing to lose.

She tried to assemble her thoughts, searching for how to cope with this. Scott, too, must be turning over different scenarios, perhaps featuring violence. He had already threatened murder. Nor did she dismiss such an option offhand.

"A hundred thousand dollars," Courtney said. "Seems like a bit much."

"Are you actually bargaining with this bastard?"

Courtney ignored the comment.

"This is business, Scott," Courtney said, turning again to Tomas. "Say half. Fifty thou." Courtney said. "Be realistic, amigo."

"I no bargain," Tomas said, shaking his head. "I go back to Mexico rich man. No more bullshit from gringos. No more curse from Harry. He thinks I 'fraid he send me back. With hundred thousand American, I go back rich. I no care about you people. You all crazy, greedy bastards." He poked a finger into Scott's chest. "Now you get me my money. Hundred thousand American. No less."

"That's a new one on me," Scott snickered. "A Mexican that doesn't bargain."

"One hundred thousand American," the Mexican persisted. "I take you out of here. You give me money. I give you camera with pictures. I wait no more than month."

"And if we don't agree?" Scott asked.

"Leave it alone, Scott," Courtney said. "He's got us by the balls."

The Mexican watched them for a long moment with feral eyes and then smiled broadly.

"*Si, amigos.* I got you by cojones." He illustrated by cupping his hands over his genitals. "I not stupid," he said. "You give me trouble, I give camera back to your father…" He smiled as if he enjoyed the repetition. "With pictures." He looked at Courtney with contempt. "You good fucker, lady," he said. "Maybe you give me some."

"You'd have to kill me first, amigo," Courtney said, staring into the Mexican's eyes.

Her comment had a suggestive ring to it. Then her mind filled with possibilities and assumptions. She knew, of course, that he was reacting to his own version of desperation, gambling on their vulnerability, seizing an opportunity that presented itself by chance.

To accept his terms, they would have to live with the possibility of more blackmail money for years until their father was gone. Then it would no longer matter. She allowed herself to contemplate other options. Old movie revenge plots unreeled in her imagination. An errant image saw him with his genitals sliced off and stuck in his mouth. She giggled then met his gaze and returned his smile.

"Now you go. We meet at dawn near horses. We take one mule for gear."

"Suppose our father won't go?" Scott said.

"You make him," Tomas said.

He turned and then turned again to face them.

"You don't fuck me, we be all okay. You fuck me, I fuck you."

"Not to worry, Tomas," Courtney said, thinking, *Not unless we fuck you first.*

"What if Harry wakes up?" Scott said, exchanging glances with Courtney.

Tomas shrugged, turned, and walked back in the direction of the camp.

He stared at them for a long moment as if he were assessing their commitment. Then he turned and walked toward the horses.

The two siblings walked back to camp in silence.

Chapter 19

—⟫•⟪—

Convincing their father to leave camp under Tomas's guidance and without Harry proved to be a tough task.

"We can't do that to Harry, leave him drunk out here by himself," their father protested. He was still half asleep. "I'm not comfortable with the idea."

"It's not a question of comfort, Dad," Courtney argued, but with careful tact. "The man can't function. There's plenty of food, and he does know the way back. He'll have his horse and the mules, and we'll be back in a day. Harry will be fine. Once he gets off his bender, he'll understand and find his way back. This is, after all, his turf."

"The least we could do is wait and try to reason with him."

"Dad," Courtney persisted. "You can't reason with a drunk, especially one on a bender. He can't function, and any hopes of him miraculously sobering up won't wash. We're at risk here, and we had better recognize it."

"Let me think about it."

"No," Courtney pressed. "We have to leave by dawn. Tomas has prepared everything. We have to sneak out of here while Harry is sleeping it off."

She shot a glance at her brother.

"I'm scared of this man, Dad. We have no choice. He could be leading us into danger. Tomas says he can get us back to the trailhead in a day. He's taking us over Eagle Pass."

"Eagle Pass?" Temple was stunned. "Talk about dangerous. Remember your Mom's experience?"

"It's the fastest way out of here," Courtney said. "Please, Dad. We're not hurting Harry. Hell, he'll be glad to get rid of us."

Temple grew silent, obviously contemplating a response.

"And Tomas is fed up with his treatment," Courtney pushed, appealing now to her father's feeling for the so-called underdog. "He has been abused terribly by this man, especially in his drunken state. And he has agreed to take us for the cash we have. How can you beat that? Please, Dad. Scott is scared. So am I. And we worry about you."

"Dad," Scott said, trying to hide his impatience. "The man has not fulfilled his obligation to us. He's been downright nasty and insulting. He doesn't deserve any consideration."

"Harry will be fine, Dad," Courtney pressed. "He's been paid. We've got to think of ourselves."

Scott watched his father's face, a beacon of indecision.

"Getting back safely should be our only consideration," Scott pointed out.

Their father shook his head and rubbed his chin. Obviously, this was a painful decision.

"Doesn't Tomas realize that he'll be blowing his job?"

"I'm sure he does," Scott said.

"He's fed up with being kicked around by a bigoted drunk," Courtney said, again playing the compassion card. "Being called a spic and treated like scum. You've seen it."

Their father nodded.

"He has been awful, I'll grant you." He was obviously struggling with indecision.

"The man's a mean drunk. You've seen it."

"The worst kind," Courtney interjected.

"So he took our offer for cash?" their father said, his businessman's instincts triggered.

"He jumped at it," Scott said, glancing at his sister.

"Does Tomas know Eagle Pass?" Temple asked. "I thought we had all agreed that wouldn't do."

"He says he's been over it many times," Courtney said.

"All those narrow switchbacks. Remember last time?"

"Any more dangerous than being guided by a drunk?" Courtney said. "Hell, Dad, we're in the middle of nowhere. It's dangerous country all around us. We need someone sober and alert to avert disaster. And we want to get out of here the fastest way and not risk being caught by Harry."

"I understand. Still—" He broke off the sentence. Scott was tempted to berate him for being soft with everybody except his own children. But that was a moot point now.

"Dad, please," Scott continued. "Let your children, for once, be put in charge of the decision. As far as we can see, there is no downside. Tomas has been over Eagle Pass before. He assures us he knows the way." He watched his father's face.

"Suppose we just found a way to keep him from the booze?" their father suggested. "Just dump all the booze."

"Ever see an addict in withdrawal, Dad?" Courtney said. She was growing increasingly panicked by his hesitation. Scott felt a sense of increasing desperation.

"I'm sure he'll be fine, Dad," Scott pleaded. He felt trapped. It was a messy business. He wanted to be rid of the responsibility, put all this angst behind him, pay off Tomas's blackmail, get back to Seattle, start a new life in a new business. Observing Courtney, he felt a sense of deep self-disgust. He no longer looked at her with affection or desire. It was over, he told himself. Enough! It was an obsession that brought him nothing but pain and bad luck.

Above all, he did not want to confront himself, to review his past, to list his mistakes or revisit his guilt, his fears, his failures. He wanted to be transported to nothingness, to dissolve and disappear. He had given his life away to stunted and forbidden desire. He hated himself for his weakness. His sister had led him into a quagmire, which recalled the image of his father's struggle to extricate himself.

His father was good and decent and truly loving. His mother, too. They were great parents, and he had betrayed them. He was beyond forgiveness, lost in his own private hell.

"You have got to make a decision, Dad. Time is running out."

They waited for his response, hearing only the night sounds of the wilderness, like a Greek chorus seconding their dilemma.

Then, as if it were inevitable, cutting into the night sounds was a piercing human scream.

Chapter 20

Another scream followed, an ear-blasting cry of extreme pain. For a moment all movement in their father's tent froze. Scott was the first to move. He peered out the tent into the darkness. Shots rang out.

The screams were coming from the direction of Harry's tent. It took Scott a moment to focus, but he could not comprehend what was happening. Harry's tent had collapsed and seemed to be alive, pulsating and moving. An odd unfamiliar stench filled the air. As the agonizing screams continued, another sound rent the night, an animal's roar. He saw Tomas crouching, moving forward toward Harry's tent, waving his arms.

"Grizzly!" he cried. "No come."

The screams continued as Tomas moved forward, shooting into the rippling canvas. A desperate roar of pain belched into the darkness. Then he saw the bear, a giant wounded silhouette, struggling free of the downed tent, swinging his massive head, his jaws holding something indistinguishable, lumbering away, dragging his load.

There was no measuring time. Scott's heart had leaped in his chest, his mind unable to fully comprehend what was transpiring.

"Stay put," he cried to his sister and father then crawled cautiously out of the tent.

He could see the bulky form of the grizzly lumbering away. The sound and image vanished quickly and silence came again.

Then he saw Tomas standing near the remains of Harry's tent. His flashlight's beam cut the darkness.

He heard his father's voice calling. The flap of his tent had opened, and Scott could make out the faces of his father and sister.

"What is it?"

"Grizzly," Scott cried. "Stay where you are."

He watched the beam of light move over the remains of Harry's tent. Tomas was standing over the tent. It had collapsed. He could make out the glint of moisture on the tent's fabric. Coming closer, he noted that the moisture was blood. Tomas pulled the canvas across the ground, revealing what was beneath. Scott could see Harry's head and torso. Below the waist there was nothing.

"What is it?" Courtney cried, her head visible in the flap of her father's tent.

"Better not come," Scott responded. He turned away from the site and dry heaved.

"Shit, man," Tomas said, avoiding the body but searching the scattered objects in the shambles. The heavy scent of booze, fecal matter, and other vile odors rose from the remains. Tomas continued to search the scene, concentrating on the scattered remains and the various objects that littered the ground.

"What is it?" Scott's father called, as he moved outside the tent.

"Stay away, Dad," Scott cried.

Courtney, notwithstanding her brother's warning, crawled out of their father's tent and came close enough to view the scene of horror, uttering a loud groan.

"Christ. I said stay away," Scott ordered.

"You listen, woman," Tomas said. Courtney turned away in disgust.

"What about him?" Scott asked, looking briefly at the terrible remains, moist and shining in the faint beams of the starlit night. Tomas, ignoring the question, looked toward the edge of their camp clearing where the bear had disappeared.

"I go find. I kill him now."

Rifle in hand, Tomas moved swiftly, following what he presumed was the grizzly's tracks.

Scott turned away from the gruesome sight and moved to where his father and sister stood. He could see their faces now. Close up they were like pale masks. By then, he had recovered somewhat from the first shock wave, and his mind was beginning to fully grasp the situation. His knees felt weak, and his nausea had not subsided. The appalling odor seemed to cover the area like a blanket.

"A grizzly attacked," he managed to explain hoarsely. "It looks like it tore Harry apart."

"Oh my God!" their father cried.

"How?" Courtney asked, her voice tremulous.

Scott shrugged, baffled by the attack.

"And Tomas?" his father asked.

"Out there. After the bear. He took Harry's rifle."

"Thank God, he's okay," their father said.

Scott, noting the irony, shrugged. So much for misplaced compassion.

Before he could explain further, a shot rang out. Then another and another, blasting through the silence.

Nobody moved, as if confusion and shock prevented any action. From the direction of the shots, they heard movement, and Tomas appeared, dragging what appeared to be human legs still in jeans. Courtney turned away in obvious disgust.

"I don't believe this."

Coming closer, Tomas dropped his burden. He had shouldered the rifle.

"He not go far. I got him before. I finish him," he said. He paused for a moment, watching them. "Soon we go. I take you back."

"And him?" Scott asked, pointing with his chin.

"We bury him first. Otherwise other animals come."

"What about the authorities?" their father asked. "They have to be notified."

"You tell them when you get back. Tell them Señor Harry attacked by grizzly. You all see what happened. You tell."

"But you're the witness, Tomas," Temple said.

"I tell you. You tell them. I illegal. They don't believe."

Temple exchanged glances of confusion with his children.

"You remember this," Tomas said, his arm outstretched toward the wreckage. His remark had the force of an order.

"Who can forget, Tomas?" Scott said, perplexed by the suggestion. "How could we possibly forget?"

The sky was beginning to lighten with false dawn. The scene, despite his reluctance to look, kept drawing his glance like a magnet.

"But why?" Temple began.

"Bear hungry," Tomas replied, showing a sinister smile. "Now we bury."

He turned to Courtney and her father, raising his hand, pointing to them with his finger, waving it in front of them.

"Now you listen. I get you out of here. You do what I say. Give me no shit. Okay? First we bury." He was aggressively taking charge. Their father looked confused.

"Bury?" Temple asked.

"We bury in shit hole," Tomas responded.

"Am I hearing correctly?" their father queried. "In the latrine?"

"We bury, then we leave."

"I don't understand. Are we just going to leave?" their father asked. "Shouldn't we do something? We have a dead man, an incident. We bury the remains in the latrine and just leave? Is that it?"

"Let's just do as he says, Dad," Courtney said. "No point in second-guessing him. We don't really have much of a choice."

"Courtney's right, Dad," Scott said.

"How could we?" their father asked, casting a brief glance at Harry's partial remains.

"You shut mouth. We bury," Tomas said. "You wait."

"But…" their father began. He appeared to be on the verge of a confused protest. Scott quickly intervened.

"Dad, please. He knows what he's doing."

"What makes you so certain—?"

"I take care," Tomas interjected. "I take you out of here. You do as I say. Hear me."

It was obvious that Temple was uncomfortable with every move Tomas made. Tomas remained silent, glancing at Scott, who took it as a signal to justify the Mexican's actions, an increasingly difficult chore.

"I don't know how to put this," their father pressed. "It's just plain wrong. Bury this man's remains in a latrine?"

"For crying out loud, Dad," Courtney snapped. "Can't you leave it alone? There would be nothing left of him if his remains were exposed."

"But in the latrine? Surely we could dig another hole."

"I'll grant you it is undignified, but the hole is already dug," Scott said, with growing impatience.

"It's insulting to the man's dignity. It's bad enough to die out here."

"Shut up, old man!" Tomas shouted. "I told you."

"But Tomas," Temple persisted. "We have to explain this to the authorities."

"No more talk, gringos. I take care. We bury Harry, then we move."

"It's just that—" Temple began again.

"Enough, Dad," Courtney cried. "The man is dead. Nothing can help him now. We need Tomas to get us out of here."

"Courtney's right, Dad."

"You listen. You want me to take you out? I do it. No more talk."

"Don't we have to report this to authorities, Tomas?" Temple asked, stubbornly persistent. "There are lots of questions here. Why this sudden grizzly attack? What set him off? This is a terrible tragedy."

Suddenly Tomas unshouldered the rifle and leveled it at Temple's chest.

"You listen, you stupid fuck gringo. I boss here now. I know what I do. You understand? I get you out. No more questions."

He looked toward Courtney and Scott. "You tell him shut his gringo mouth." He jabbed the rifle into Temple's chest.

"Cool down, Tomas," Scott said, on the verge of panic. "He means no harm. We're cool. Right, Dad? Tell him we're cool. And, Tomas, please don't point that rifle at my father. It will spoil everything. "

"No more questions, Dad," Courtney said. "Please."

Tomas lowered his rifle and motioned with it to Scott.

"You help." Then he looked toward Courtney and Temple. "You no move from here."

"I still don't—" their father began.

"Damn it, Dad, stop," Courtney screamed.

Despite his revulsion and periodic gagging, Scott helped Tomas drag Harry's remains to the edge of the camp where he had dug the latrine. He was carrying the upper torso, Tomas the lower.

He followed Tomas, stopping at the edge of the latrine pit.

"I hate what we're doing," Scott said, gagging, his stomach lurching.

Without answering, Tomas flung his burden into the latrine pit.

"It's the latrine for chrissakes."

"Why dig new hole?"

"It's so…" Scott searched for words. "Disrespectful." He looked at what he was carrying and dry heaved.

"Throw in," Tomas ordered.

"I can't."

Tomas grabbed the remains and flung it into the pit. Tomas had left a spade stuck in an adjacent pile of dirt and scooped out the hole. Scott watched as he dug into the pile and threw dirt back in the hole, filling it then patting it down.

Dawn had begun to break, lighting the area in dull daylight. As he stood beside the pit, watching in horror, Scott saw a reddish rectangle detach itself from a fabric surface. It was imprinted with a word, but in his distress it did not register as the rectangle floated downward into the pit.

"Now we clean camp," Tomas said.

Trancelike Scott followed. Courtney and her father had sat on a log awaiting their return. He noted that Tomas inspected the area with deep concentration, picking up scraps of what he assumed might have been part of Harry's remains. He gathered what remained in the canvas of the tent and rolled it up. Then he ordered Scott to help him take down the three other tents, which he assembled near the cooking fire and proceeded to throw into the still-glowing embers. In a short time they began to burn.

"I don't get it?" Scott asked.

"We travel light. I put food in cantle bags for trip."

"Aren't we destroying evidence?" their father said.

Tomas paid no attention but continued to add fuel to the fire. The fire blazed. Then he started to throw in their possessions. The heat became oppressive, but Tomas made certain that the edge of the fire was contained.

"This is crazy," their father muttered. "He's burning everything but the clothes on our backs."

"For crying out loud, Dad. Leave it alone. Let him just get us the fuck out of here."

It was becoming clear that Tomas had worked out a plan. He had no intention of facing the authorities and would leave it to them to deal with the authorities.

Something continued to linger on the edge of Scott's mind, a missing something. Finally the fire banked as they watched. As Tomas inspected the site, Scott noted that the meat pole had already been dismantled. What remained was put in the flames.

When the fire burnt low enough, Tomas dug another hole and pushed in the ashes and remains, then covered it up.

"I don't believe this," Temple muttered.

"Let it go," Scott warned.

"I am still confused," their father said. Despite attempts to placate him, he remained fixated on his suspicions. "What would prompt a grizzly attack on only Harry, an expert on evasion of such a predator?"

"You'd have to ask the grizzly," Scott said, hoping humor might deflect his questions.

"Now we go to horses," Tomas ordered. He started to walk to the meadow where the horses were hobbled.

"I don't understand any of this," their father said.

"Neither do I," Scott admitted.

"Just follow the fuck," Courtney muttered.

It seemed too appalling to understand. Scott's mind felt numb, but he could not find the courage to protest. Besides, it would be pointless. It was obvious that Tomas had his own agenda, and they had no choice but to obey him. There was no point in second-guessing him.

Scott urged himself to deal only with his own priorities, like survival, his future, protecting his secret. They were outlanders here, aliens. Other rules applied. The wilderness was an arena of brutality, where animals killed each other to survive. Man is just another animal, he assured himself, flesh and bones.

"It's getting hairy," Scott said, as Tomas moved quickly to the meadow, not looking back.

"Don't question it. Go with the flow," Courtney said. He could see the fear in her eyes.

"Have we a choice?" Scott asked.

"It seems somehow as if he's destroying evidence," Temple muttered.

"Evidence of what?" Scott asked, offering a cynical smile. "Are you implying there is a crime here?"

"Crime? There is no crime here, Dad," Courtney said. "Clearly Harry was killed by a bear."

"Surely there has to be an investigation to determine the facts. Yes, Harry was quite obviously killed by a grizzly. Wouldn't they need evidence to determine the facts? Is that an irrelevant question?"

"Not our worry, Dad," Scott said, determined to change the direction of the discussion. "If asked, we tell them only what we know. The man was killed by a bear, period." Still, something nagged at him. He remembered the red label that had stuck to the fabric. He had seen it before.

"Poor man. Deprived of a decent burial."

"Dad, let's just go with the flow," Courtney reiterated. "We'll be home in another day."

"Sorry, kids," Temple said. "It's not what I expected."

"Not your fault, Dad."

When they reached the area where the horses were hobbled, they noted that Tomas had already saddled four horses. There was no sign of Harry's horse or the mules.

Scott asked about their whereabouts.

"They gone," Tomas said impassively.

It was not a satisfactory explanation. Temple shook his head and exchanged troubled glances with his children.

"Don't ask, Dad," Courtney said. "It will only complicate matters."

Tomas and Scott helped their father mount his horse. It proved far more difficult than previously. His energy level seemed diminished, and he could not get a firm grip on the pommel. Nevertheless, Scott encouraged him, and he finally was mounted, although he looked somewhat exhausted from the strain of it.

"Why Eagle Pass?" their father asked, as Tomas and Scott lifted him into his saddle.

"Because I say," Tomas said, impatiently.

"Because you say?" their father questioned, obviously offended by his tone. He glanced at Scott and Courtney. "Am I missing something here?"

"Apparently we get back faster over Eagle Pass," Scott said.

"Dad, please," Courtney said. "The quicker we get out of here, the quicker we can report it. Isn't that right, Tomas?"

"*Si,*" Tomas muttered, with a shrug.

"There is a mystery here, children—"

"Damn it, Dad," Scott said, loud enough for Tomas to hear. "Why can't you just accept Tomas's actions? He knows the turf, we don't. Frankly, I have one thing on my mind: Let's just get the hell out of here!"

After their father was seated, although somewhat precariously, Courtney and Scott prepared to mount the other horses that each had rode before.

"You'd think Tomas was responsible for the bear attack," Courtney whispered, a remark that struck a discordant note. Scott did not challenge the idea, but it did trigger an uncomfortable notion. Was it possible?

"You okay, Dad?" Scott called out to his father.

"Fine," he replied, flashing a wan smile. "But very confused."

"He looks like hell," Scott whispered, after walking out of his father's hearing range.

"Yes, he does," Courtney agreed. "Considering our situation, we probably all look like hell."

"We go now," Tomas called.

A chill swept through Scott. But he could not deny that the stakes suddenly had become higher. His fear soared. The Mexican had shown himself to be a lethal combination of cunning and desperation. He was also a blackmailer, and he held the evidence of their incestuous relationship. Denial was becoming increasingly difficult to maintain.

Observing his father closely in the quickening daylight, Scott noted that his complexion was ashen. He looked older, the expression in his eyes troubled, his general demeanor sickly. His body seemed less jaunty and bent, which had little to do with the light. His persistent questioning, too, made him seem more irritable and petulant. Probably the shock of events, Scott reasoned.

"Who could have predicted this?" their father said.

"All that matters is that we get home safely," Courtney said.

"Focus only on that," Scott said. He was also concerned with the aftermath: the required payoff. They had given Tomas all their cash as agreed. Scott did not dwell on the other demand. One obstacle at a time, he told himself.

"We go now," Tomas said, kicking his horse forward. He had arranged the string so that Temple followed him. Courtney and Scott brought up the rear.

Without a word, Tomas led the train through the meadow and away from the camp.

But something continued to nag at Scott. He remembered what Tomas had told him last night.

"I take care," he had said. The words echoed in Scott's mind. Take care of *what?*

For the next hour they moved through the empty trails as the sun rose in the sky. In the background beyond the steady thumping of the horses' hoofs, the symphony of the wilderness rose and ebbed in a steady rhythm. Scott could hear the trill of birdsong, the quiet swish of leafed branches, and the occasional bleat of a running animal.

An odd serenity encompassed him as if all the pain and angst of what they had experienced in the last few hours had disappeared. Then, as swiftly as it had come, it vanished as memory kicked in. He could identify the red label that he had seen affixed to the fabric of Harry's lifeless corpse. It was the wrapper from the bacon packages that had been hoisted up and down the meat pole.

It explained in sharp clarity the presumption of what had occurred. Tomas had used it as bait to draw the grizzly, and he embellished its meal with the flesh of the outfitter. Scott felt the sudden rise of bile in his throat, and it took a massive effort of will not to vomit.

Chapter 21

⟶⊷⟵

George Temple was never one to believe in omens. But what had happened so far in this abortive trek sorely tested his denial. And yet, he could not say that it was a total disaster. He had bonded with his children, reinforced certain conclusions about his own future and theirs, and generally reduced some of the psychological burdens that were inhibiting his future life with Muriel.

Heading home now, he felt enervated and physically and mentally diminished by the improbable events that had suddenly occurred. What he feared most at this moment was that he would not be able to make it over Eagle Pass. It was increasingly obvious that at seventy-odd years he did not have the strength and fortitude of a younger man, and he had greatly exceeded his own physical capacity.

Another by-product of this strange trek is that it forced him to face the reality of his mortality. All the cosmetic surgery, hair dye, and Viagra, all the dieting and exercise, all the vitamins and prescription elixirs to cope with or postpone disease, all the careful routine recommended to theoretically prolong life could not undue the stark fact that the curtain of his life's drama was descending faster than he had realized.

It was true that his relationship with Muriel raised hopes for an expanded, albeit limited, future. She had forced him to look ahead with courage and discard the baggage of past years, and he had dutifully followed her sage advice. At this moment he felt too debilitated and beset by signs of physical and mental weakness to project his thoughts beyond the moment.

His short-term memory, for one thing, seemed failing. Misplacing his camera had been a profound loss, and he had wracked his brain to retrace areas where it might have accidentally landed. Years earlier it might have seemed a small thing, the result of simple carelessness, but in the context of the aging process, it suggested the beginning of mental decline. Sharing those camera images would trigger memory, validate a milestone, offer evidence of a bonding experience with his children, and as it was on their first trek, offer proof and pleasure of a transcendent experience.

Why couldn't he remember what he had done with it? On the earlier trek he had not lost his camera. He rarely misplaced anything. In his business, he was always razor sharp, often boastful about his ability to remember the weight and quality of every gemstone in his inventory.

What he hadn't told his children this morning was that, in the hubbub of his quick exit, he had forgotten to retrieve, of all things, his blood pressure pills from his possessions Tomas had ordered to leave behind. The shocking event of last night had simply crowded out all the little details of daily living.

He was secretly embarrassed by his forgetfulness concerning the pills, and he did not wish to tell his children. He was ashamed of these episodes and all that they implied about his mind. His children might think Alzheimer's had begun its nasty work.

Perhaps that fear was why he had been so persistent in his questioning of Tomas. It took on the aspect of an exercise in mental gymnastics, one question leading to another, a kind of hysterical mind game.

He continued to review the details of this weird event. Why had Harry been attacked and not one of them? Was the odor of booze a grizzly seducer? Was Harry giving off a scent that attracted bears? Sober, Harry would have known how to handle the situation. And what of Tomas's burning of everything in the camp? And his show of power with the rifle? And leaving behind the mules and Harry's horse?

These were puzzles to ponder. Keep at it, he willed himself. It will tell your brain that you are still alive and functioning. He pondered the craziness of these events. They seemed beyond logic. He wondered if Tomas had simply been pushed beyond sanity by Harry's abuse.

He wondered, too, if they would notice that he was having difficulty sitting upright on his mount, although he did muster the strength to hold on to the pommel and look as if he was properly seated in the saddle. It took all his willpower to accomplish this feat.

They moved forward in silence, Tomas leading them through trails that they had not traversed on the first day, although the topography seemed the same. They moved through forests of evergreens, then upward through snaking trails that took them high over deep canyons. The sun rose in the cloudless cerulean blue sky. His horse was second in the line of the train, behind Tomas. Scott rode in the rear.

About two hours into the ride, Tomas stopped the train abruptly. They were traversing a high path over a shallow canyon. Tomas's attention was directed at the canyon floor, where even from that distance Temple could see a rider moving in the opposite direction from where they were going. Tomas lifted binoculars to his eyes and peered into them with deep concentration.

"What is it?" Courtney asked.

A ranger perhaps, Temple thought. "We should flag him down."

"No," Tomas said. "We go on."

Temple turned to his son.

"Did I hear correctly? Did he say go on? Could be a ranger down there, an official. He might have a radio with him to get help. If not, he could come with us back to the camp and start to assess the situation."

"I don't know, Dad" Scott said.

Temple turned to Tomas.

"Let me have the binoculars, Tomas," he said.

"We go on," Tomas said.

"Obviously, he wasn't a ranger, Dad," Courtney said.

"Then why won't he give me the binoculars?" Temple persisted. Tomas started to move forward.

"No," Temple cried, keeping his horse reigned. "We've got to get his attention, Tomas. He could be someone to help us."

Tomas turned in the saddle and looked menacingly at Temple.

"You old man. Hear me. You follow," he said.

Temple peered into the distance. He could barely make out a tiny figure below and a horse bent over a stream.

"I'm going down," Temple said, ignoring Tomas's order. He saw a trail that could lead him down. A charge of adrenaline shot through him. He kicked his horse's haunches and started to move.

"You no go down," Tomas said. He unshouldered his rifle, cocked it, and pointed it at Temple. "You no go down. You listen."

Scott kicked his horse's belly, caught up to his father, and grabbed the reins of his father's horse, stopping it.

"Don't, Dad," Scott said. "He means business."

"But it could be someone to help us. Maybe a ranger," Temple said. He looked at Tomas, who still held the rifle pointed directly at him. "Why is he reluctant? It makes perfect sense." He addressed Tomas. "Why not?"

"You go. I shoot."

Courtney brought her horse around so that it was between Tomas and her father. The rifle was now leveled directly at Courtney. Scott tensed.

"Okay. Okay," Temple said, panicked, seeing his daughter at risk.

"Don't be an asshole," Courtney said. "What's the point? Put it down."

Tomas continued to point the rifle.

"He no go," Tomas sneered.

"Okay then," Temple said, his heart pounding. "Just put down that rifle."

"Makes no sense," Scott interjected.

"He's right, Tomas," Courtney said. "It won't get you anywhere. Do I have to spell it out?"

It struck Temple as an odd response, but he dismissed it. He turned toward Scott who still held the reins of his horse.

"Okay, Tomas," Temple said. "We'll do it your way."

Slowly Tomas lowered the rifle. Temple was relieved. But the excitement of the brief confrontation took its toll. He felt fatigued by the experience.

"I'm not sure I understand," Temple shrugged.

"He's illegal, Dad," Courtney said, turning to Tomas. "Isn't that right, Tomas?"

"No talk. We go."

Temple looked downward again to where he had seen the rider.

"He's gone now," Temple mumbled. "You've made a big mistake here, Tomas."

Tomas slung the rifle over his shoulder and moved his horse forward.

"This man is a menace," he muttered to Scott.

"Just keep going, Dad. He's got his reasons. Let's just get the hell out of here."

"It makes no sense."

"Don't fight it, Dad, please," Courtney begged. "We'll be out of here soon, and all will be just fine."

Temple felt trapped and followed in line. He could not understand Tomas's logic.

The sun grew hotter, and they continued to move to higher ground. Temple began to feel dizzy. He called out weakly and slumped over the pommel. Scott rode up to him. His breath came in gasps.

"Rest," Temple whispered.

"You no stop," Tomas shouted, continuing.

"No way," Scott called. "He's having problems. I don't think he's well. Could be the altitude."

Temple felt completely exhausted and suddenly very weak. A cold sweat began to pour out of him. Tomas galloped up to him, and both he and Scott helped him dismount, then they helped him walk to the nearby shade of an evergreen. They propped him against the trunk and gave him water.

"Rest for a while, Dad," Scott said, turning to Tomas, who moved away and squatted nearby.

"The heat is all," Courtney said. "And you're probably dehydrated. Drink up and rest. You'll be fine."

"Probably his blood pressure," Scott said. "We've moved pretty high up."

Temple took deep breaths. His head ached, and he felt awful.

"I'm fine, Scott," he lied. "Just let me rest a moment."

"It's all the excitement," Courtney said. "It's been a tough few hours."

Temple nodded weakly. "And confusing." He looked at his children, observing their faces. They looked concerned. It crossed his mind that maybe he would not survive this trek and worried that if he did die here, he could not make good on his promises to his children.

The idea began to prey on his mind. *I'm being morbid,* he told himself. In a few more hours, they would be back to civilization. He'd see a doctor, replenish his blood pressure pills. Besides, this was no place to die, in the middle of nowhere.

The trek, he acknowledged, might have seemed like a good idea at first, but it had gone awry. He was too old for it. Who was it that said, *You can't go home again?* They were right.

"Have to move," he whispered, rising unsteadily.

"You should rest, Dad," Scott said.

His father shook his head.

"Help me up," he said. Courtney came forward.

She joined Scott in helping their father mount up again. It was a chore, but he was determined.

"He be fine," Scott mumbled, with an angry glance at the Mexican. "You Mexican piece of shit," he mouthed under his breath.

If the Mexican heard, he made no comment. They got Temple into the saddle and put his feet into the stirrups.

"Hi ho, Silver," he said weakly. Stay alive, he begged himself.

Chapter 22

Courtney's thoughts churned with plans and methods to achieve them. She had no illusions about where she stood and what she wanted. It was about money, only money. Money to fund her career. This was her total focus. What was transpiring offered her both an opportunity and a rationale.

Accept the reality, she told herself. Life was finite. Her father was near his end. In terms of time, she had a lot more left on her lifetime clock than he did. Thus, the act she now contemplated would merely reduce a tiny portion of his allotted time.

She had carefully weighed the alternatives. If he died on this journey, she and Scott would share their inheritance. There would be no need for his generosity. And Tomas would be deprived of his blackmail ploy. It could be the perfect solution.

The idea had accelerated in her mind with greater force after the grizzly attack on Harry. The episode embellished the idea from a mere abstract wish to a real possibility. When Tomas leveled the gun at her father, she felt a strange exhilaration. If he pulled that trigger, it might have been the perfect solution.

On that idea, dire speculation had intruded. It would be clearly murder, requiring wasted time, long investigations, perhaps a trial. She rejected such an outcome, but it did not stop her imagining other scenarios.

In this wild place, danger was practically institutionalized. It was everywhere. Harry had illustrated a number of possibilities, one of which resulted in his own death. Every act required a cautionary note. A fall from a horse meant injury or death. A slip in a stream or lake could mean drowning. A tree might fall and crush a living creature. One could trip in a hole or on a boulder. A sudden fire might move too swiftly in the wind. A freak rainstorm could start a mudslide. There was no order out here, no police, no protection, except what could be devised by the rules of caution.

One was totally dependent on a horse's instinctive desire to stay alive. A false step on a narrow trail that ran adjacent to a high canyon was a real possibility, especially on the many narrow switchbacks of Eagle Pass. In her thoughts, Courtney catalogued and narrowed the possibilities.

The point of the exercise was finding a way for death to happen to her father without consequences to her or Scott, although her brother was becoming more and more of an annoying obstacle. As she pondered, alternatives appeared. Was it possible?

She was increasingly certain that she could overcome her moral inhibitions and would be strong enough to withstand any attack of conscience or guilt. She knew she was seriously weighing both the method and the consequences. The point of the exercise was to get away with it, collect the inheritance, and get on with her career plans.

Of course, her father was a good man. He had been an adoring and caring father, had protected, supported, and loved her, for which she would be grateful as long as she lived.

She could say with absolute candor that she had loved him once in a daughterly way. His adamant refusal to continue his generosity had been a trial for her, but it appeared that he had reversed his decision and would put it into practice when he returned. She had no doubt, considering his history, that, if he arrived home safe, he would keep his word. But was that enough?

She could see obvious pitfalls ahead. Dear Muriel would surely find a way into his pockets. It was a natural progression, and while she welcomed her father's current promise of generosity, she speculated that his sudden death would leave what she believed was his original intent intact. Muriel would be aced out.

Indeed, she could not imagine that he would have yet changed his estate plan in defiance of their mother's wishes, which meant equal distribution between her and her brother. Even in their most bitter argument at her mother's funeral, he had averred that he had followed their mother's wishes. At this point, she knew there was only one way to assure that outcome.

Others, she acknowledged, if they knew her thoughts would think of her as cruel, heartless, selfish, cold-blooded, and monstrous. Thankfully, they didn't know her thoughts, although she had provided subtle hints to her brother. Of course, he would never go along. He was weak, and he hadn't the guts or the temperament.

She hadn't yet figured out a way to act on a plan, although she had taken a tiny first step. She had deliberately stolen her father's blood pressure pills, but she could not be certain whether the brief deprivation was having an effect. He looked terrible, pale, wan, sickly, but she couldn't be sure she could attribute this condition to this lack of medication. It was not a pretty picture, and while she could not summon the requisite compassion, she would prefer a quicker resolution.

As for the scheming Mexican, he was needed to get them back to civilization, although she remembered, from their earlier trek, that once over Eagle Pass, they would follow the path through Shoshone National Forest, which should bring them in contact with people. She hadn't yet figured out how she would handle that. Her first priority lay elsewhere.

These thoughts continued to circulate through her mind as they proceeded up the path to the Eagle Pass trailhead. They had been traveling for more than an hour since her father had first shown signs of flagging. A quick glance showed him looking exhausted and slumping over the pommel.

"Maybe we should stop for a while," Scott called to Tomas, who looked back and shook his head in disgust.

Scott's shout alerted his father, who straightened in the saddle but said nothing.

"Are you okay, Dad?" Courtney asked, noting his declining condition as a good sign.

"Fair to middlin'," her father said, offering a thin smile.

"I really think we should stop," Scott said. Then addressing himself to his father, "Maybe if we ate something."

"Good idea," their father said, pulling on the reins of his horse, the effort an obvious trial.

"A few miles more we get to Eagle Pass," Tomas said.

"No, Tomas. We rest now, if you don't mind," Scott demanded.

Tomas started to protest, then shrugged, and dismounted. He continued to keep the rifle slung over his shoulder. Scott and Tomas helped Temple to dismount. His legs were obviously shaky, and he had to be helped to a nearby tree, where he slumped to the ground, using the tree as support. Scott offered water and unwrapped the food in his father's cantle, mostly candy bars and crackers. He gave them to his father.

"Eat up, Dad. You'll feel better."

Their father took a sip of the water and unwrapped one of the candy bars. He bit off a piece and chewed with little appetite. Tomas squatted nearby, eyeing them with narrowed hostile eyes. He had unslung his rifle and laid it across his legs. He did not eat.

Courtney motioned to Scott, and they moved out of earshot of Tomas, who watched them with obvious suspicion.

"I'm really worried about him," Scott said. "He seems to be going downhill fast. It's just too much for him. "

"The excitement probably," Courtney said, hoping he would see her response as sincere. "Poor guy."

She had moved toward a realization that Scott needed to observe her concern. She knew now that she was moving forward on her, as yet, unfocused plan. Observing her father's condition, she speculated that, with luck, any action on her part would be avoidable. Perhaps, she thought, nature would take its course.

"And we have to contend with that crazy Mexican," Scott said, between clenched teeth. "You think he would have shot Dad?"

"Or me."

"He's not that stupid. He's too shrewd for that. His only chance for filthy lucre is to get Dad back in one piece."

Their father's head lay back against the tree trunk, his eyes closed. Opening them briefly, he observed them, smiled, and closed his eyes again.

"He'll be fine, Scott."

"You think so?"

She noted a touch of belligerency in his voice, which disturbed her. Was he reading her thoughts?

"Remember, Scott," she said archly, deliberately testing the waters. "It was his idea. Not ours. He can't blame us."

"Who said anything about blame?"

"I mean if something happened to him up here."

"Like what?"

"You know what I'm saying," she said.

She watched his reaction, knowing that she had sent a clear message. He shook his head and spat on the ground.

"You are one fucking cold-blooded bitch," he sneered.

"Cold-blooded? I'm being a realist, Scottie."

No alliance there, she thought. He was too sentimental, too weak.

She turned away, her anger rising, and shifted her gaze to where her father was sitting. The old man's eyes were closed. His mouth was open, and he seemed to be sinking into a deep sleep.

"Don't be so self-righteous. I'm merely stating the obvious, whether you want to hear it or not."

"If you must know, I don't want to hear it."

"Your choice, brother mine. But this I'll tell you. If it does happen, you will better understand the risk/reward reality."

"You're off the wall, Courtney. Considering all he's done for us, for you, you should kiss the ground he walks on."

"And so I did. Other places as well."

"You sure turned out to be one scummy bitch," he sighed, turning away.

"Sticks and stones, Scottie boy," she muttered. It was time to write him off. So much for family solidarity. For a moment their eyes met. She wondered if his much-professed love for her had disappeared. But then, she acknowledged, she had never quite understood it and the power it held over him.

"Now we go," Tomas said, rising, cutting short her speculation.

At the sound of his voice, their father opened his eyes. He started to rise, using the tree for balance. Scott and Courtney helped him up.

"Feeling better, Dad?" Courtney asked. Scott looked at her with obvious contempt but said nothing.

Their father nodded, forcing himself to rise with the assistance of the tree for support. They helped him to his horse, and Tomas joined them to get him mounted. He gave them a thin smile when he was seated.

"Hi ho, Silver," he murmured, but without much force. "Where's Kemosabe?" He looked at Tomas. "Ah, there he is." The stoic and humorless Tomas looked at him briefly with indifference.

They mounted their own horses again, but this time Courtney managed to change the order of the string, maneuver her horse behind Tomas, and put her father's horse behind her and in front of Scott's. Tomas looked back but made no move to change the order. He looked at her and nodded his approval, perhaps thinking it would speed up the string.

They began to move up the trail. It was past noon, and the heat from the sun was relentless. In the distance, they could see black rain clouds gathering.

What she needed here, Courtney decided, was a twofer. If both her father and brother were…well…eliminated, she would be the sole heir, unchallenged. Easier said than done. Her father, as anyone could see, teetered on the brink. Her brother's demise would take some ingenuity.

What she needed now was a new beginning, free of all tangible entanglements, a clean slate. In the end we are all alone, she told herself with philosophical authority, as if such a thought might justify any future action. Courage, girl! God helps those who help themselves. She felt her resolve morph into a sworn commitment.

Ideas of method jumped into her mind, but she had not yet focused on a single course of action. The only thing she had determined thus far was venue. The narrow switchbacks made ideal possibilities for a contrived accident. They were narrow and hazardous paths over high canyons, a perfect recipe for creating a disaster. The tiniest disruption of concentration could send a slow-witted horse over the edge. Of one thing she was dead certain: she would never have this opportunity again.

Such speculation did not deter her from contemplating the aftermath. After all, to take such drastic action required justification and a plan. Hell, she thought, she was an actress. She could play her part as bereaved daughter and sister with ease. She knew all the contrived ticks and moves of a distressed witness. Piece of cake, she decided.

She speculated on the career-enhancing projects that she would be able to fund. She would option books, commission screenplays, hire staff. She had been educated by her failures and mistakes. She would no longer be a supplicant. She would pay her multimillion-dollar entrance fee into the Hollywood-insiders club. This meant that she would have the means and the contacts to do whatever was required to move a project to the next level. She would invest in herself.

Money would automatically empower her. After what she intended here, no act would be too difficult, too offensive, too cruel. She would dispense mental anguish to those who opposed her or offer rewards to sycophants and enablers.

If she had to humiliate people as she had been, torture people as she had been, lead people on as she had been, she would not hesitate. She would demand favors for career moves, manipulate wannabes to serve her cause. She would use any means to achieve her goal of stardom. Money would make her bulletproof. She told herself she was having a kind of *All About Eve* epiphany. Old movie and theater plots buzzed in her head. She became Barbara Stanwyck in *Double Indemnity,* albeit in a new ending.

Lines from her Shakespeare performances echoed in her head. Lady Macbeth, Goneril, Regan. She could get into their mindsets. People told her she was great, believable. She knew these roles.

First things first, she urged herself, trying to recall how it had been the first time they traversed Eagle Pass. She remembered numerous switchbacks, narrow winding ribbons of dirt that wound round and round the mountain, some barely two feet wide. Her mother, she remembered, was paralyzed with fear. They had had to dismount and lead the horse by its reins for fear a misstep might send the horse and rider careening into the air in a sheer and killing descent.

At some point, she speculated, a mistaken heavy pull on the reins or some variation of the gesture might spur the deed, the idea being to use the drop as the weapon of choice. Her task, she acknowledged, was to come up with the means, exactly the right action to accomplish her purpose without making it obvious to the prying eyes of investigators.

They moved through the forest on a rough up-and-down path lined on either side with grass. Occasionally, her horse would lower his long neck and stop to munch, and she would pull on the reins to get him focused again and continue to follow the lead horse on which Tomas was mounted.

When the gap between horses became too wide, the horses would canter to catch up. This meant a sudden burst of speed to narrow the gap. For inexperienced riders like them, this was a strenuous physical annoyance. Such antics would certainly have a negative effect on her father, who was having trouble enough to keep upright at the most plodding pace.

From time to time, she would deliberately lead her horse off trail and allow him to eat the grass, causing a copycat effort by her father's horse and Scott's. This would catch the attention of Tomas, who would call out for them to catch up and get the horses back in formation. The resultant effort of starts and stops might accomplish the hoped-for effect on her father.

After nearly an hour of this, she was pleased to see her father slump exhausted in his saddle, listing further and further to the right. Noting this, Scott called for Tomas to halt the train. The Mexican looked back in disgust, dismounted, and walked back to where Scott was helping his father down from the horse.

"Sorry I'm such a bother," their father said weakly as he was helped to a log, where he lay down using it as a headrest.

"Let him rest," Courtney said, noting that her plan seemed to be bearing fruit. Perhaps, she speculated, she would not have to devise the accident she had been contemplating.

"All that bouncing around," Scott said, his tone edged with anger as he addressed her. "Can't you keep that horse of yours moving?"

"He's hungry. I can't stop him," Courtney replied, studying her father. She bent down and gave him water from her canteen. He barely wet his lips.

"We'll rest here for a while, Dad," Scott said. "We still have to go over that damned mountain."

Courtney looked toward the mountain and Eagle Pass. It was afternoon now, and the sun was angling toward the west. She calculated that if they stalled enough, there might be a chance that darkness would descend when they were on Eagle Pass. Although she hadn't come up with a plan as yet, she was certain that darkness could be an ally.

"Yes, I'll just close my eyes for a bit," their father said.

"I no like," Tomas said. He studied the sky. "Bad rain come soon."

"He needs the rest," Scott said, shifting his eyes from Tomas to Courtney.

"Apparently," she echoed, looking at her brother with clear contempt.

Scott squatted down beside his father.

Seeing them together, Courtney felt, for the first time in her life, a sense of jealousy, of sibling rivalry. Wasn't it she who had always occupied the favored spot in her parents' admiration? Wasn't she the apple of their eye, certainly their father's favorite, his little girl?

Together, the two men seemed inordinately intimate. She felt shut out, marginalized. They were talking, whispering, which further inflamed her. She moved away, still observing them. Why had they locked her out? Her father, looking pale and exhausted, lay with his head on a log. His lips were moving slowly. Scott had his ear cocked against his father's mouth, listening, concentrating, his face oddly troubled. Occasionally, he looked toward where Courtney stood, his eyes narrowing then turning away.

She felt infuriated by being left out of this conversation. What were they saying? Were they talking about her? She looked toward Tomas who squatted beside his horse, watching them with obvious annoyance. Rather than just stand by and observe, she walked into the adjacent stand of trees, dropped her pants and urinated, thinking of the act as a statement, her mind focusing instead on her deadly mission.

The idea expanded in her mind. She decided she needed that concept to keep her focused. She fully understood her objective, although the means was still uncertain.

She pulled up her pants and walked back to the trail. Her father's eyes were closed, but his lips were still moving. Something conspiratorial seemed to be going on, stoking her anger. She moved forward but when she had reached them, her father stopped talking and closed his eyes.

"Let him sleep for a bit," Scott said.

"What were you two talking about?"

Scott shrugged. She detected a kind of whimsical smile as he lay back, brim over his eyes, offering a farewell motion with his hand.

The gesture stoked her anger, and she moved toward where Tomas squatted. A new idea had begun to hatch in her mind. Tomas watched her as she came forward. She bent down beside him.

"My father looks bad," she said.

Tomas nodded.

"He may not have the stamina to make it," she continued cautiously, watching the Mexican's bronzed flat features to assess his understanding of the prospect.

"Means no money, Tomas. Face it. He dies, you have no hold on us. You catch my meaning?"

"He no die," Tomas said, his eyes narrowing.

"You think so. Hell, you were going to shoot him. And me."

"I no shoot. I not stupid."

"He dies, your little blackmail scheme goes down the drain," she pressed, hoping she was reaching deeper, putting a needle into the balloon of his dreams. "No going back to your village rich, Tomas. Nada. You wouldn't want to go back a peon with empty hands." She paused, watched his face. "Would you?"

"He no die." He looked over to where her father lay sleeping. "He not that bad."

"He be fine," she mimicked. "It's time to stop bullshitting yourself, Tomas. You got a problem." Her eyes met his. She read his suspicion in them, waiting for the message to sink in. "So have I. Two problems."

His reaction seemed attentive. He cocked his head in concentration and suspicion. At the same time he touched the stock of the rifle that lay secure across his lap, as if it were a gesture to emphasize his authority.

"Them," Courtney said, glancing toward her resting father and brother. She knew she was about to make the most crucial and life-changing statement of her life. Tomas's brow wrinkled. He glanced toward Temple and Scott.

"If they both were to have say…" She paused. "…an accident."

His eyes narrowed and met hers. She was certain that she had gotten his full attention.

"You would get, say…" She had wanted to say a million, but stopped herself. A million would be beyond his wildest dreams, a figure he would surely mistrust. "Five times a hundred thousand. In your village it would last a lifetime. Maybe two. You would be a…a *patrono*, a man of deep respect."

She noted a nerve begin to palpitate in his jaw. His tongue licked his lips. His eyes appeared feral, alert. The message had been received.

"I listen."

She sucked in a deep breath, expelled it with a sigh. Unfortunately, she could only offer an objective, not a means. Again, she looked toward her father and brother.

"There are ways, Tomas. Horses slip on the narrow trail." She paused, watching him. "It's a long way down." She paused, waiting for some sign of his understanding. "They die, my father's money comes to me. Do you get my drift?"

He swallowed hard and rubbed his chin.

"You say die," he whispered, moving his face closer to hers. She nodded.

"By accident. It must be an accident." She paused, then wet her lips and smiled. "Like Harry."

His eyes narrowed and met her gaze. She could tell even from the briefest rearrangement of his facial muscles that she had struck pay dirt. From her standpoint, it was a wild guess, but she knew she was onto the truth.

"You understand what I'm saying Tomas?"

He nodded.

"You *perra*. Kill your *padre*? And your brother who you fuck?"

He spit on the ground and chuckled, his lips curling in a sinister smile. She let him contemplate the idea through a long silence. Her heartbeat accelerated, and her pores opened in a copious sweat. Her mind clogged suddenly with doubts. Had she gone too far? How could she possibly trust this venal Mexican?

"Where the trail is narrow," she persisted. She wondered if such an accident had precedent.

He rubbed his chin again, his smile fading.

"A misstep by a horse," she pressed. "Something as simple as that." She watched and waited. "An accident. Only you and I would know the truth. And for that…five hundred thousand dollars, American."

She felt a sudden laser look as his gaze met hers. His eyes narrowed, as he seemed to look deeply into her thoughts.

"Five hundred thousand." He seemed to hiss the words through clenched teeth.

"You bullshit me?" He broke his gaze and looked toward her father and Scott.

"He rich like that?"

"Yes. And when he dies, it goes to me and my brother. All to me if my brother is not around…you get my drift, hombre?"

He lowered his head and studied her with a laserlike look.

"When I get that money?"

"When I get mine. He has to die first."

"How do I be sure?"

"Trust, Tomas. We would have to trust each other."

"I kill you if you fuck me over."

"I have no doubt."

"Maybe I just shoot them?" He chuckled and lifted the rifle, aiming it but not to the suggested targets.

"Don't be ridiculous, Tomas. I told you it must be an accident. It must stand scrutiny. There could be an investigation. It must look like an accident." She paused, watching his face, and repeated her previous subtle accusation. She paused for a moment then took a shot in the dark. "Like Harry."

"Harry killed by a grizzly," Tomas snapped. It struck her as oddly defensive.

"You think we're dumb gringos, Tomas? Something about it is very strange. Very strange."

Tomas, in a quick reaction and still seated, moved the rifle into firing position. Courtney moved the barrel with her hand. She met no resistance, but the act confirmed her suspicion.

"Don't be an idiot, Tomas. As far as I'm concerned, a grizzly killed Harry. End of story. As for the others…" She shrugged.

"They don't believe no wetback. I go far from here."

"Without a doubt. Of course, I'll tell my version of what happened, a series of unlucky accidents. Believe me, I can be very convincing. I'm an actor, Tomas. I make people believe. I'll make sure no suspicion of any wrongdoing falls on you, Tomas."

She was working it out in her mind now, filling in the blanks based on what she could recall of all those suspense movie scripts she had read over the years. Tomas would split as soon as they arrived back at the trailhead. She felt certain that he would hook up with some secret system that illegal Hispanics had established, a kind of underground railway like in the old American-slave days. Besides, they might break him down and spoil her scenario.

"Then how I get my money?"

"Believe me, Tomas. I won't be hard to find. Frankly, I expect to be a known figure. Maybe a celebrity. You trust me. I trust you." She pulled a card out of her pocket. "Believe me, I'll be easy to find."

He looked blankly at the card and slipped it in his pocket.

"You don't give me my money, I kill you."

"Of that, I have no doubt."

Yes, she told herself, I will be happy to give him the money. Of course, there was always the chance he would, like most blackmailers she had encountered in movie scripts, be asking for more and more. She would cross that bridge when she came to it.

Tomas grew silent for a long time. He looked over to where her father and Scott lay. Temple had dozed off, and Scott, using his arms as a pillow, was staring into the sky. The weather was becoming more and more overcast. In the distance, they could see bursts of lightening and hear the echoing sound of thunder. Tomas grimaced as he inspected the sky. He shook his head and made no comment.

The impending bad weather seemed a sign that her plan might gain traction in Tomas's mind. A slick, soft, and muddy trail could make the consequences more believable. Rain was yet another movie signal anticipating ominous events approaching. She imagined she could hear the background music.

She felt little pity or remorse for what she was planning. Like a true actor, she had immersed herself in the character of the person she was portraying: ruthless, unsentimental, focused, and determined. Impatient, she broke into the Mexican's silence.

"We got a deal, Tomas?"

His response was a blank look and a snarl.

"How I know you not fuck me?" he muttered.

"Why would I do that?"

"You gringo. Gringo's fuck Mexicans."

She looked into his eyes. He was obviously wary and uncertain.

He shook his head, cleared his throat, and spat out a wad of phlegm on the dirt in front of her.

"Of course, you could refuse," she said. "If he lives, you'll get your hundred thousand as promised. If not..." She shrugged.

He glanced to where her father and brother were reclining.

"Business, Tomas. Why settle for one hundred when you can have five hundred thousand. Why would I not meet my end of the bargain?"

"Me dumb Mexican wetback. You crazy lady."

"Dumb, Tomas? What I see is the shrewdest fucking Mexican on the planet. Look what you pulled off. Go ahead. Consider your options. I'm offering you a fucking future, fella. *Dinero*. Lots of *dinero*. You want to be a peon for the rest of your life, taking orders from bastards like Harry? Don't sell yourself short, hombre. You're one smart fucking Mexican. Listening. Watching. Looking for the main chance. Don't give me that humble poor dumb wetback shit. I've seen you in operation." She pointed with a gesture of her head toward her father and Scott. "You give a fuck about them? No way. What do they mean to you? I'm offering you the deal of a lifetime. And remember. I'm on the line, too. I've got to convince the authorities that everything that happened was purely accidental, a bad string of tragic events. That's my job. That's my risk."

She knew she was running at the mouth, slightly hysterical, maybe even illogical, but enraged at his resistance. Besides, she wasn't certain he even understood what she was getting at. He shook his head and showed her a thin smile.

"Tell you what, lady," he said, lowering his voice. "I got idea."

She grew hopeful.

"Okay, Tomas. I'll buy."

He moved closer, his mouth near her ear.

"You fuck me like you fuck your brother, and I decide."

She had vaguely considered such a proposition and had actually pondered a reaction, then dismissed it. Instead she contemplated yet another stance, insult and indignation. Then discipline prevailed, and she held back her pose of scorn, assuming yet another role requiring the usual clichéd movie dialogue.

"I guess you could call that a sweetener, Tomas. Okay then, you do this deal, and I'll give your Mexican dick a ride to paradise. Not before." She looked toward her sleeping father and sibling and grabbed his crotch. "And that's another promise. And it'll prove that I keep my promises."

She could tell the Mexican was startled by her response. He rubbed his chin and grabbed her breast. She brushed his hand away. His expression betrayed nothing. He had not committed himself. Opening her mouth, she showed him her tongue.

"Bet you're horny as hell, baby," she whispered between clenched teeth. He offered a tiny smile and looked away, leaving the question up in the air. She waited for a response, and when none came, she said, "Deal?"

"We see."

"That's no fucking answer, Tomas," she said sharply.

He scowled and turned away.

Frustrated, she shook her head. By her lights, she was making him an offer he could not refuse.

For a long time, she sat, slumped against a tree, her mind raging with possibilities. Perhaps, she conjectured, she might find a way to perform a triple accident, do away with all three. Like a chain reaction on a highway. Such an outcome intrigued her.

In that action, there would be no witnesses, no obvious evidence, and she felt certain that she would be able to concoct a credible story. Her role would be that of sole survivor, a sympathetic grieving figure, a perfect candidate for a headline story on the world media.

She was sure she could pull it off, complete with tears. Hadn't she auditioned for such roles, over and over again? Think of the publicity. She chuckled. It was one way to become a celebrity. The media were suckers for sole survivors.

The problem, of course, was the method. She glanced toward her father stretched out, snoring lightly. If only he would die of natural causes. This would eliminate any possibility of blackmail, but it would not eliminate her brother. She had become fixated on that new idea. Of course, now that she had announced her intentions to Tomas, he would possess damaging information about her attempt to eliminate her brother. It had become a conundrum.

She felt as if she were having a movie story conference with three sides of herself, coming up with plot points. She tried out numerous scenarios, none of which seemed foolproof. She wished she could wave a magic wand and eliminate all three of the male protagonists. Unfortunately, nothing she could think at that moment seemed adequate to the task, meaning foolproof and untraceable to her.

Think hard, she urged herself. Imagine, conceive, conjure.

Chapter 23

Through his almost-closed eyelids, Scott saw tiny slits of light and felt little dabs of cold moisture on his skin. It took him a few moments to become conscious of his surroundings. His brief sleep had been dreamless but deep and disorienting. With awareness came clarity and remembering. It had started to rain, and in the distance he saw black clouds gathering.

Beside him, his father stirred. He studied his face, pale, unshaven, sickly. Still, he could see the outlines of the younger face, Dad's face, the face that dominated his memory. Earlier, his father had conveyed to him the anguish and guilt that lay just beneath the surface.

Lifting himself on his elbow, Scott watched the oncoming clouds clotted with rain and accompanied by bolts of lightning, together with the frightening sound of rolling thunder. A sharp breeze shook the branches of the trees, and the temperature had dropped precipitously. A few yards away Tomas squatted. His head had dropped to his chest but rose now as he watched Scott move. Courtney was sitting on the ground, her back against a tree, watching him.

Scott noted that the horses had been tethered to nearby aspens. Occasionally they would lower their heads to graze. He looked toward his father and gently shook him. The old man grunted and opened his eyes, showing some confusion.

"Jeez," he said. "Went out like a light."

"All the excitement, Dad. How do you feel?"

With some effort, his father got himself into a sitting position. He held out his hand. Scott rose and helped him up. He was shaky and not too sure of his footing. His nostrils quivered as he sucked in a deep breath. Courtney stood up and came over to them.

"Big storm coming."

"We go now," Tomas said, standing.

Courtney rose and came over to her father.

"Think you can make it, Dad?" she said.

"I have to," he said, cutting a quick glance at Scott, who nodded then looked at his sister, certain that she was merely paying lip service. He saw her with new eyes now.

Scott looked toward Tomas, who had already donned a poncho, then at the sky.

"Won't it be dangerous? In this weather?"

"In cantle is poncho. It will pass."

Scott pulled the ponchos from his father's cantle and his own while Courtney donned hers. The rain was beginning in earnest now, putting a glistening shine on the horses.

Oddly, he saw the rain as a cleansing force. His deep conversation with his father had helped unburden his spirit. While not a full confession, it had soothed his conscience.

He felt suddenly like a fly that had managed to break out of the sticky web that had trapped him for years. Feeling the strange sense of freedom, he felt an inner exultation, enjoying the delicious irony of knowing what his father had imparted.

He would tell his sister at a moment of his own choosing. His father, out of his own perceived guilt, had assigned him the task.

Tomas observed them and came over, studying Temple, obviously assessing his prospects to continue. He, too, had an investment to protect.

"We go now," Tomas said, looking up at the sky.

"The rain?" their father muttered. "On Eagle Pass. With all those narrow switchbacks, won't the ground get soft?"

"We be fine," Tomas said.

"Like Harry," his father mumbled.

Temple seemed somewhat worse. The rest hadn't done him much good.

Scott whispered to Courtney, who had come towards them. "Tell him he looks better," he commanded. She looked at him, wide-eyed and confused, then nodded.

"Oh yes, much better."

Her father leaned against Scott as they moved toward his horse. Then he and Tomas helped their father to remount. Mounted, he looked precarious.

"We go now," Tomas said, mounting his horse and moving forward. Courtney followed and then Temple, hunched over his horse's neck. As before, Scott held up the rear. The rain grew in intensity, but the horses moved forward, stoic and seemingly oblivious to the elements.

Once mounted and watching his father with consternation, Scott recalled their conversation.

What his father had imparted was a startling revelation, a secret uncovered from deep inside his memory. Why now? Scott wondered. Was his father being prescient?

"Please, Scott," his father had pleaded. "Get me through this. I have to fix things. A father's duty is to protect his progeny. I was wrong. Forgive me."

Temple had reached out and squeezed his son's arm. "You may think I'm a foolish dodo, but I have not got the strength of conscience to let the matter rest. A father's love and responsibility comes with the territory. I'm scared son. I'm failing. My strength is ebbing. I need to get home, make the correction, and fulfill the promise I made to you here. If I don't make it, things stay as they are. Do you understand what I'm saying? Don't let me die out here."

The effort had winded the old man. He was clearly panicked, and despite his ebbing strength, his words had tumbled out in a burst of hysteria.

"You're being morbid, Dad. You're going to make it home and to your new life. You've got to stop worrying about us."

"But I promised to help in your and your sister's new ventures. If I don't make it, that would be another promise unfulfilled."

"Why are you so worried, Dad? So what?"

Despite the promise that his new venture would be funded, his own response was a revelation to himself. Suddenly it didn't matter, and he said so.

"It matters to me," his father said. "It's unfinished business."

"Unfinished business? That's ridiculous. We're undeserving. We've done nothing except put our hands out. Besides, you've done enough. We're losers, Dad. That's the long and short of it. Getting you back in one piece is all that matters. You still have a life to live. A new chapter is beginning. But yes, I would be grateful for your help, and this time I won't let you down."

He felt exalted by the opportunity to tell his father what he really felt. He meant what he said, deeply, sincerely, ardently. From out of the corner of his eye, he had seen his sister studying them. She seemed puzzled. A lump formed in his throat. Without any signs of contrition, she would gladly see her father dead and gone, to get possession of her inheritance.

He wondered whether his father had sensed this. Or was he so blinded by fatherly love? Suddenly Scott felt emotionally overwhelmed. He felt the urge to tell his father the truth, the total truth, but held back, fearing that the revelation would kill him.

"I love you, Dad," he whispered. "Please, Dad, hang in there. You'll be fine."

He saw his father's face through a veil of tears.

"Please, son. I owe this to myself. I am the father. It is not a question of your and Courtney's being undeserving. That is not the issue, not anymore. I'm talking here of responsibility. As your father, I need to do this. It is necessary to validate that I am your father and protector. Do you understand?"

"I'm not sure."

Scott paused, unable to get the words out. He wanted to say that whether or not they received this largesse, it would change nothing. Love, he was certain, could never be purchased. Your daughter wants you dead, he was tempted to say.

"I need this for myself," his father continued. "I owe this to myself. You are my children. That is the point of it all. I gave you life."

Was he being overly sentimental, Scott wondered? If he knew what they had done, would he still feel the same sense of responsibility? Or would he be insulted and disgusted? He had the urge to argue, to confront him, to point out the error of his judgment, but he feared weakening him further.

"You're overwrought, Dad," he said, holding back what he really wanted to say. We are undeserving of your protection. We have crossed over the line of sibling propriety. We have betrayed your honor. We are not who you think we are. We are liars, secretive voluptuaries. We have disgraced you. We have cheated your aspirations, wasted your money. Worse, we have stolen from you. We are thieves. Your guilt is misplaced.

He looked toward his sister, no longer feeling any sense of attachment, either as sibling or lover. The idea of endless love that had dominated his brotherly passion and had very nearly destroyed his life was over, dead and gone. A weight had been lifted from his psyche.

"Just promise that you'll do all in your power to get me back," his father had reiterated.

"That's a given, Dad. Why would you think otherwise?"

His father nodded but did not offer an answer. A long silence ensued. Temple had closed his eyes and seemed on the verge of sleep, then opened them again.

"Son," he said. "I have lived with another burden. I know what you and your sister did."

Scott had felt his heart thump in his chest. He swallowed hard and tried to respond, but his voice would not come. His father's hand reached out, held his arm as he raised himself on his elbow, and whispered into his son's ear.

"I know about the diamonds. Your mother and I knew that they could only be taken by you and your sister."

Scott made every effort to respond but could not find words. The revelation stunned him.

"And you know why?" his father continued. "Just hear me out. We knew what you did with it. No need to respond,

Scottie. We found out. Don't ask how. It began with a call from a customer in New Jersey. Then your mother and I hired an investigator. We learned about the abortion, and we found out where you sold the diamonds, which we bought back. We knew, too, what a heroic effort it was on your part to help your sister! Obviously Courtney was in trouble. Believe me, we agonized about revealing what we knew, but we promised each other never to tell. Your mother went to her grave with this secret. But I feel compelled to confess it, to clear the slate. Now is the perfect moment. No one else knows. I did not tell Muriel."

"You knew?" Scott felt himself on the verge of blacking out.

"No need to explain, son. In the end, we felt you had done something to help your sister out of her dilemma. We did not know how she had gotten herself into that situation. We could never find out who had impregnated her, but when the matter was closed, we just let it go. It was pointless to pursue it further. We knew it had to be an act of desperation. We were parents after all and did not want you to submit to our judgment. We were hopeful that it was the end of it, and thankfully it was. You never stole from us again, and your sister went on with her life."

"Why now?" Scott had whispered, wondering if knowing it earlier would have changed his mind about going into the business. No, he thought. There were two parts to that guilt. He wondered what his parents would have done if they had known who had impregnated his sister. A wave of nausea had gripped him. "Does Courtney know?"

His father shook his head.

"No need," his father sighed. "Leave it be. Not now. Why bring back a memory like that? She has other things on her mind. Maybe some day after I'm gone."

"You'll be around for a long time, Dad. Just rest now."

Despite his concern for his father, the irony was telling. After a while, his father opened his eyes again.

"I'm losing it, Scottie," he mumbled.

"That's crazy, Dad."

"No. I misplaced my camera, and this morning…" He paused and swallowed. "My damned blood pressure pills. I can't find them. I think I left them back in the camp. The altitude. I think I'm paying the price."

Scott felt himself on the verge of confession, but he held back. There was no way he could tell him about Tomas and the camera. Dismissing the idea, he focused instead on the blood pressure pills.

"Where did you keep the pills, Dad?"

Beyond the question was a small tingle of suspicion.

"Usual place, my toiletry kit, where I always kept them. I guess I must have forgotten to put them back when I took them yesterday morning."

"Maybe they dropped out."

"I can't understand it. I'm usually so careful about them."

"Just get some rest. It's been a rough day."

His father closed his eyes again, and soon he had fallen asleep.

Suspicion grew in Scott's mind. Courtney had made no secret of her desire. Had she become so fiendish and diabolical, that she had chosen to steal their father's pills as if it were an obvious weapon of choice? A sudden chill made him tremble.

Peripherally, he had noted that she was deep in discussion with Tomas. Why? They had seemed conspiratorial.

His father was a good man, and his revelation had moved Scott profoundly. His children had disappointed him, but the bond had not been broken. He had been set adrift by the loss of their mother and was finding a new life. They should be supportive and respectful.

Of course at this moment, his own guilt pummeled him: the stealing of the diamonds years ago, the incestuous relations with his sister. Studying his father's face, he had contemplated that this might be the moment of his own confession. He felt himself on the verge, in need of this final expiation. But just as he sensed himself ready, his father had closed his eyes and drifted into deep sleep. He allowed the moment to pass.

Another issue intervened as well. His father had begged, cajoled, nudged but not demanded that he enter the business. Scott had demurred for reasons that suddenly, in the light of reality, seemed ludicrous. Here was his father agonizing over family, fairness, and continuity, and he had eschewed the legacy of taking over his business because of what he had done decades ago. Yes, in fact, he was ashamed.

Wasn't it equally as honorable to embellish what his father and his father before him had created? Business was, after all, business. Trading in gemstones was no different than trading in food. Why had he been so adamant? He sensed in himself a life-changing moment. Had he made a turn on the wrong path? He suddenly felt a growing sense of obligation.

Again and again, his father's words echoed in his thoughts. Soon, he seemed to have tranced out, lost in his ruminations, as they moved closer and closer to Eagle Pass. The rain continued steady and relentless, softening the ground.

The pain in his knees awoke him to reality. He had already popped four ibuprofen tablets, and he found he needed more. He took the vial from his shirt pocket and took two more. As he did so, he noted that again his father, who was riding ahead of him, was beginning to list in his saddle.

"You okay, Dad?" he called out.

His father lifted his hand and nodded his head, clearly suggesting that he was hanging on. He looked at his watch, noting that they had been riding for nearly two hours.

Tomas lifted his hand, and the train stopped. Scott noted that they had reached the trailhead of Eagle Pass. Tomas dismounted and moved forward on foot assessing the pass.

From the perch on his horse, Scott looked upward. A fog was beginning to settle on the mountain, and the rain was continuing in a steady downpour.

"Are we going up in that mess?" Scott asked.

Tomas observed the sky.

"We go over. We be okay. Horses take us. No problem."

"We can't very well stay here," Courtney said, pulling up her horse. "Tomas is right. Let's move. We're wasting time."

Scott remembered how it had been on their earlier trek, how they had to dismount to traverse the narrowest of the switchbacks. Again he observed his father, who was hunched over and listless. His complexion was ashen.

"My father is beat," he said. "This is not a good idea."

Courtney reined her horse to pull up beside her father.

"You okay, Dad?" Scott heard her say. Her hypocrisy filled him with contempt. He turned his attention back to Tomas, who had mounted his horse.

"He won't be able to walk on the narrow switchbacks," Scott said. "It will be too dangerous."

"He stay in saddle then," Tomas said. "I lead his horse."

"That means you have to lead two horses."

"I tole you. I take care."

He remembered Tomas's words in referring to Harry earlier. A chill ran through him. He looked up at the sky.

"Just be careful."

"No worry. I take care."

Tomas nodded and turned away, his eyes scanning the ascent. Scott returned to where his father sat on his horse. He looked wan, enervated.

"We're going to start the ascent," Scott explained. "You'll stay mounted. Tomas will lead your horse in the tight spots."

"He knows what he's doing," Courtney interjected. "We'll be on the other side in no time."

Tomas signaled that they were ready to move out. He had changed the order of the string with Temple's horse directly behind him, followed by Scott, and Courtney holding up the rear. As Tomas moved his horse forward, Temple followed, but Scott held back and let Courtney pull abreast of him. He leaned toward her.

"I know about the pills," he hissed, watching her expression. He hadn't been certain up to that moment. Her expression clearly revealed her guilt.

"Fuck you," she said, her teeth clenched, her jaw raised belligerently. Suddenly he saw it all, her intent.

He had glanced her way while having his intimate conversation with their father. She and Tomas were in deep conversation. He and his father were so thoroughly involved that he had paid little attention. Only now, watching her, the memory of them together, their odd intimacy suggested something conspiratorial and ominous. An epiphany exploded in his mind, a sense of danger so compelling that it prompted an instant reaction. As if by rote, he knew what had to be done.

"And something else, little sister."

Her eyes narrowed. She cocked her head, waiting. Intuitively, he sensed that Tomas and Courtney had conspired about taking some action, although he could not be certain.

"He changed his will," he blurted. "We've been virtually cut out. He will change it back to where it was when he gets home. And he will instruct his bankers about our stipend. It means that if he doesn't survive this, we're shit out of luck."

"I don't believe you."

"I didn't ask you to."

"But he had promised Mother—"

"Broke it, kiddo. He reassessed."

"Are you bullshitting me?"

She looked toward her father, who was already out of hailing range, following Tomas who was not looking back. Temple was slumped over the saddle. The rain had become more intense with the wind shifting, so that it came at them from the summit in slanting gusts.

Scott shook his head, fearing that any further explanation would reveal his sudden ploy.

Courtney replied but a burst of thunder prevented Scott from hearing her response. Suddenly, as if it were a fit of temper, she kicked her horse and tried to put it ahead of his. He quickly blocked her and turned into the pelting rain to begin the ascent. He could barely see ahead of him. Looking back, he saw Courtney following. The trail was narrowing, and it would be impossible to get ahead of him.

Looking into the oncoming rain, he could see no sign of Tomas or his father.

Chapter 24

⟫⟪

Tomas had navigated the twenty-three switchbacks on ten-thousand-foot Eagle Pass numerous times. Often he had shut his eyes and dozed as the horses lumbered steadily and carefully upward then downward through the terrain. He had been here through heat, cold, rain, and snowstorms and was familiar with every turn and potential hazard.

Harry had led a horse train over the pass for years without a single mishap and was proud that he could give his clients this touch of danger, which he exaggerated in his effort to prove that he was giving them their money's worth. To many it was the highlight of the trek and gave them lots to talk about for years.

Tomas had been a cook in a broken-down motel at the outer edges of West Yellowstone. Harry had found him the day his boss announced that the motel was being bought by developers, who were putting together a pricey resort for upscale people who wanted to enjoy the Western experience and the newly developed ski slopes beginning to dot the area.

By then, Tomas had been in *El Norte* for two years, having jumped the border from his village in central Mexico. He had worked on a ranch in Mexico and was familiar with horses and the hard life it entailed with little compensation. He was the middle child of seven children, and because he had done well in school, his parents had hopes that one day he would return from the states a rich man and rescue them from a life of poverty and drudgery. His girlfriend had promised to wait.

In desperation, he had followed the well-worn trail to the States, hoping to make enough money to send back home to his impoverished family and build a nest egg for marriage to a girl he had known almost all his life.

He had learned all the survival skills of being an illegal alien in a country that offered better wages, opportunity, and upward mobility while dodging the authorities that viewed him as a renegade and interloper. He had learned by the example of others in his predicament to camouflage himself, fade into the background, armor himself against any insult or abuse, and use silence to obliterate any expression of understanding from his features and body language.

He had quickly learned all the back alleys and secret pathways to negotiate through the spiderweb of interconnecting strands among his outcast countrymen that kept him free to earn wages triple what he could earn in Mexico. Working his way from Los Angeles to Montana, he had acquired cooking skills, learned from watching chefs at various restaurants where he had done menial labor in LA, and easily found work at various short-order rural beaneries eager to employ illegals with useful skills at low wages.

Since he had no family ties and because of his circumstances, he was wary of any relationships with men or women. He could work long hours to earn more money even at below-legal wages. Because he was alone with his thoughts and observations most of the time, he had learned to study the Anglo people with whom he had to interact. He had self-trained himself to listen and watch them carefully and adapt himself to what he imagined was the way he should be safely perceived by them.

In the little spare time he had, he had taken up reading fiction, finding used paperbacks in both English and Spanish, mostly mysteries and thrillers, that gave him a broad picture of what he assumed was an accurate depiction of human nature in all sorts of circumstances.

Reading filled his mind with plots, images, and ideas about pitfalls he might encounter and of what was realistically possible to achieve in his own life. Although the English editions were difficult at first, they eventually improved his vocabulary, however not his accent, and they had developed in him an understanding of the American idiom.

Through the treks with various clients, he had learned the ways of the gringo, who could be observed intimately in the isolated setting of the wilderness. Many, he had discovered, were arrogant and spoiled and would ignore his presence as if he wasn't there. Admittedly some were pleasant and kindly, like Temple, but the bulk seemed to take him for granted, a working prop for their gratification.

His strategy was to make himself absolutely indispensable to Harry, whose alcoholism was cutting into his expertise as an experienced outfitter. But Tomas had watched him and listened carefully until he was able to absorb all the wilderness skills that Harry had acquired. He already knew a great deal about horses, mules, and other animals, and he quickly learned to do any chore assigned to him and was able to carry out any order that Harry or his clients could command, without visible complaint.

He knew he was treated as someone alien and practically invisible but had intuited that a display of competence as an employee in whatever capacity and a willingness to obey orders and do whatever was required to please his employer would insure his employment. Harry had offered a perfect marriage of what he required, long stretches away from prying eyes, work that he could do with competence, a knowledge of horses, camping skills, hardships, and living under minimum conditions of comfort. In his tent away from Harry and his clients, he read his paperbacks by searchlight.

In addition to adopting a silent expressionless persona, he was an extraordinarily skillful cook and all-around wilderness handyman who could easily adapt to Harry's escalating abuse. Short, with a dark complexion that was a sure sign of his Indian antecedents, he knew exactly the way he was perceived and had developed a stance that could skillfully put himself in the same category as a pebble, to be hardly noticed and largely ignored.

In the four years he had worked for Harry, the man's drinking had changed what was once a tolerant personality to a cruel and mean-minded person, whose abuse of Tomas had escalated in direct proportion to his growing alcoholism. By making himself indispensable to his drunken boss, he had begun to sense his own growing domination over his employer, for whom he could play the role of lackey and actually encourage his drinking by burying large quantities of booze in designated spots at various campsites.

Occasionally there were perks. Forced by circumstances to be largely celibate, he occasionally visited prostitutes in those parts of Montana that were safe for illegals to fornicate among their own, and it was not uncommon to fuck a horny, usually older, female client who stayed back in camp while Harry took the others on his various side adventures. He had learned, by careful observation and surreptitious listening to the conversation among Harry's clients, intimate details about their lives and what kind of people they really were.

Stripped of the amenities of civilization, he had learned that people tended to reveal more of their real selves than they did in their more orderly lives in urban environments. Lately, he had begun to realize that while he was sending money home, his own life was passing swiftly by and his vague hope of financial independence was an empty dream. Worse, his last phone call to Mexico had revealed that his sweetheart had tired of waiting and had married someone else.

With eyes wide open and attuned to find a way out of his static circumstances, he waited for the moment, meaning an opportunity to better his life. In his mind, that meant money. He had come to *El Norte* for money. He had grabbed at every miserable employment for money. Money was the route to his salvation. Money was the manna from heaven. He had learned that only money could free him from this forlorn and lonely life. Nothing was worse than being without money. In Mexico this had been the perpetual condition of his family.

Then the Temples had arrived: a rich man hoping to restore the bonds of fatherhood with his two weird adult children. It startled him to see the brother and sister fucking, but it put the idea of blackmail in his head. He knew they saw him as just another dumb faceless illegal, an ignorant wetback, an abused and put-upon piece of human shit. He listened carefully to their intimate talk and knew he had found the possibility of a golden opportunity.

Blackmail was a well-worn plot in his paperback reading. He had gambled on their fear of exposure, and it had seemed to work. He had panicked them and got them to react to his threats. It gave him the impetus as well to settle the score with his employer. For a long time he had contemplated the method, and his success with the Temples had goaded him to put his plan into action.

He had no illusions about what he was up against. Despite his attempt to make it seem as if a grizzly had accidentally killed Harry, he knew that an investigation by experts might eventually uncover his ploy, and the authorities might figure out how it had occurred. The woman had already hinted that she suspected what had happened.

He had decided to take off as soon as they reached West Yellowstone, using the money he had collected from the Temples. If the woman attempted to screw him out of the hundred thousand, he would find her and kill her. Now he was faced with another decision that he turned over in his mind as he led the sickly old man up the pass, deliberately moving up ahead of the man's two children, prodding his horse forward in the blinding rain.

After the first switchback he had grabbed the reins of Temple's horse to be certain it would keep the pace he had set. He needed to put distance between them and the others. Above all, he needed time to think.

He knew, too, that his principal deal was with the woman, a miserable ruthless bitch who would stop at nothing to get her own way. He had determined that her brother was a cowardly weak idiot that had been led around by his cock by the rotten sister. As for the father, he was a nice man but a sentimental old fool, who was being set up to part with as much of his money as the two terrible children could get. He had encountered similar situations in the various books he had read.

Now, as he made his way upward on the switchbacks of Eagle Pass with the rain pelting his face, he was contemplating an offer that was too tempting to refuse offhand. The bitch was asking him to murder her father and her brother and make it look accidental in exchange for a half-million dollars.

The idea of murder, despite what he had devised for Harry, was of deep concern. Harry was an evil man who had abused him without mercy. In that case he had caused the conditions for his death, but it had not been done by his own hand. One might say that Harry's death by a grizzly was God's will.

While he rarely went to church and had been to confession only a couple of times since entering the United States, he had been taught the catechism and was aware of God's mercy and the concept of heaven and hell, which had been drilled into him as a child by the village priest.

Despite all the tough talk of killing, he had not entirely lost his sense of salvation and his fear of eternal damnation. He could kill an animal by his own hand and had done that numerous times, but this was more out of mercy for the animal and for food to survive. This was justified, not sinful and not, in his mind, worthy of punishment.

But killing anther human being was a troubling idea, despite the temptation to free himself from poverty and perhaps do good things for himself and his family. Harry's death had been another matter. These people he had been asked to murder had done him no harm and except for the fact that they were gringos, he was having trouble justifying such an act. Actually, his hesitation surprised him. The temptation was awesome.

He had devised the manner in which they could die: by deliberately laming the horses that they rode and pushing horse and rider over the narrowest switchback. The long fall would undoubtedly kill the rider and probably the horse instantly. He admitted to himself that he would not be able to avoid the pangs of conscience, although he was hopeful that he might confess the act and be forgiven.

He would, of course, have to flee the area, perhaps hook up with another outfitter in another state far from Montana, maybe New Mexico or Arizona. No one in authority would believe any version of his alibi even if the woman who clearly benefited from the deaths backed it up. He did not believe she could be that good of an actress. What he hoped was that the wildlife would destroy the identity of the bodies before they were found.

Even that would not end the matter, since Harry was registered as an official guide and had reserved the campsite in advance. Sooner or later, the park administration would have to investigate his disappearance.

He knew the ropes of the underground and the various ways to get around the authorities, and he was well aware that the bitch was not to be trusted. On that issue, he would have to gamble. If she didn't come across with her end of the bargain, he would certainly consider killing her, but in that case—as in Harry's—he might find justification and forgiveness. She was, after all, a mean lady who had sinned against God by fornicating with her brother.

She might, of course, deny the deal she had made with him. In that case he felt certain that he would find her and make her comply. Like the characters he had encountered in the many mysteries and thrillers he had read, he would devise ways to get what he wanted. If not, he would be justified in killing her. What would another death matter? Still, he continued to wrestle with his decision and remained conflicted and unsure about taking action.

Looking behind him, he could see the old man listing precariously on his horse, which managed the soggy switchbacks with increasing difficulty. In this situation four legs were better than two. He noted that the rain was gaining in intensity, and the thunder and lightening seemed to be heading their way.

It was impossible to hear or see any sign of the others. But there was no escaping that he had reached that place where the trail was at its narrowest point, overlooking the sheerest drop near the summit. It was the prefect spot to do the deed. He slowed his horse and dropped the reins of Temple's horse.

His plan was to dismount, tether his horse to a tree, lame Temple's horse with the axe affixed to his saddle, and push horse and rider into the valley below. Then he would lie in wait and repeat the action with the son's horse. It was all worked out in his mind. Still, he hesitated.

As he reached the point in the trail that he had designated as the perfect spot, a sudden lightening strike split a tree less than ten feet from where he stood, followed by a teeth-shattering blast of thunder. Both horses in the train bellowed and rose on their hind legs, panicked by the explosive noise. Tomas himself was stunned and frightened by the sound, which grew louder and closer as the rain intensified and fell in what seemed like solid sheets of water.

He had smashed his axe into the nearest tree and held on to its handle while the lightning and thunder continued its cacophony echoing through the valley below. Is this the voice of God warning him of what he was about to do? He felt his body shake and his heart pound with fear.

Through the solid screen of rain, he could see the vague outline of Temple's horse, restless and frightened and rising on his hind legs. Between lightening strikes and the loud beat of thunder, he peered through the wall of water and saw that Temple's horse was riderless. It was obvious that the old man had been unseated. Leaving the balanced safety of the buried axe, he rushed toward the horse and pulled the reins, steadying the horse with the security of the tension.

Searching the ground near the horse, he could find no sign of Temple. Noting that he was close to the precipice, he moved with the horse as far as he could get to the tree line no more than a yard or two from the edge. It was only then that he could assess what might have happened. The frightened horse had thrown Temple, and since there was no sign of him on the trail, it was obvious that he had fallen into the valley below.

The first idea that crossed his mind was that God had intervened and had rescued him from the devil. He fell to his knees and crossed himself, murmuring remembered prayers in his Spanish. He lost track of time, searching the sky, as if looking for a further sign of God's staying hand.

After a while the rain eased and the heavily laden black thunderclouds passed on. Hearing sounds of clanking horse bridles, he turned and saw the two following horses and their riders moving slowing round the turn of the switchback. He stood up, watching them with dumb concentration, and then he untethered his horse and waited for them to reach him.

He was not thinking clearly, caught between a desire to continue moving and waiting for the impending confrontation.

The brother's horse rounded the bend first. His eyes squinted into the scene then inspected the nearby area. Tomas could tell that he had rightly interpreted the situation. Courtney's horse had not yet rounded the bend.

"No, amigo," Tomas screamed. He raised his hand, pointing to the sky. "The horse—"

"You fuck," Scott cried, jumping off his horse and bounding the few steps toward Tomas, grabbing him by the shoulders.

"I no kill him, amigo. I swear to Jesus. He fall. The storm—"

"You murdering bastard," Scott cried, banging his fists into Tomas's face, drawing blood, which streamed out of his nose. "You fucking killer. You did Harry, now my Dad. You fucking miserable bastard."

Tears running down his cheeks, his face twisted into a mask of profound desperation and rage, he pummeled Tomas with his fists. At first, disoriented and confused, Tomas did not resist. Then, in a knee jerk act of survival defense, he realized that the man was acting out of murderous rage, and he began to fight back.

He kicked Scott in the groin, forcing him to double up in agony and fall to his knees.

"I no kill him, I swear to Jesus. I no kill him."

He met Scott's gaze, repeating his words like a mantra.

"I no kill him. I swear, amigo. I no kill him."

He raised his hands, palms up in a gesture of both denial and supplication. With effort Scott stood up, still in pain, his breath coming in gasps.

At that moment Courtney riding round the switchback bend, moved toward them, obviously puzzled by the scene of the two men confronting each other.

"She," Tomas pointed to Courtney then turned to Scott, whose complexion had turned dead white as the tears continued to flow. "That she-devil whore sister, she wanted me to kill your *padre*—"

"Shut your stupid mouth, asshole," Courtney cried.

"Your *padre* fall. I do nothing."

"You should both rot in hell," Scott cried, his eyes shifting between Tomas and his sister.

"She is devil, amigo. She promise me half a million from your *padre* if I kill him. But I no kill him. I swear, amigo."

Scott, breathing heavily, looked toward his sister, who had dismounted, burning with obvious rage.

"Don't you believe that fucking Mexican lying bastard. He's making up a story to save his own ass." She turned toward Scott, whose eyes shifted between his sister and the Mexican, obviously confused and uncertain.

"You murdered Harry," Scott muttered, charging Tomas again, hysterical with anger. "And my father."

Both men fell to the muddy ground, twisting and turning in the muck, rolling precariously toward the edge of the narrow switchback.

Tomas felt the man's hands clasping his throat, pressing hard, beyond his own capacity to loosen the grip. He knew he was choking, losing air, on the cusp of oblivion, blackness descending like a curtain closing. Hysteria had given the brother focus and strength. They were on the very edge of the precipice.

From the corner of his eye, he saw the woman moving toward his horse where the rifle was encased in a leather holster. He saw her remove the rifle, point it toward them, and then heard the blast. He heard the man's brief cry of pain and the panicked sounds of the horses as they fled. He felt, too, the clamping hands around his neck loosen and the air rush into his lungs. But his strength had ebbed, and he could not find in himself the power to rise.

Looking up, he saw the woman's face, smiling, a fearful image of what he was certain was the face of the devil.

The woman kneeled, and he felt the lunging pressure on his body, as he and the dead weight above him locked together in an embrace of death fell into space.

In the seconds it took for him to rush downward into the bottom of the valley, he was not certain whether he heard the musical trill of a heavenly sound or the ominous drumbeat from the burning pit of hell.

Epilogue

——◆——

I n the report of the first ranger on the scene where a group of trekkers had found a wandering woman, he described her as disoriented and deranged, obviously suffering both mentally and physically from a long episode of exposure. Apparently, from identity papers found in her possession, she was registered as a client of Harry McCabe, whose body had not yet been found.

Human bones were found scattered over some distance in the valley below Eagle Mountain. A New York driver's license that could have come from one of the McCabe party identified someone as George Temple, aged seventy-two, giving his address in New York City.

There was a curious paragraph in this very preliminary first report that was listed as an addendum by the first ranger. He apprised his superiors of the fact that he had been an English major at the University of Wyoming, and he noted that the obviously deranged woman was muttering repetitive lines from what he recognized as the famous scene from Shakespeare's *Macbeth* spoken by Lady Macbeth before she commits suicide. Perhaps to impress his superiors, he quoted:

"Out, damned spot! out, I say.—One, two;—why, then 'tis time to do't.—Hell is murky! Fie, my lord, fie! a soldier and afeard? What need we fear who knows it, when none can call our power to account?"

It is reported that the superior was impressed. The woman died before she could be hospitalized. The investigation is continuing.

ABOUT THE AUTHOR

⟹⋅◆⋅⟸

Warren Adler is a world-renowned novelist, short-story writer, poet, and playwright. Over the past 40 years the prolific writer has published nearly three dozen books and more than a third of them have been sold to Hollywood. His most famous book, *The War of the Roses,* a masterpiece fictionalization of the ugliest divorce ever, was turned into a box office hit with Danny DeVito, Michael Douglas, and Kathleen Turner. *Random Hearts,* starring Harrison Ford, was a major motion picture, and *The Sunset Gang* was a PBS trilogy. His books have been translated into 25 languages and have been reviewed or featured in *The New York Times, LA Times, USA Today, Wall Street Journal, Cosmopolitan, Newsweek, Variety, Glamour, Washington Post, W, Time, Rolling Stone, Gannett News Service,* and the *Hollywood Reporter.* He has also appeared on the *Today Show* and *Good Morning America.* Adler writes several times a week for *The Huffington Post.* He resides in Manhattan and can be found at www.warrenadler.com.